Praise for Jan Watson

"This is a settle-in-and-savor type of a read. . . . With rich texture and detail and unforgettable characters that lodge themselves in your heart, Jan transports us to a world without modern convenience, where we live with the people of the land. Danger, tragedy, faith, romance—it's all here in spades."

JERRY B. JENKINS, coauthor of the Left Behind series

"Watson's success lies in her ability to create characters that are enjoyable, endearing, and timeless . . ."

ROMANTIC TIMES* MAGAZINE ON *WILLOW SPRINGS

"Colorfully descriptive language, engaging characters, and words that flow like honey make this a rich, satisfying historical novel. As charming as its predecessor and easily as good; highly recommended."

LIBRARY JOURNAL* ON *WILLOW SPRINGS

"[*Troublesome Creek* is] one of the best books I've read all year. I couldn't put it down."

EVA MARIE EVERSON, author of the Cedar Key series

"This first-time novelist captures the reader's heart as pages quickly turn to reveal plot twists and a story of real-life family love."

CHRISTIAN BOOK PREVIEWS ON *TROUBLESOME CREEK*

"Jan Watson has a true gift for weaving in details that make the mountains of Kentucky almost like another character in the story."

"*Torrent Falls* is a great story demonstrating the reward of remaining faithful to God and His laws."

"Watson brings forth intimate characters with a strong sense of family, obligation, and faith and evokes sensitive and realistic issues. Readers will enjoy the latest journey set in the mountains of Kentucky."

"Packed with characters full of feminine strength, *Still House Pond* paints a picture of nineteenth-century rural life, while offering a hint of romance and a dash of suspense."

"[In *Still House Pond*] Watson brings together lovable and unforgettable characters, a small-town feel, and suspense that gently grips the heart."

"*Still House Pond* spins a charming tale. There were moments where I could not wait to turn the page and discover where the story went next."

Tattler's Branch

Tattler's Branch

Branch

JAN WATSON

Tyndale House Publishers, Inc., Carol Stream, Illinois

Visit Tyndale online at www.tyndale.com.

Visit Jan Watson's website at www.janwatson.net.

TYNDALE and Tyndale's quill logo are registered trademarks of Tyndale House Publishers, Inc.

Tattler's Branch

Designed by Stephen Vosloo

Edited by Sarah Mason

Published in association with the literary agency of Benrey Literary LLC, P.O. Box 12721, New Bern, NC 28561.

Scripture quotations are taken from the *Holy Bible*, King James Version.

Tattler's Branch is a work of fiction. Where real people, events, establishments, organizations, or locales appear, they are used fictitiously. All other elements of the novel are drawn from the author's imagination.

Library of Congress Cataloging-in-Publication Data

Watson, Jan.
  Tattler's branch / Jan Watson.
    pages cm
  ISBN 978-1-4143-3915-3 (sc)
1. Women physicians—Fiction. 2. Rural women—Fiction. 3. Coal miners—Kentucky—Fiction. 4. Abandoned children—Fiction. I. Title.
  PS3623.A8724T38 2013
  813'.6—dc23   2013015405

Printed in the United States of America

19	18	17	16	15	14	13
7	6	5	4	3	2	1

In memory of dear friends gone before:

Julie A.

Marcia W.

Myra R.

Jinny M.

Judy C.

Elizabeth R.

I will see you in the morning.

CHAPTER I

1911

Armina Tippen's muscles twitched like frog legs in a hot skillet. She leaned against the deeply furrowed trunk of a tulip poplar to wait out an unexpected change in the weather and to gather her strength. The spreading branches of the tree made the perfect umbrella. Gray clouds tumbled across the sky as quarter-size raindrops churned up the thick red dust of the road she'd just left.

The rain didn't amount to much—it was hardly worth the wait. Armina kicked off her shoes, careful to not disturb the kerosene-daubed rags she'd tied around her ankles to discourage chiggers. She didn't have to fool with stockings because she wasn't wearing any.

Back on the road, she ran her toes through the damp dirt. It was silky and cool against her skin. The only thing better would have been a barefoot splash in a mud puddle. There should be a law against wearing shoes between the last frost of spring and the first one of fall. Folks were getting soft, wearing shoes year-round. Whoever would have thought she'd be one of them? Knotting the leather strings, she hung the shoes around her neck and walked on.

Clouds blown away, the full force of the summer sun bore down, soothing her. She poked around with the walking stick she carried in case she got the wobbles and to warn blacksnakes and blue racers from the path. Snakes did love to sun their cold-blooded selves.

She hadn't been up Tattler's Branch Road for the longest time. For some reason she'd woken up thinking of the berries she used to pick here when she was a girl and living with her aunt Orie. Probably somebody else had already stripped the blackberry bushes of their fruit, but it didn't hurt to look. There weren't any blackberries like the ones that grew up here.

After she crossed the narrow footbridge that spanned this branch of the creek, she spied one bramble and then another mingling together thick as a hedge. Her mouth watered at the sight. Mayhaps she should have brought a larger tin than the gallon-size can hanging from her wrist. Or maybe two buckets . . . but then she couldn't have managed her walking stick. Life was just one puzzle piece after another.

Armina stopped to put her shoes back on. It wouldn't do

to step on something unawares, although the sting from a honeybee sometimes eased her aches and pains. You'd think she was an old lady. She couldn't remember the last time she felt like her twenty-year-old self. But if she stopped to figure on it, it seemed like her health had started going south in the early spring while she was up at the family farm helping her sister plant a garden. She'd caught the quinsy from one of the kids, more than likely her nephew Bubby. He was the lovingest child, always kissing on her and exchanging slobbers. When her throat swelled up inside, her sister had put her to bed with a poultice made up of oats boiled in vinegar and stuffed in a sock that draped across her neck to sweat out the poison. It was two days before she could swallow again.

The rusty call of pharaoh bugs waxed and waned as she pushed through the tall weeds and grasses growing along the bank. She'd loved playing with the locusts' cast-off hulls when she was little. She would stick them on the front of her dress like play-pretty jewels. Not that she liked adornments—she mostly agreed with St. Paul on that particular argument. But she did like something pretty to fasten the braid of her hair into a bun at the nape of her neck. At the moment, her hairpin was a brilliant blue-jay's feather.

The blackberry vines tumbled willy-nilly over a wire fence. She disremembered the fence; it seemed like there'd been easy access to the fruit. To her right was a gate free of creepers, but she wouldn't trespass. There was more than enough fruit this side of the hindrance for the cobbler she aimed to make for supper. Doc Lilly loved her blackberry cobbler, especially with a splash of nutmeg cream. Ned did too, but he wasn't at home. Just like Doc Lilly's husband, Ned was off doing whatever it was men had to do to make their precarious way in this old world. Armina missed her husband and his sweet ways.

She walked down the line of bushes to the most promising ones and let her stick rest against the branches. With one hand she lifted a briar and with the other she plucked the fruit, filling the bucket in less than five minutes. The berries were big as double thumbs and bursting with juice, so heavy they nearly picked themselves. She didn't have to twist the stems at all. In another day they'd be overripe, fermenting; then the blackbirds would finish them off, flying drunkenly from one heavily laden bush to another.

Her mind was already on the crust she'd make with a little lard and flour and just a pinch of salt. Maybe she'd make a lattice crust, although a good blackberry cobbler didn't need prettying up.

Armina slid the container off her wrist and bent to set it down. When she raised her head, specks like tiny black gnats darted in and out of her vision. Lights flashed and she lost her balance, falling backward through the prickly scrub. She landed against the fence with her legs stuck straight out like a lock-kneed china doll.

"For pity's sake," she said with a little tee-hee. "I hope I didn't kick the bucket."

A scratch down her cheek stung like fire, and one sleeve of the long-tailed shirt she wore open over her dress was torn, but otherwise she reckoned she was all of a piece. There was nothing to do but wait a few minutes for her head to stop swimming. Then, if she could get her knees to work, she could crawl out.

It was cool here behind the bushes—and peaceful. A few feet away, a rabbit hopped silently along. A miniature version of itself followed closely behind. Their twitching whiskers were stained purple. Brer Rabbit and his son, Armina fancied as she watched their cotton-ball tails bob.

Suddenly the gate slammed against the bushes. Blackberry fronds waved frantically as if warning her of a coming storm. Startled, Armina parted the brambles and peered out. A couple wrestled silently toward the creek. A man with long yellow hair slicked back in a tail had a woman clamped around the neck with his forearm. He pulled her along like a gunnysack full of potatoes. The woman bucked and struggled to no avail as they splashed into the water this side of the footbridge.

The woman broke free, gasping for air. She was going to make it, Armina saw; she was going to escape. But instead of running away while she had the chance, the woman charged back toward the man, swinging on him. The man's hand shot out and seized a hank of her disheveled hair. He reeled her in like a fish on the line and they both went under. When they came up, the man held a large round rock that glinted wetly in the sun.

Armina opened her mouth, but the rock smashing down and the water arcing up in a spray of red stilled her voice, which had no more power than the raspy call of the molting locusts.

The man bent over with one hand holding the rock and the other resting on his thigh. His chest heaved in and out like a bellows. The rabbit zigzagged out of the bushes, leaving the little one cowering behind. The man straightened, looking all around out of stunned eyes.

The world had gone still as a churchyard greeting a funeral procession. Armina didn't dare to breathe. If he saw her feet sticking out from under the bushes, she was dead. She felt sick to her stomach, and her brain spun like a top. She willed the spinning to stop, but it paid her no mind as everything faded to black.

When Armina awoke, it was like nothing untoward had happened. Birds chirped and water burbled in the creek. The little rabbit's whiskers twitched nervously as it munched on white clover.

Armina was ravenously hungry and bone-dry thirsty. She could never get enough to drink anymore. She picked a handful of the berries and ate them. If she wanted water, she'd have to get it from the creek. No way could she do that after what had happened. She'd been more than foolish not to bring a fruit jar full.

She felt like she'd wakened from a nightmare. Lately she'd been having strange dark spells and bright-colored auras. Doc Lilly would be mad that she hadn't told her, but Armina didn't much like sharing. Besides, if she told, Doc would list a bunch of preventatives that Armina wouldn't pay any mind to. She liked being in charge of her own self.

Pulling her knees up to her chest, she tested the strength in her legs—looked like she was good to go. She crawled out from under the brambles.

She wasn't one bit wobbly as she marched to the footbridge and went straight across, looking neither to the right nor to the left. The bridge felt good and solid under her feet, just like it should. The sun shone brightly, as it would on any normal July day. Her legs were sturdy tools carrying her along toward home just like legs were made to do. It was fine. Every little thing was fine—except she was missing her red berry bucket and her strong white sycamore walking stick. She'd have to go back.

A trill of fear crept up her spine. From under the bridge, the rushing water called for her to look—look there, just on the other side. Look where the smooth round rock waited in judgment. She swallowed hard and heeded the water's call.

Armina felt faint with relief. There was no body in the branch. Her mind had played a trick on her just as she thought.

It was going to be a trick of another sort to find her stick, which had surely fallen among the brambles. She nearly laughed aloud. It was so good to have such a simple problem.

If she hadn't stopped at the water's edge—if she'd gone on home—she would never have seen the trail of dark-red splotches. If she'd gone on home, she would not have followed them up and beyond the garden gate. It was blood;

she knew it was. It smelled metallic, like your palm smelled if you ran it over the frame of an iron bedstead. She wished she'd never stopped. Now she was compelled to follow that ominous trail.

Armina heard the baby's cry before she saw the cabin. It was a mewling, pitiful cry, nothing like the lusty bawls her niece and nephew had made when they were newborns, but still she knew that sound.

The house sat nestled in a grove of trees, as cozy as a bird's nest in thick cedar branches. The place was neat, the yard free of weeds and the porch swept clean. Merry flowers blossomed in a small garden beside the porch steps. Armina could make out zinnias and marigolds from where she lurked behind a tree. A zinc watering can lay overturned on the top step. In the side yard, a wire clothesline sagged beneath the weight of a dozen sun-bleached diapers. She didn't see a body but there had to be one somewhere close. That woman from the creek just didn't up and walk away—not after losing all that blood.

The man with the yellow hair came out the open door and hurried down the steps. He picked up some tools that leaned against the porch railing—a shovel and a pickax— then paused for a moment in the yard and rubbed his chin, keeping his back to the door. The baby's cry persisted. He turned like he might go back inside, but he didn't.

Armina hunched her shoulders and pressed up against the tree, praying he wouldn't come her way. After a while, she could hear the distant sound of the pick or the shovel grating against rock. When she peeled herself away from the tree, she could feel the print of black walnut bark on her cheeks.

As quick as Brer Rabbit, she ran to the near side of the cabin and stooped down under an open window until she dared to look inside. Just under the window sat a Moses basket holding an infant with dandelion-yellow hair and a strange foreign face. A nearly full baby bottle rested on a rolled towel, the rubber nipple just shy of the baby's mouth.

What sort of mother would try to feed a baby this young from a prop? No wonder it cried so piteously.

Armina listened for the sound of digging. If the man was grubbing a grave out of this unforgiving earth, it would take a while. She figured she was safe as long as she could hear the scrape of metal against stone.

"Legs, don't fail me now," she pleaded under her breath.

Taking hold of the window ledge with both hands, she clambered over the sill. She didn't hesitate, just grabbed the handles of the woven basket and with one swoop set it in the thin grass outside the window. She climbed out and went to the clothesline in the side yard. With quick jerks that popped the clothespins off, she helped herself to the dozen diapers. If she was going to steal a baby, she might just as well steal its diapers.

Clutching the basket to her chest, she ran back the way she had come. Even over the sound of her feet pounding across the bridge, she fancied she could hear the swing of a pickax rending the air, bearing down on rock.

Dr. Lilly Still hung her stethoscope on the hall tree in the great room, set her doctor's kit on the oak side table, pulled off her work shoes, and went to the kitchen. It was odd to find no supper ready when she came in from the clinic. She put her palm against the enamel front of the oven door. It was cold.

She found her sister Mazy in the back bedroom.

"Have you seen Armina?"

Mazy slowly lowered the book she was reading. "Um, no. . . . I helped her wash the breakfast dishes; then I guess I got lost in this." She waved the Elsie Dinsmore novel around before placing a crocheted marker between the pages. "I'd like to be an author like Martha Finley. How hard could it be to write a book?"

Disturbed from his nap, a small, short-haired terrier jumped from Mazy's lap and rushed to greet Lilly.

Lilly bent to ruffle the fur of Kip's head. "Did you have lunch with her?"

Mazy lowered her feet from the ottoman that matched the linen-covered chair she was sitting in, stretched, and stood. At the mirror over the dresser, she plumped her hair. "She was going berry picking. I didn't want to go. The sun causes freckles, you know."

"That's why we keep umbrellas in the stand by the front door. They're not just for rainy days."

Mazy frowned. "I'm not going to climb up some mountain carrying an umbrella like an old lady. I don't even like blackberries."

"Did you go to the Tippens' for the laundry?"

"Armina said she'd pick it up after she got back."

Lilly sighed. Why her mother had sent Mazy to help her this summer, instead of her more industrious twin sister, Molly, she'd never understand. She couldn't be aggravated with her sister for long, though. Mazy was really a sweet and thoughtful girl, if a tad bit lazy. "Would you go across the road and check on her?"

"Sure." Mazy twisted a spiral of her blonde locks around her finger. "I want to try some of that new solution I read about in *Woman's Home Companion*."

"And what would that do for you exactly?" Lilly asked.

"Straighten this mess!" Mazy picked up a hand mirror and turned her back on the dresser. She shook her head to watch the curls on the back of her head tremble, then slammed the looking glass down and threw herself across the bed. "I hate the way I look. I'll never get a fellow."

"You're seventeen. There's plenty of time for fellows."

"Almost eighteen," Mazy said, sticking her lower lip out in a pout. "You don't understand, Lilly. You're old already, and besides, you have Tern—if he was ever home, that is."

Her sister's statement gave Lilly pause. Did she look old at twenty-six? What a dreadful thought. She stole a look at the mirror, rearranging her hairpins. Maybe she could use a new updo.

Mazy left the bed and came up behind Lilly. She rested her chin on Lilly's shoulder and stared at their reflection. "What we need is a trip to the city. There's no fashion here in Skip Rock."

Lilly couldn't help but laugh. Mazy was right—there was no fashion sensibility in the coal camp. The women who lived here were more interested in survival. Lilly wore white shirtwaists and lightweight wool or linen skirts every day as befitted a physician. Instead of fashionable pumps, she laced on sturdy shoes. The last time she'd had a chance to dress up had been in early spring when she'd accompanied her husband to a charity affair in Washington, D.C. After the event, he'd taken her to the opera. The opera! Her dove-gray watered-silk gown had fit right in.

She slipped an arm around her sister. "A trip to Lexington

would be wonderful. We could shop, and I could visit some colleagues. Catch up on the latest."

Mazy squealed, jumping up and down. "You're the best sister in the world." She flipped through a stack of magazines. "I'll have to plan our wardrobe. We don't want to look like hoboes on the train."

Lilly took the magazines from her sister and put them back on the ottoman. "You have plenty of time. We can't even think of a trip until Ned gets back to take my place at the office."

"Oh yeah," Mazy said, scooping Kip into her arms. "Where is he exactly?"

"He's finishing nurse's training in Boston. Don't you remember Armina talking about it?"

"Alls I remember is how crabby she is. Good grief, if I were her husband, I'd never come back."

"Mazy Pelfrey! Bite your tongue."

Mazy giggled as Kip licked her chin. "Lilly, you sound just like Mama. You both would try the patience of a saint."

Gauzy white curtains danced in a quick breeze. Lilly lowered the window. "Looks like a storm is brewing. Be a good girl and run on over to Armina's for me. I'll fix a bite of supper."

Back at the dresser, Mazy dabbed carmine on her lips. "Just let me freshen up a bit."

Lilly might as well go herself. "Mazy, I don't think Mama would approve of your coloring your lips."

Mazy smacked her lips together. "What Mama don't

know . . . ," she sassed as she straightened her collar. "There. I'll be right back."

"Leave Kip here," Lilly said. "We don't need him running off if it storms."

Lilly went from window to window, closing them. She loved the simple geometry and horizontal lines of the prairie-style house Tern had built after they'd married. He'd modeled it after the designs of the famous architect Frank Lloyd Wright. At first, Lilly resisted a house so different from its neighbors. Especially after Tern confided he'd once witnessed Mr. Wright zipping around the streets of Chicago in his custom yellow raceabout, married mistress at his side. But Tern wore her down, going so far as to show Lilly two issues of *Ladies' Home Journal* featuring the architect's modern design and promising her that he'd not line the iniquitous Mr. Wright's pockets with any of their hard-earned money.

He'd kept his promise, although he'd fretted that the stained-glass windows he had specially made would have been much cheaper if purchased in Chicago. Lilly had requested that the long, low windows have sashes and the lower half be plain and fitted with screens. Now they were a delight to her. She loved how the air circulated through the house in warm weather and how the morning light shone through the leaded glass, casting beautiful patterns on the hardwood floors.

The house was built on the outskirts of town, putting her at some remove from the clinic. Tern didn't want people thinking they could just drop in anytime. Her husband was a wise man.

Armina and Ned lived in a cottage across the street—or road, as they called it here in Skip Rock. Ned was Lilly's distant cousin as well as her assistant. Although the practical nurses and nurse aides she'd hired for the clinic were competent, she missed Ned sorely. She hadn't been aware of how dependent she'd become on him until he left to finish his schooling and take his boards. When he came back, he'd have his degree as a registered nurse—a huge accomplishment considering his background.

In front of the open icebox, Lilly stared at an array of leftovers and mused about her first meeting with Ned three years before. She'd been the brand-spanking-new doctor fresh out of medical school and interning at the rugged coal camp dubbed Skip Rock. He'd assisted with her first surgery—patching up a young miner injured in a roof fall—and championed her through long-held superstitions about the bad luck caused by having a woman in the mines. She and Ned made a perfect switched-around team—she was doing what most considered a man's job, and he was becoming a nurse.

After slipping on an apron, she selected a ham butt and a bowl of potato salad and carried the food to the counter. Armina had left a colander full of cucumbers and one ripe red tomato in the deep sandstone sink. She must have worked in the garden before she went berry picking. Lilly held the tomato to her nose. It smelled of summer. She laid it on the wooden cutting board and reached for a knife. Juice spilled over the edge of the board with the first cut. A small salad of tomato and cucumber would be delicious with the ham and potatoes.

Lilly's stomach grumbled. She couldn't remember if she'd eaten lunch. It had been a busy day at the clinic. Along with other problems, Timmy Blair had a greenstick fracture of his radial bone and Mrs. Cooper's three-year-old had the measles. She'd had to quarantine the family—never a popular choice, but measles could spread like wildfire. She must remember to notify the health department, a job Ned usually took care of. No wonder she missed him.

What was keeping Mazy? Lilly leaned across the sink to look out the only window she hadn't closed. Heavy gray clouds draped over the roof of Armina's house like a giant bolster pillow, spitting raindrops instead of feathers. She watched heat lightning flash in the distance.

Kip tugged at her skirt tail. She cut him a bite of ham and put it in his bowl. His stumpy tail wagged in appreciation.

Lilly poured hot water into the sink, added a bit of Gold Dust dish powder, and washed the knife and cutting board. All the while she watched through the window for Mazy. Her sister was probably talking Armina's ear off. That was funny to think of because Armina wasn't given to chatter. She tolerated Mazy, though. Mazy charmed everyone.

Mama was concerned that Mazy didn't seem to have a sense of direction. Molly had known she wanted to be a teacher since the twins were four years old, but Mazy flitted from one interest to another like a butterfly in a garden of delight.

Although her mother hadn't said so in the letter she'd sent prior to Mazy's coming, Lilly suspected there was a fellow in the woodpile somewhere. She'd caught Mazy drawing hearts and arrows in the fog of her bathroom mirror. *T. M. + M. P.* She'd wiped the letters away with the curve of her hand when she saw Lilly watching.

"Is T. M. someone important?" Lilly had asked.

"Not anymore," Mazy had sighed.

Lilly dried her hands on the red-checked tea towel and twisted the black cap from the bottle of lotion she kept on the windowsill. It was hard to keep her hands soft when she washed them so many times a day, but she was determined. She'd seen too many doctors with cracked and bleeding knuckles. Besides, Tern liked a soft touch.

Just thinking of her husband made Lilly's heart skip a beat. She missed him dreadfully. It seemed he was away more than he was home, always boarding a train—off to another mine site or a directors' meeting, instigating inquiries into the safety practices in coal mines.

In the dining room, she set the table for three, tucked linen napkins under the heavy monogrammed silverware, and lit the candles. She liked a civilized dinner. As a girl, she'd often visited her aunt Alice in Lexington and admired the careful way her aunt laid a table. At her mother's house it was "grab a fork and find a seat." There'd be a dog begging at the door, babies sitting in laps, and strangers helping themselves to the pot of pinto beans and the skillet of corn bread ever ready on the wood-burning cookstove. Her mother tried to feed the world.

Kip whined at Lilly's feet and she had to laugh at herself. Her mother might have a dog begging at the door, but she had one begging at her feet. She supposed she was a mix of her mother's easy hospitality and her aunt Alice's social consciousness.

"One more bite," she said as Kip ran circles around her.

At the sink, she cut meat from the bone, making sure to include a bit of marbling. A little fat each day made Kip's fur shiny and kept him from getting dreadfully itchy hot spots. Armina gave him half a teaspoon of bacon grease every morning.

"Help!" she heard her sister's voice call through the open window. "Lilly, help!"

Lilly ran outside and crossed the road, wiping grease from the ham on the skirt of her apron.

Mazy was backing out of Armina's front door, dragging something with her.

"Mazy? What happened? What's wrong with Armina?"

CHAPTER 3

MAZY KNELT under the deadweight of Armina's body, letting Armina's head rest in her lap. "I don't know what happened. I called her name, but she didn't answer, so I sat down at the table and waited. Then I heard this awful gurgling sound. Armina was lying on the floor in the parlor by the sofa. I couldn't just leave her there, so I was bringing her with me." Mazy mopped her brow with her forearm. "Who'd have thought Armina is so heavy?"

"We need to get her inside," Lilly said, noting Armina's pale color and the pulse that beat faintly in the curve of her neck.

Like an answer to prayer, Turnip Tippen came up the

road, carrying a bundle of laundry. "Do you need some help? I was just bringing your washing by before the rain sets in," he said.

"Thank goodness you did. Help us get her into my house."

Turnip scooped Armina up. "She's light as air. What happened to her?"

Lilly pulled Armina's door closed and followed with the bundle of linen. "We don't know. Mazy just found her like this."

In the house, Turnip gently laid Armina on the sofa. "I saw her earlier today. I think she was going berry picking— probably got too much sun."

Lilly placed two fingers on Armina's wrist. "Fetch my stethoscope, Mazy, and wet a cloth to put on her forehead."

At the touch of the wet cloth, Armina stirred. Her eyelids fluttered open, and she tried to sit up.

"Looks like she's gonna be okay." Turnip turned up the collar of his jacket and put his hat back on as hard rain began to pound on the roof. "Me and Tillie's just down the road if you should need us tonight."

"Yes, thank you again, Mr. Tippen. Tell Tillie I'll pay her when I pick up the ironing tomorrow."

"Sure thing," he said. "You ladies take care."

"Well, if this ain't a pretty how-do-you-do," Armina sputtered. "Me laying stretched out like the dead in front of who knows who."

"Didn't you recognize Mr. Tippen, Armina?"

"Whether I recognize Turnip or not is beside the point.

I don't like people staring at me." She collapsed against the couch cushion. "I'm all swimmy-headed again."

"Mazy, bring me the honey," Lilly said.

Mazy brought the jar and a spoon. Lilly propped Armina up. "Take this," she said, bringing the honey to Armina's lips.

"Right out of the pot? I ain't a heathen. Least you could do is put it in some tea."

"I'll put on the kettle," Mazy said, hurrying from the room.

Lilly set the spoon back in the little earthenware container. She'd best go slowly with Armina. If she got angry, she'd clam up and Lilly would get no answers from her.

"Do you want to tell me how you were feeling before you fainted?" Lilly asked.

"Is that what I did? Huh. I got them black squiggles in my eyes. I sat down quick right on the floor in the front room. Next thing I knowed, Turnip Tippen was taking my measure."

"Did you have a headache? Were you short of breath?"

"Maybe a little. Seems like I was in a hurry to get somewheres. Probably I was rushing around too much."

Lilly nodded, letting Armina take her time. "Maybe it was the heat. Mazy and Mr. Tippen said you'd been berry picking."

"Turnip Tippen thinks he's the mayor of Skip Rock. He don't know nothing about my whereabouts."

"What did you do today? Mazy remembers washing the breakfast dishes with you." Lilly wasn't about to mention berry picking a second time. She didn't want to set Armina off again.

"That girl," Armina said. "She tries but she can't do nothing but dry. She can't seem to get the egg off the forks. I would say something, but I don't want to discourage her from learning."

A sense of unease captured Lilly. Armina was talking around the subject because she couldn't recall most of the day. Perhaps she'd suffered a mild stroke. "Take my hands and I'll help you sit up."

With Armina's hands in hers, Lilly tested her grip. She noted a minute tremor, subtle as a gentle rain, in the left. "May I look at your eyes?"

Lilly moved one finger side to side and up and down. Armina tracked perfectly, and her pupils were normal. "One more thing—I'll need you to sit in a straight chair for this, okay?"

Armina grunted dismissively, but she walked to the library table and sat down on a rush-bottomed chair as Lilly watched. There seemed to be just the slightest stiffness in her gait. "You gonna hammer me like you do them folks comes by the clinic?"

Using a small rubber hammer, Lilly tested her friend's reflexes—normal on the right with some weakness on the left. Armina had always been a puzzle. When Lilly first met her, she'd been fractious as a feral cat. At the tender age of seventeen, she was living up the mountain past Swampy

Creek seeing to the needs of her medically fragile aunt and her sister's two abandoned children.

Lilly knew well the snare of being a caregiver; that's why she was a doctor practicing in a coal camp when she could be working in a research lab as she'd intended to do with her medical degree. The study of disease, its causes and cures, was her first love, but duty had called, and she came to Skip Rock and then couldn't leave. Maybe someday she and Tern could live elsewhere. For now, she felt she was where the Lord wanted her to be.

It was surprising to Lilly when Ned Tippen and Armina fell in love and married. Maybe it shouldn't have been, for Ned was as patient and kind as anyone could be. And he was smitten with Armina from the moment he first saw her. Nobody had ever given much thought to Armina's needs until Ned. He was determined to make her life easier. And he had, but still Armina could be cantankerous if rubbed the wrong way. She was like an ornery old lady in a young woman's body. Lilly couldn't imagine how she'd be at eighty.

"You have a nasty scratch on your face, Armina."

"Huh." Armina raised her hand to the wound. "I wondered what was stinging me."

Lilly caught her fingers before she could touch the scrape. "Best leave it alone. It's already scabbing."

"That's a good sign, right? It means your blood's good if it scabs quick?"

"Yes, that's generally a good thing, but right now it's more important to determine what caused the injury." Lilly stood back, examining her patient with her eyes—always a physician's best tools. Armina had recovered her senses without the use of honey. So she could probably rule out the dreadful diabetes.

"Have you been ill at all that you can remember? Even the slightest bit? It could be important."

Armina opened her mouth to speak but then closed it. She repeated the motion a couple of times before she answered, like she was giving up state secrets. "Back in the spring, when I was at my sister's, I got the quinsy, but that's weeks ago. I don't have a bit of sore throat anymore." She elongated her neck and swallowed as if proving her point.

"Hmm," Lilly said, pondering Armina as Armina had pondered the question.

Mazy brought a tray laden with cups of tea and ham sandwiches cut in small squares. She'd trimmed the crusts from the bread and arranged slices of cucumbers on a saucer. "I thought we could eat in here," she said, setting the tray on the library table.

"This is perfect," Lilly said.

Armina nibbled the edge of her sandwich. "Where's the crust? It seems wasteful to throw them away."

"Oh, I saved them," Mazy said, beaming with satisfaction. "Tomorrow I'll toast croutons and make a salad for lunch. I love to cook. I might be a chef one day."

Lilly exchanged a look of amusement with Armina. As far as she knew, Mazy hadn't touched the stove since she'd been here.

She brought two more chairs to the table and they ate in companionable silence, listening to the rain, while Kip played musical chairs, begging at each knee in turn.

"Mr. Still ain't gonna appreciate how you're spoiling this dog," Armina said, pinching a piece of bread from the corner of her sandwich and offering it to Kip.

Lilly pushed back her chair and patted her lap. Kip jumped up, right at home. "I know," she said. "Tern thinks dogs belong outdoors, but Kip's my weakness. Tern will have to adjust." She rubbed the sweet spot between Kip's ears with her knuckles. "Isn't that right, Kippy?"

Kip licked Lilly's chin in agreement. Lilly turned her face away and laughed. "Give a dog an inch . . ."

A roll of thunder muffled the sound of Armina's teacup shattering against the floor. Armina slapped the top of the table with an open hand in jerky, irregular movement. The muscles of her face contorted ridiculously as if she were making mouths at somebody.

Mazy shot up from the table, her eyes wide with fear. Her chair tipped over. The back bounced once, then settled. Kip whined and leaped from Lilly's lap, beating a path to the couch, where he disappeared under the skirt.

Lilly steadied Armina. "Mazy, help me lower her before she falls."

Once Armina was on the floor, Mazy went for pillows and blankets, which Lilly used to cocoon Armina.

"I know what she has," Mazy said. "I read about this in one of your medical books. It's called epilogue—or something like that. We should stick a spoon in her mouth so she doesn't swallow her tongue."

"A spoon?" Armina said. "Make sure it's a silver spoon." She giggled, then began to sing: "'By the light of the silvery moon, we're gonna spoon. With my baby, I'll . . .'"

"Armina doesn't sing, Lilly, not even in church. I think she's gone stark, raving mad."

Lilly held a finger to her lips to hush her sister. "Mazy, don't be so dramatic. It's nothing of the sort." She laid the back of her hand against Armina's fevered brow. "You'll be fine, Armina." How many times had she said that very thing to other patients while praying it was so? Now she sent that silent prayer upward again.

Motioning for Mazy to follow, Lilly led her sister to the foyer closet and took a rain slicker from a wooden hanger. "I need you to go to the clinic and get one of the nurses. Have her bring a bottle of salicylic acid." She tied a scarf firmly under Mazy's chin.

"Acid?" Mazy said, narrowing her eyes seriously.

"Sorry, I'm being obtuse. Have her bring a bottle of aspirin and some alcohol."

Mazy buttoned the jacket up to her throat and opened the door. Wind and rain whipped around her. "This is so exciting, Lilly. This is like something Elsie would do."

"Elsie?"

"From the book—Elsie Dinsmore. Her life is *so* interesting," she said, unfurling an umbrella against the storm.

"Go straight there, Mazy, and don't tarry."

CHAPTER 4

FINALLY HER HOUSE was at rest. Lilly rubbed tired eyes as she went for one last check on Armina.

The night nurse, Hannah, sat under a dim light. Her fingers worked a skein of blue yarn with two needles. "She's resting well, Dr. Still," she whispered. "The aspirin and the alcohol bath did the trick."

"Temp?"

"It was 99.6 fifteen minutes ago."

"Very good. I'm going to catch some sleep, then."

Hannah laid her knitting aside and followed Lilly to the bedroom door. "So what's wrong with her, Doctor?"

"There's a history of severe sore throat—now with the

fever and the odd movements, I suspect Saint Vitus' dance brought on by untreated rheumatic fever."

"Oh, poor thing." The nurse shook her head sympathetically. "So we're in for the long haul."

"I'll go over her treatment plan more thoroughly in the morning, Hannah." Lilly covered her mouth against a yawn. "You know she must be kept quiet to avoid agitation."

"Yes, ma'am, Dr. Still. My sister had the very same thing. I'll take good care."

Lilly's head had barely dented the pillow before Kip started whining. "Lie down, Kip. You've had your walk already."

Kip moved to the end of the bed. Taking a guarding stance with ears alert and tail straight out, he growled low in his throat.

Lilly sighed as her feet sought her bedroom slippers. "I give up," she said, tightening the sash of her robe. "This had better be important."

At the front door she fished a dog lead from the four-gallon crock that held Kip's things: leashes, brush, worn towels for feet wiping, and such. She kept a carbide lantern sitting on a shelf there as well, and now she switched it on.

Kip's little body trembled in anticipation, and he cast a hurry-up look over his shoulder at her. She fastened the lead to a ring on his collar even though the bad weather had passed. Despite Tern's opinion, the dog was well-behaved and would not stray far from her unless it was storming. Thunder and lightning released something primal in the animal, as if he were in charge of chasing the tempest away.

Now it was she giving hurry-up looks as Kip strained against the lead, wanting to cross the road instead of using his favorite spot under the lilac bush. Lilly released the lead—maybe he needed a bit of privacy. As soon as he was free, Kip shot across the road to Armina's house, traversing two mud puddles on the way. He pushed his nose against the front door, his whole body wagging. When she caught up with him, he rewarded her with a shake of dirty water.

Lilly positioned the light from the lantern on the doorknob. What could be in the house that had Kip in such a state?

There was only one way to find out. She turned the knob.

The door creaked open. The inside of the house was pitch-dark and smelled faintly of spoiled milk. Lilly trained the light on Kip. Along the ridge of his backbone, a line of fur stood stiff as the bristles on a boar's-hair brush. He whined again, urgently this time.

Then Lilly heard it—the weak, almost-ineffectual cry of an infant. Lilly could hardly believe her ears. How very strange. "Good boy, Kip."

Armina's house was small—just the living room with a kitchen to one side and a bedroom in back. Kip led Lilly to the bedroom.

She found the baby lying in a basket made of rush that sat in the middle of Armina's perfectly made bed. Beside the basket she saw a stack of folded diapers and a tin of Cashmere Bouquet talc.

Kip jumped up on the bed and peered into the basket.

"Are you this baby's mother?" Lilly asked as she scooted him aside and unfastened the diaper pin. A cloud of talc wafted her way. A girl, clean and dry—Armina must have changed her before her own befuddling incident occurred. Lilly would have much preferred to find a wet nappy. Dehydration was a killer of infants.

"Sh, sh," she crooned as she wrapped the baby again and gathered her up. The little girl lay limply in her arms as she rushed to the kitchen and pulled the string to the bare overhead bulb. She laid the baby on the table and opened the blanket around her, taking in the child's sloping fore-head, the flat nose and low-set ears. The baby barely gripped Lilly's finger when she stroked her tiny palm. "Poor dear little thing."

Leaving the baby where she lay, Lilly went to Armina's pantry and got a can of condensed milk. At the sink she filled the teakettle. Thankfully, Armina was not one to let her stove grow cold. Lilly lifted a stove lid with a prong, shoved a chunk of hickory down the eye, and set the kettle to boil.

Kip pawed something on the floor. Keeping his nose low to the ground and his rump in the air, he watched as a bottle spun in circles toward Lilly's feet. He barked expectantly—like he'd found something necessary.

"My word, Kip, it's a baby bottle. The baby's bottle. What's it doing on the floor? But then why wouldn't a bottle full of curdled milk be on Armina's kitchen floor?"

Kip cocked his head as if giving thought to Lilly's question.

"After all," Lilly said as she popped the rubber nipple from the bottle and poured its contents into the slop bucket kept under the curtained sink, "we've just found a baby on her bed. It all makes a strange kind of sense."

The baby whimpered from her nest on the table as Lilly washed the bottle and nipple. The teakettle roiled. She poured a cup of the water and set it aside to cool, then sterilized the bottle, the nipple, a mason jar, and a zinc lid. While she waited, she dropped a tea ball into a white mug and fixed herself a strong cup of tea. She needed it. This night might never end.

After her tea had steeped, she punched a hole in the top of the tin of milk. She stirred a spoonful of the creamy liquid into the cup of water and mixed the baby's formula. Upending the can, she let the rest of the milk drip slowly into the canning jar.

A cushioned kitchen chair comforted Lilly as she sat holding the baby in her arms. She teased the baby's lips with the nipple, but she would not suck. A stream of milk leaked from the corner of her mouth and dribbled onto her gown. Tiny embroidered yellow ducks paddled across the front of the long white sleeper. "Somebody loves you," Lilly crooned. "Somebody loves you to have dressed you in a gown so fine."

The baby looked at Lilly through weary, fading eyes. Lilly had seen those deathbed eyes before but never on one so young. "Don't give up," she said, giving the baby a gentle shake. "Don't you give up on me."

Babies were not Lilly's specialty. Oh, she could turn a breech or wield a set of forceps with the best of them, but once babies were delivered, the mother or a midwife was the expert. Lilly much preferred a full-blown heart attack or a compound fracture to the ills of the newborn. If only her own mother were here. She would know exactly what to do. As the only baby catcher on Troublesome Creek, Mama had probably delivered a thousand infants by now. She would be a great help when Lilly had children of her own.

Lilly pinched the baby's cheeks to make a seal around the nipple. Milk gushed out her nose, and in mere seconds her pale face turned a dusky leaden color. Upending the infant, Lilly let the milk drain, mopping it up with a tea towel.

With one finger she examined the roof of the baby's mouth and found the hidden cleft that allowed communication between the cavity of the nose and mouth.

"Two strikes," she said as the baby made a snuffling sound and the color returned to her face. "Let's pray there's not a third."

Lilly bundled the baby, the bottle, and the remainder of the condensed milk, then said, "Come on" to Kip.

The dog stuck close as they walked down the road to the clinic, using the lantern for light until they came closer to town, where the sidewalk was lit by gas lamps. The door was locked and her key was in the bag left at home. She rapped sharply on the door.

"Dr. Still?" Anne, the other night nurse, said as she opened up. "What have you got there?"

"A very hungry baby," Lilly said. "I'm guessing she's two weeks old."

Anne took the baby into her ample arms. "She's scrawny for two weeks, Doctor. She should be gaining weight."

"Yes, but she has a cleft palate. Obviously she's been getting some nourishment but not enough to thrive."

"Dear, dear," Anne said, her forehead knitting in a frown of worry.

"I've brought her formula, but don't attempt a feeding. I'm going to get a length of India-rubber tubing. I'll be right back."

Lilly stood in the walk-in supply closet and perused the stacks. She saw skeins of gauze, rolls of tape, dozens of thermometers, brown-paper packages of sterilized linens and autoclaved instruments, but no tubing. Her ire rose as she rummaged around. A body could never find anything when she needed it.

"Top shelf, right-hand corner," Anne said behind her. "You'll find a tube just there—a little to your left. There you go."

"Thank you, Anne," Lilly said, more than a little discomfited. A nurse could put you in your place quicker than anybody. *I should have asked,* she thought as she cut the tubing to size and inserted it into the opening she'd widened in the nipple. "Pray this will work," she said.

Anne settled into a rocking chair and held the baby in a sitting position. "Let's give her a try."

Fifteen minutes later, the baby had gotten no more than a tablespoon of liquid from the slapped-together feeding system. "This takes much too long. She'll starve to death with the bottle in her mouth," Anne said, raising the baby to her shoulder for a burp.

"What we need is a wet nurse. The human breast makes the best seal."

"Well, why didn't you say so?" Anne said. "My Amy's nearly two, but she ain't weaned yet. Likes her ninny, she does."

"Would you be willing?"

"Of course," Anne said, settling deeper into the chair and unbuttoning her blouse. "Little thing needs all the loving she can get."

Lilly closed the window blind and draped a blanket over Anne's shoulders. The bit of milk the baby had received from the bottle had piqued her interest. Finally she began to feed.

Anne patted the baby's bottom as she rocked and nursed. "Mongoloid, ain't she?"

"Yes, I'm afraid so."

"Mongoloid and harelip. Don't seem fair."

"Cleft palate—not cleft lip. You can't see it from the outside, which is why I nearly choked her to death." Lilly stirred honey into the mugs of tea she'd made for herself and for Anne. "You'll need extra fluids if you're nursing two," she said, taking a seat close by.

"Where's her mother anyway?" Anne's face fell. "No! Don't tell me. She's dead—ain't she?"

"I'm going to trust your discretion, Anne. I want nothing repeated."

Anne crossed her heart right over the baby's head. "I

took the Nightingale Pledge, Dr. Still. I never talk about my patients, though I admit it's hard sometimes."

Lilly leaned forward. "It seems Armina found her this morning, but now she's sick herself."

"Is that why your sister came for Hannah?"

"Yes, but they don't know about the baby. I expect someone will show up asking about her. After all, someone is missing her daughter."

"What's your gut saying, Doc?"

"I think something has happened, something terrible enough to cause Armina's system to go into shock."

"Must be bad. Armina's tough as a pine knot." Anne took a drink before setting the mug down to shift the baby from one side to the other. "What do you aim to do?"

Lilly rubbed her eyes with the tips of her fingers. "I'll talk to the sheriff, of course—"

"Chanis Clay! Ha, he's still wet behind the ears. He won't have a clue."

"Probably not," Lilly said, leaning forward in her chair, "but since his father was killed, he's all the law we have. I don't think it would be right for me not to say anything to him. What if a crime has been committed?"

"I get your point. Meanwhile, why don't I take this little gal home with me? Amy won't mind to share, and we can trust my husband. He don't talk to anybody. The most you can get out of him is a grunt."

"You're an angel, Anne. Let me run home to get dressed and check on Armina; then I'll come back and man the clinic until the day-shift nurse arrives. You'll have to take some time off, but I'll see that you get your full salary."

"Good thing it's a quiet night. We only got the two patients in-house. Guy in bed two is going home in the a.m. You already wrote his discharge."

"Gracious, I didn't even ask about the others."

"The others are my department, Doctor. I'd of told you if they was in need."

Lilly picked up the lantern. She nudged Kip from his slumber by the door. "Thank you, Anne. I'll be back shortly."

CHAPTER 5

LILLY HAD BARELY FINISHED breakfast when she heard knocking at the back door. She wiped the corners of her mouth, folded her napkin, and pushed her chair back.

A workman in striped coveralls stood on the kitchen stoop, holding a rectangular wooden box under one beefy arm. Kip, fresh from his solo morning walk, sniffed at the man's shoes.

"Where you want this thing, missus?" the workman asked.

With all the turmoil of the day before, it had slipped Lilly's mind that she and Tern had ordered the installation of a calling system. "I'm sorry. I have a patient here. We'll have to arrange another time."

"A telephone? We're getting a telephone?" Mazy said from behind her. "Don't make him go away, Lilly. This thing could change my life."

"Just pick a place, little lady," the man said, looking at Lilly. "The mister done paid for it."

Lilly extended her hand. "I'm Dr. Still—and you are?"

"Jim Jones, at your service. Sorry; didn't mean to be rude." He leaned the device against the doorjamb and doffed his cap before taking Lilly's hand. "I didn't realize this was the doctor's house. The work order just says Still."

"That's quite all right, Mr. Jones, but I have a patient who can't be disturbed." Lilly pulled a watch fob from the pocket of her skirt and checked the time. "Would it be inconvenient for you to come back this afternoon? Say around two?"

"No, ma'am, no inconvenience at all. I've one to install at the clinic and one at the mine office. I'll just switch the times around."

"Thank you," Lilly said, moving to close the door, but the man stayed on the stoop turning his cap around and around in his hands. "Is there something else, Mr. Jones?"

"Well, seeing as you're a doctor and all . . . would you mind to take a look at this?" He turned his right hand over, palm up.

Lilly saw a raw, reddened wound in the flesh at the base of his thumb. "Splinter?"

"Yeah, from a pole. I tried to get it out with a needle, but no luck."

"Did you sterilize the needle?"

"Yes, ma'am, I dipped it in a bottle of 80 proof."

Lilly took a magnifying glass from a box of supplies she kept in a drawer of a kitchen cabinet. "It's fairly deep, Mr. Jones. Let's try an old-fashioned remedy."

"I'm game," he said.

Lilly doused the area with iodine, laid a square of fatback over the wound, bound it with brown paper, then secured it all with a looping figure-eight bandage.

"You'll need to wear gloves," she said.

"Got them in my pocket," he said while examining the dressing. "This reminds me of something my grandma would do."

"Sometimes old ways are the best ways. You might have to reapply this tonight. It might not stay put while you're working."

"Good thing I'm left-handed," he said as he slid a glove on. "I appreciate it, Doc."

"Come by the office tomorrow," Lilly said. "I'll want to check for infection."

Mazy closed the door behind the man, then leaned on the drain board as Lilly washed her hands at the kitchen sink. "I'm so excited I can't stand it. I'm going to call up everyone I know."

"Who do you know with a telephone?" Lilly asked while drying her hands. "Someone has to be on the other end of the line."

Mazy's face fell. "I never thought of that. So then why are we getting one if I don't get to use it?"

Lilly put the box of supplies back inside the cabinet drawer. "It's for business, Mazy. It's so I can have contact from home to the clinic and so Tern can stay in touch when he's away."

"What else is in here?" Mazy said, opening the wide upper cabinet door and pulling the flour bin down. It was clean as a whistle. "You know, Lilly, most women keep flour and spices and stuff in their Hoosier cabinet, not iodine and gauze."

Lilly laughed. "Not much of a housewife, am I?"

Mazy gave her an appraising look. "No, but I like the way you are, Sister. Anybody can put flour in a bin, but not just anyone can do what you do."

"I can do what I do more easily because Armina cooks and cleans for us and because Mrs. Tippen does our laundry. One job is not more or less important than the other."

"You sound just like Mama," Mazy said, turning away. "Always a sermon."

Lilly let the comment go. Maybe she did sound like Mama. "I have a job for you this morning. I need you to tidy up Armina's house, air out the rooms, and put fresh linens on the bed. Will you do that?"

"Sure, I don't mind. Does that mean she's well, then, if she's going home and all?"

"No, not yet, I'm afraid, but Hannah will stay there with her. I think she'll do better in her own surroundings, and it's much too hectic here."

"Poor Hannah. I wouldn't like her job, all that bathing and bedpanning."

"I appreciate that you helped her with Armina's care this morning so I could get a bit of sleep."

Mazy wrapped a length of hair around her finger. "Yeah, I helped, but then I got to leave. Hannah's like a prisoner or something."

"I'm sure she doesn't feel that way. She's very good at bedside care, and that's how she supports herself."

"How did she learn all that stuff?"

"She went to the Women's Institute for her training, as did the other nurses. The hospital board members provided scholarships."

Mazy cocked her head and pursed her lips. "So Ned couldn't go there because he's a guy? That doesn't seem fair."

"Ned's training is more exact than that offered at the institute. Besides, I don't know that a man has ever sought schooling there."

"I think I'll just marry rich," Mazy said.

"Would that be before or after you become a chef and write a bestselling novel?" Lilly teased.

"Depends on when he comes along," Mazy said, flashing a devilish smile before skipping to the door. "Let's go, Kip. We've work to do."

"Mazy," Lilly called after her sister.

"Yes?" Mazy said through the screen door.

"You'll find a basket and some folded linens on Armina's bed; just set them on the kitchen table."

Mazy saluted sharply. "Aye, aye, cap'n."

Kip ran circles around Mazy. Lilly smiled and watched

them go. Mazy could entertain, but could she pull her weight? That remained to be seen.

The wheeled invalid chair bumped across the graveled road. Armina was weak and mentally logy but compliant. Mazy met them at the door and helped Lilly and the nurse lift the chair over the stoop and into the kitchen.

"Thank ye for bringing me home," Armina said, trying to lift herself from the chair, her arms about as useful as wet noodles. "La, I don't know what's come over me. I've got so much that needs doing."

Lilly knelt down, face-to-face with her friend. "Armina, you've been ill. That sore throat you thought you got over has weakened your system. You need lots of rest. Hannah will stay with you for a few days." She patted Armina's hand. "Understand?"

"I ain't a child who needs telling what to do," Armina said with a flare of temper that seemed to clear her mind. "I'll just set here a spell and then I'll be good as a coon in a holler log." She shooed them with one hand. "You all can go on now."

What Armina didn't know, and was not ready to hear, was that the possible upshot of her illness was heart damage and even total mental collapse. "Armina," Lilly said, putting words to what she thought was necessary, "would it be better if Ned were here? I can call for him to come home."

Armina's face clouded. "No, you'll not disturb his studies. He's nearly done." She grabbed Lilly's hand fiercely. "Promise me."

Fine tremors passed from Armina's hand to Lilly's own. Another storm was coming. Lilly motioned for the nurse, and between them, they managed to transfer Armina to her bed.

"Will you let Hannah and me take care of you, then, Armina? So I won't have to call Ned?"

Armina could barely nod before the convulsions commenced, her arms shooting out like lightning strikes. The nurse dodged but not quickly enough to prevent a fist to her jaw. She captured her patient's flailing limbs. "It's okay," she said. "I've got her."

The storm blew over fast, leaving Armina spent and helpless on the bed.

Lilly took a canvas supply tote from the handle of the wheeled chair. She padded Armina's limbs with cotton wool, leaving long strips for Hannah to tie to the bedframe the next time Armina was violent.

"Watch for the little tremors and then act quickly," Lilly said. "You're protecting her as well as yourself."

"I understand," Hannah said. "I've had to do this before with other patients."

"I don't want to dope her, but I'll give her some laudanum tonight. You'll both need to sleep."

CHAPTER 6

IT WAS NEARLY DARK before Lilly finished her charts, capped her fountain pen, and set the bottle of navy-blue ink in the inkwell of her desk at the clinic. Moving Armina and all that entailed had given a late start to her workday. Careful as they were, the stress of the move had caused Armina to have more of the jerky irregular movements and mild mania that marked Saint Vitus' dance. Who would have suspected that Armina knew the words to so many silly songs? "She'll Be Coming Round the Mountain" still rang in Lilly's head.

When Lilly once again mentioned notifying Ned, Armina had leaped out of bed, threatening to run into the woods if Lilly did any such thing. She wouldn't hear of it.

Now Lilly was between the proverbial rock and hard

place. She stood up from her desk and stretched. Her back popped and her neck released its knot. Ned was not going to be happy if this was kept from him. What was Lilly to do? Armina was her patient and Armina had rights. . . .

She'd let it play out for a couple of days—if Armina didn't worsen.

Taking a ring of keys from the desk drawer, Lilly selected the one needed to lock up. The clinic was empty tonight. Her patients had been discharged. She tapped the key against her chin. What was she forgetting?

Oh, forevermore, her hat! She laid the keys back on the desk, retrieved her hat from the hat rack, and stepped into the private lavatory off her office, another thoughtful gift from Tern. She was probably the only coal camp doctor anywhere to have her own bathroom.

She hung her stethoscope on the towel rack and then, despite herself, removed her hairpins and combs. Her dark hair cascaded in waves nearly to her waist. She looked closely into the mirror over the washstand, making sure there was still only the one streak of platinum in her locks—the one she'd been born with, the one that started at her widow's peak and ran like a vein of mercury to the very tips of her hair. Tern loved that oddity, and admittedly so did she.

"Well, Dr. Still," she chided her reflection, "it seems you have an unsightly streak of vanity to go along with the streak in your hair."

Lilly had been particular with herself and her things since she was a girl, the need for perfection as tenacious as a weed growing in a garden of daisies. She longed to be more like her mother, whose natural beauty had not faded with time because it came from within, or like Armina, who didn't even own a mirror.

Turning away from her reflection, she secured her hair in a familiar chignon but looked back as she stuck a long jet-beaded pin through her hat. She just couldn't bring herself to go out into the world with a cockeyed hat on her head.

A verse from Philippians memorized in her Sunday school days came to mind. *"Let nothing be done through strife or vainglory; but in lowliness of mind let each esteem other better than themselves."* Or as Mama would say, *"Pretty is as pretty does."*

Lilly knew she wasn't guilty of thinking she was better than anyone else, but vanity—caring too much about appearances—was definitely a weakness she needed to work on.

Still, she couldn't leave the bathroom without first straightening the wire soap dish on the counter and adjusting the cotton towel on the rack so that all its corners were even. Lastly, she draped her stethoscope around her neck. There, everything was in order. Her mind was filing a list of things still needing to be done as she stepped back into the office.

She was startled to find a man standing at the window, staring out into the darkening night. He wore a blue shirt tucked in on one side and rumpled suit pants.

"Excuse me?" she said. "This office is closed."

The man turned slowly toward her. "The door was unlocked." He tipped his brown felt fedora but did not take it off. "Is the doctor in?"

Lilly suppressed a sigh. She should take to wearing a sign around her neck. Obviously her stethoscope was not marker enough. "She is."

Sweat beaded just below the band of his hat. His set lips were a slash of pain, the skin around them white. "I figured to see a man," he said.

"On the one hand, you've got me," Lilly said. "On the other, I'm all there is."

He swayed on his feet and steadied himself against the desktop. "If you don't mind."

"One moment," Lilly said, going past him to open the door wide. Just yards away, the street was busy with folks coming and going. The commissary was within yelling distance. She didn't feel unsafe, just cautious.

"What seems to be the problem?" she asked.

Standing where he was, the man began to inch his stained chambray shirt upward, not bothering with the buttons. He grimaced as he ripped the bloodstained fabric from his side, revealing two distinct wounds in his right upper quadrant.

"Take a seat." Lilly patted the end of an exam table.

"I can stand."

"A seat," Lilly directed, as much to take command of the situation as to make the exam easier for herself. She was glad she had just washed her hands. She would rather not turn her back on this patient.

"Doc Still?" she heard from the doorway. "I saw your door standing open and came to check on you." Timmy Blair looked in from the small back porch.

"How's your arm, Timmy?"

The boy lifted the sling that cupped his fractured limb. "I was a-wondering, Doc: will I ever play ball again?"

"You'll be back at bat and good as ever in a few weeks."

"Maybe could I go in the front room and play with the forewarning bird? Mommy's shopping in the commissary. It'll take forever."

Lilly kept the canary she'd once rescued from the mines in the clinic's waiting room. It served to entertain her patients while they waited.

"You may, Timmy, but don't forget to put the cloth back over the cage when you finish. Tweety was already covered for the night."

Timmy sauntered through the office, his sharp brown eyes taking everything in. "You need to take your hat off," he said to the man.

"Timothy," Lilly warned.

"But my teacher says a gentleman don't wear a hat indoors. He's being disrespectful."

Pain flashed across the man's face when he raised his arm and removed the brown felt fedora. His hair uncoiled like a snake, spilling a long blond braid halfway down his back.

"Wow," Timmy said. "I never seen a man with braids before. Are you an Indian? But no, then you wouldn't have yellow hair, would you?"

Lilly could almost see the gears turning in Timmy's brain. Maybe the boy would elicit some history from the stranger.

"I know! I know!" He waved his arm as if he were the only

student in school who had the correct answer. "You're like that girl that was kidnapped by the Indians—Daniel Boone's daughter." A satisfied look played across Timmy's freckled face. "Do you live in a tepee?"

"Timmy," Lilly said, "Daniel Boone was a long time ago. Now either go play with Tweety or go find your mother."

"Sorry," the boy said. "I was curious is all. Can I give Tweety a bedtime snack?"

With a flip of her wrist, Lilly waved Timmy away.

The boy hopped on one foot down the hallway that led to the waiting room. "I'm a champion at hopscotch."

"Lie back," Lilly said as she prepared to examine the stranger's gaping wounds. "I want to see how deep these are."

"I think I stuck my gut," the man said.

"More likely your liver. How did this happen?"

The man's hands tightened on the edges of the table as Lilly probed the first puncture. "Cleaning a fish—" he grunted in pain—"and knife slipped."

"Twice?"

"I'm clumsy. Sue me."

Lilly ignored his condescending manner. Pain brought out the worst in people. "Your wounds are clean—no sign of infection. Your ribs probably deflected the blows. Have you had any trouble breathing?"

"No—just weak as a sore-eyed cat." He let out a small groan. "Can you sew me up?"

"These need to heal from the inside out," Lilly said while packing sterile gauze soaked in hydrate of chloral into the sites. "We'll need to change this twice a day for a week or so. Come by during office hours and one of the nurses will take care of it."

"I ain't likely to get the gangrene, then?"

"No, I wouldn't think so."

The hard lines of the man's face clinched as he sat up and slid off the end of the table. "What do I owe you?"

"You can pay when your plan of care is complete."

He straightened his shirt and flung a gold piece onto the desktop. "I thank you kindly, ma'am." With that he was out the door.

Lilly watched his fading back. She wondered about his story and about what brought him to this particular place. Was he a stranger just passing through or a transient looking for a few days' work in the coal mines around Skip Rock? In any case, she would bet he wouldn't return for wound care.

She put a vial of laudanum in her bag, switched off the light, stepped out the door, and turned the key in the lock. It was getting late. She'd have to wait until morning to check on the baby. Armina needed her attention now.

As she walked toward home, her mind whirled with thoughts of the day, especially the stranger. Lilly did not for one minute believe his story. Most likely he'd been in a bar brawl—fighting over a card game gone wrong or over a woman done wrong. Why wait so long for treatment, though? The wounds were not fresh. And why the stealth? Unless he'd killed someone—and she thought she would have heard if that were so. Gossip and rumors swirled around the coal camp like dead leaves in a dust devil.

Besides that, Chanis Clay, the sheriff, kept her abreast of shootings, stabbings, and family feuds. He knew she might see the results of mayhem before he did. The folks who lived up the hollers of the high mountains were secretive and clannish—not given to call in the government and not given to calling on doctors unless there was no other option. Like the stranger whose fear of gangrene flushed him out.

He'd probably be all right, though. His rib cage had deflected the one stab that might have killed him, and she'd treated him the best she could with chloral hydrate to prevent tetanus. It was not a sure cure—nothing was against lockjaw. But he'd bled freely, and that was the best preventative. It amazed her how God had provided the body with healing properties. A person almost had to go out of his way to circumvent them.

Lilly was halfway home when she remembered Timmy. Good grief, she'd locked the boy in the clinic! Key in hand, she hurried back. What was happening to her mind?

There was Mrs. Blair standing under the porch light and there was Timmy looking out the window beside the door.

"Mrs. Blair," Lilly said, twisting the key in the hole. "I am so sorry. I didn't mean to lock Timmy up."

Mrs. Blair laughed. "His daddy says lockup might be in that boy's future—might as well get him used to it."

Timmy sidled out. "You ain't mad, are you, Mommy? I was figuring to spend the night."

"But why, Timmy? I told you to wait on the commissary porch. I've spent half an hour looking for you."

Timmy hitched up his pants. "I was figuring to protect Doc Still from bad guys. Me and Tweety had settled in for the night."

With a sigh, Mrs. Blair ruffled her son's hair. "You and your imagination. What am I going to do with you?"

"It's my fault, Mrs. Blair. I don't know what's happened to my mind lately. I can't remember anything. I found some papers I needed in the icebox the other day."

Mrs. Blair gave Lilly an appraising look. "Go ahead, Timmy. Your father's waiting in the buggy."

Timmy hugged his mother around the waist. "I ain't getting a whipping, am I?"

"No, your daddy's not mad. He was once a boy. Now go on." Once Timmy had run off, Mrs. Blair said, "I don't know why that boy's talking about a whipping. He's never had more than a swat on his backside."

"He's a good boy," Lilly said. "It's obvious he's well raised."

"You're looking a little peaked, Doc. Are you all right?"

Lilly smiled; she knew where Timmy got his curiosity. "Just tired, Mrs. Blair. It's been a long day."

"You're not in the family way, are you? That would explain why you're forgetful and why you look peaked. My husband says I lose my mind every time I have a baby. Last time he said I never got it back. Ha."

"I'll be right as rain after a good night's sleep."

"All right then. Why don't you let us run you home in the buggy?"

"Thank you, but I enjoy the walk—clears my head."

Timmy waved when the buggy rattled past, headed for the Blairs' farm outside of town. Lilly waved back. Timmy's family was one of Lilly's favorites. Mrs. Blair had two older children, Timmy and his sister, and now two little ones. Lilly had delivered both the last babies.

Hidden under her loose-fitting jacket, Lilly rested her hand on her stomach. The ladies of Skip Rock had been speculating about a pregnancy since the day after her wedding. It might be a harmless pastime, but Lilly found it irritating. It was as if one would score a point if she guessed correctly before anyone else.

Just this morning, Lilly had checked her reflection from the side in the full-length cheval mirror in her bedroom. She looked like she'd gained a few pounds, but she hoped it wasn't obvious. She was almost twelve weeks. So sure her baby was a boy, she whispered his name against her fear, as if the naming would somehow anchor him and keep him safe.

She hoped against hope to share her news with Tern before anyone else voiced it. The fear of loss had kept her from telling him the last time he was home—that was selfish on her part.

Longing for Tern washed over Lilly. She needed him here. Who would have guessed she would marry a man who was busier than she was as a doctor? Before Tern had walked back into her life, she'd intended to marry another man—a fellow from medical school. Paul lived in Boston, where they'd planned to practice together. It had bothered Lilly greatly to break her engagement to him, but love won out—as love will do. Paul had been good about it. And after a time, he became a friend and colleague who was never too busy when she needed a consult on medical matters.

She had made the right decision for everyone involved, including the people of Skip Rock, who so badly needed a physician. Regardless, the die had been cast, and here she was in a place she never intended to be, married to a man she rarely saw. Yet she smiled just thinking about Tern. Perhaps that old saw "Absence makes the heart grow fonder" was correct. Maybe if they were regular old married folks, she wouldn't still get butterflies every time he crossed her mind. Judging from the frequent complaints she heard from her female patients, a husband's constant presence could be a wearying cross. "No woman needs a husband seven days a week," one who was pregnant with her fifth had said.

She couldn't imagine that being with Tern would ever grow old. The way she felt right now, if her husband were home, she'd not only put his dirty socks in the hamper without a murmur, she'd wash his smelly feet.

Hannah was resting when Lilly stopped to call on Armina. Earlier in the day she'd had a cot delivered, and the nurse had set it up right outside the open bedroom door.

"Hannah," Lilly whispered, "are you asleep?"

"Oh!" She startled awake and sat up. "Sorry, Doctor."

"No, no—rest whenever you get the chance. That's why I

sent the cot." Lilly peered into the darkened bedroom. Light snoring filled the space around them. "Did you have to use the restraints at all?"

"No, she's been quiet most all day. If she gets fractious, I talk her down."

"Good. I won't wake her. I'm very pleased we won't need more laudanum yet."

Lilly motioned for the nurse to follow her into the kitchen. She needed to fill Hannah in about the baby in case Armina said anything. "Don't question her, though, Hannah," Lilly said after she'd relayed the facts. "We need to let her remember on her own, else she could have a setback."

"Anne must be in seventh heaven," the nurse said. "That woman does love babies."

"I very much appreciate both of you," Lilly said.

"But what about you, Doc? Having us tied up puts quite a strain on you."

"Thankfully, there are no admits in the ward right now. The day-shift staff can handle the front office unless there's an emergency. I suppose I should think about hiring a secretary type to man the desk."

The nurse pulled her robe tightly around her. "When it rains . . ."

Lilly nodded. "It seems so."

"A secretary might help out lots in the long run."

Thinking back over the day, Lilly silently agreed. Tomorrow she would take Mazy along to the clinic. She could man the waiting room and keep things orderly.

They both jumped at the sound of scratching at the kitchen door, then laughed to find Kip, come to see Lilly home. "I'll be back at 3 a.m. to check on you," Lilly said.

"We'll be fine. You sleep. I'll come fetch you if things go awry."

At home, Lilly found Mazy sitting at the kitchen table, spreading peanut butter on a thick slice of light bread. "I tried to wait supper, Lilly, but my belly was growling. Want a sandwich? Mrs. Tippen sent this delicious bread." She waved her arm toward the stove. "And those disgusting beans. I could dish you up a bowl."

Mazy had spread a crocheted cloth on the scarred oak table. Fresh-picked daisies with centers like daubs of sunshine brightened the table. Mama had sent the table to Lilly so that she would have memories of home in her new house. Even though Tern preferred modern furnishings, Lilly welcomed it. She had but to close her eyes to see Mama ensconced there, reading her Bible or feeding a baby—sometimes both at the same time.

She didn't know how famished she was until she took the first bite. Surely simmered on the back of the stove all day, and fragrant with smokehouse bacon, the beans were just what the doctor ordered. "I didn't know you don't like pintos, Mazy."

Mazy sliced the crusts from her bread with a butter knife. "Bean soup is so common. I'm trying to lighten my palate."

Lilly nearly choked on her beans. "With peanut butter?"

"Well, there's not much fine cuisine to be had here."

"Mazy Pelfrey, don't get above your raising."

A tear slipped down Mazy's porcelain cheek. "There you go, just like Mama again."

"Honey," Lilly said, reaching across the table to take her sister's hand, "I didn't mean to hurt your feelings."

"Oooh, Lilly, I'm so homesick. I thought Troublesome Creek was boring, but this place has it beat. There's nothing to do here, and you're gone all day."

"I know. I'm sorry. But I have a plan. Would you like to go to the office with me tomorrow? I could use an assistant."

"I don't like nursey stuff. I might just as well pick daisies."

"Not patient care, more like secretarial duties. You'd be good at that."

"Do I have to know shorthand? Molly and I took it in tenth grade. She was good, but it made me squeasy." She shuddered at the thought. "Ugh."

Lilly quickly spooned up more beans to hide a smile. *Squeasy?* "No shorthand, but you could organize the office and say which patient is to be seen next, that sort of thing."

"What would I wear?"

"I should think you could dress up. You'll be a business person, after all."

A smile as bright as the daisies lightened Mazy's countenance. "Oh, this could be fun." She pushed away from the table. "I'm going to pick out an outfit."

Lilly went to the icebox and poured a tall glass of buttermilk, then foraged in the breadbox for a wedge of corn bread. Back in her chair, she crumbled the bread into the milk and ate it with a long-handled spoon. Her little one needed nourishment.

Mazy's outburst made her wistful. She wanted so much to share her news with her mother face-to-face, not with a few pages of stationery sealed in an envelope. Mama would be so happy, and her stepdaddy, John—why, he'd bust his buttons. Lilly pushed back the edge of the crocheted cloth and caressed the surface of the table in a familiar way. The tips of her fingers read each dent and ding as if it were braille. Here was a smooth triangle shape from when she'd heated her playhouse iron on the stovetop, then dropped it because it was too hot. And here the crisscross marks from chopping twigs to make a robin's nest for an abandoned baby bird.

As a girl, she was always bringing in some creature in distress—a grinning possum with a broken leg, a turtle with a cracked shell, a blacksnake missing an inch of tail. Even when she brought home the only survivor from a litter of albino skunks, so tiny its eyes were fused, her mother didn't fuss but patiently taught her how to feed it with an eyedropper. It was about the time of the skunk that Daddy John had cleared a space in the washhouse for Lilly's growing obsession.

She circled a pockmark with her index finger—such warm memories. Her childhood had been nearly perfect. Could she make it so for her own children? With a father so often gone and an untraditional mother, would her baby have such a strong sense of family?

Upending her glass, Lilly drank the last dregs of mushy bread. For the moment, all she could promise was sturdy bones.

CHAPTER 7

ANNE'S SQUARE ONE-ROOM HOUSE was easy to find when Lilly went calling the next morning. The Beckers lived on a few rocky acres just past the Coopers' house. Chickens flocked around her feet, pecking at her shoes as she walked across the yard. From under a shade tree, a short-haired red dog barely raised his head in interest. A fat sow rolled in a mud bath and grunted contentedly from the area underneath the raised porch. Lilly wondered if the chickens had cause for alarm. Daddy John always said if a hog caught a chicken, it would eat it, and once a hog had the taste for blood, it would kill anything, including humans, given a chance.

Anne welcomed Lilly with a big smile before laying the

baby on the bed for an exam. "I'm calling her Glory," she said. "A baby's got to have a name."

Lilly listened intently as she auscultated the tiny chest. Anne's own daughter, Amy, pulled herself up on the edge of the bed and played with the baby's toes.

"She's so good with her," Anne said when Lilly finished, "and not one bit jealous."

"How are the feeds?"

"La, she eats all the time." Anne laughed. "My breadbasket is overflowing—just like when Amy was first born. You know how it is before you get their take-out regulated with your put-out. I wake up soaked in milk."

Lilly took the baby in her arms. "You're so good to do this, Anne."

"She's a sweet little mite and hardly any trouble." Anne gently scratched the infant's scalp with her fingernails. Glory stretched and gave a goofy grin just like a normal baby would do under such stimulation.

Using a tongue depressor, Lilly examined the inside of the baby's mouth as she had done the other night. "I've seen worse clefts," she said.

"Is it a thing that can be fixed?" Anne asked with the air of a worried mother.

A weary sadness filled Lilly's heart. It was the hardest part of being a doctor—answering such a question with truth couched in hope. It didn't take a woman long to bond with a baby—hers or someone else's. Anne's demeanor was proof of that. Unlike a cleft lip, which could have been repaired in infancy, a palate repair could not be done until the baby was several months old. It was a difficult surgery requiring great care afterward—the baby could not be allowed to speak and must be fed with a spoon for a long duration. Even then the results were rarely favorable.

It wasn't the cleft that might snuff out this little life, however. It was the ominous murmur she'd just heard through the bell of her stethoscope that gave Lilly pause. The third strike she'd hoped not to find—a weakened, ineffective heart.

Lilly laid the baby back on the bed and sat down beside her. When she stroked the baby's palm, the tiny hand curled around her finger. No, it didn't take long for a woman to bond with a baby.

Lilly lifted Amy onto her lap and laid her cheek against the top of the little girl's head. Amy's skin smelled fresh and pure as Ivory soap. She wiggled around in Lilly's arms until they were face-to-face—so much energy in such a small package.

"She'll be okay. Won't she?" Anne asked again.

Lilly hedged. She hesitated to spread doom and gloom until she had to. "There is a murmur, but often murmurs go away. Continue what you're doing, Anne. We'll reassess the time for a surgical repair of the cleft when she's several months old. In the meantime, perhaps her mother will show up."

"Have you heard anything?"

"Not a word," Lilly said.

"Armina's not talking yet?"

"I saw her last evening. She was calm but still very confused."

"My, my, the things that can happen to a body."

"Indeed," Lilly said, handing Amy to her mother. "I'll see you tomorrow."

On the way to the office from Anne's, Lilly widely skirted the Cooper place. A *Quarantine* sign was tacked to the wall between the window and the front door. Although measles was a disease most commonly contracted in childhood, persons well along in years sometimes came down with it. She wasn't taking a chance unless she had to.

Two little children pressed up against the windowpane, waving enthusiastically to her as she walked by.

When Mrs. Cooper brought her brood into the office, only one had broken out. The mother had been in a panic. She was sure little Johnny's rash meant scarlet fever. He'd had a high temperature followed by chills and languor for three days before a dusky-red rash erupted on his forehead and gradually spread all over his body. He also had weepy eyes and a runny nose. Lilly had been secretly appalled to think Mrs. Cooper would bring the boy into the office if she suspected a contagious disease, especially one as dangerous as scarlet fever. It would have been much safer for the community at large if she had requested a house call.

Johnny's mother had been relieved when Lilly taught her how to tell the difference between the two diseases. In measles the spots were not as deeply colored and were differently shaped, grouped in crescents, and rougher to the touch. In scarlet fever the spots appeared on the second day of illness, in measles on the third or fourth, and the irritation of the nose, sneezing, and discharge that were prominent symptoms of measles did not occur in scarlet fever.

Thankfully, Mrs. Cooper's children were otherwise healthy. Lilly didn't expect there would be complications. She'd provided a care plan for the mother to follow: spare diet, including baked apples to keep the bowels gently open, plenty of diluted drinks, sponge baths with tepid vinegar and water to cool the skin and relieve the itching, and a darkened room to soothe the eyes.

Mrs. Cooper appeared in the window behind her children. Soon the little ones were throwing kisses Lilly's way and Mrs. Cooper mouthed, *"Thank you."*

Poor dear, Lilly thought, waving back. *She's in for a long haul.* It was not uncommon when there were several children in a family for the cases to succeed each other in fortnightly intervals. She suspected Mr. Cooper had moved out of the house for the duration. A man couldn't afford to be caught up in quarantine. Someone had to make a living. *I should have sent her home with a bottle of Lydia Pinkham's. She might need a bit of uplifting tonic to keep from pulling her hair out.*

Lilly slipped in the back door to her office. The clinic was an L-shaped building. The short arm held the waiting room and her office/exam room, which backed up to a wide hallway that led to the small hospital and the surgery. She'd learned never to go in through the front room, where patients would be waiting. Long minutes seated on hard wooden benches—not to mention whatever ailment had brought them there—tended to make folks impatient. If she went through the front room, someone was sure to demand her attention even if they were out of turn.

She seated herself behind the desk and pulled the string that would ring a bell at the nurse's station to signal that she was ready for the first case of the day.

"The doctor will see you now," Mazy said as she escorted old Mrs. Hill to the chair facing Lilly's desk.

Lilly caught her sister's eye, and Mazy gave her a thumbs-up. Dressed in a coffee-colored linen blouse and coordinating glen-plaid skirt, she was cute as a bug.

"Everything going okay out there?" Lilly asked.

Mazy's hand strayed to plump her hair, but she jerked it back as if she'd been caught admiring herself in a mirror. "Yes, thank you, Doctor. Nurse says I'm a fast learner."

"It's not so well with me," Mrs. Hill said with a huff. "I've been waiting since eight."

Behind the patient's back, Mazy rolled her eyes. Lilly wished she could roll hers. The office didn't even open until nine. There was not a single solitary thing wrong with Mrs. Hill. But she showed up every Wednesday morning like clockwork—always the first patient of the day.

"What seems to be the problem, Mrs. Hill?"

And so the day progressed. By lunchtime, Lilly had seen a slew of patients, and now a dozen metal-backed charts were stacked at her elbow. Most doctors charted as they went, but

Lilly kept notes that she later transferred. She liked her logs and graphs to be neat and precise and always in navy-blue ink. Thankfully, Wednesdays were half days.

"Whew," Mazy said as she plopped into the empty chair. "You never told me it would be so busy."

Lilly leaned back in her chair, taking a minute for her sister. "What do you think? Did you enjoy your morning?"

"I did. This was almost fun—except for the sick people. All that sneezing and snorting. I didn't like that so much. You know the best part?"

"No, what was the best part?"

Mazy straightened her shoulders. "For once in my life I got to tell people what to do."

"The first time ever? Surely not," Lilly teased.

"Oh, Lilly, you don't know what it's like to be the second-in-line twin. Molly was born superior."

"Well, Nurse said you did very well. I hope you'll take the job."

"Do I get paid?"

Lilly opened a chart. "Yes, I think a stipend is in order."

"I'd rather have money," Mazy said, her face as guileless as a two-year-old's. She jumped up and went into the washroom, leaving the door open. "I'll bet you didn't know there's a beauty parlor here in Skip Rock," she shouted as water splashed into the basin of the sink. "When I get paid, I'm going to get an appointment." Drying her hands, she leaned around the doorframe. "Getting this mess of hair straightened will be money well spent."

Lilly uncapped her fountain pen, but she didn't say a word. There were some things a girl had to learn on her own.

Mazy smoothed lotion on her hands, releasing the scent of almonds and cherries into the room. "This smells just like Mama."

Lilly looked up from the line she'd just penned. "I think that every time I twist the top off the bottle."

Caught in a beam of sunlight streaming in through the window, Mazy's golden curls framed her face like a halo. "Do you have any other jobs for me?"

A fissure of disquiet fractured Lilly's concentration. Her sister was so lovely in her innocence—still so unmarred by the vicissitudes of life. Sometimes Lilly wanted to put her in a box and store her on the top shelf of a closet like a fine piece of china too precious for everyday use.

"Would you like to get us some lunch from the diner? Their chicken salad is really good."

Mazy's eyes lit up. "Oooh, yes, how fun. Mama would never pay for lunch. Do you want an iced tea? And oh, they have that machine that makes potato chips while you watch. I want some of those. We could share."

"Sounds good," Lilly said, fishing a bill from her wallet. "And, Mazy, stop by the sheriff's office on your way. It's two doors up from the diner. Tell Sheriff Clay I need to speak to him."

"The sheriff's office? Really? Are we in the midst of a crime spree?"

"Hardly. Now just ring the bell and wait until he comes to the door. Don't go inside. Understand?"

"Well, yes, but why?"

"It's an unbecoming place for a young lady. Sheriff Clay won't mind taking a quick message."

"All right." Mazy patted her hair. "Be right back."

"This cold sweet tea is so good, Mazy," Lilly said after a long sip through a soda straw. "Don't forget to rinse the thermos."

"Mmm, okay." Mazy wiped a bit of mayonnaise from the corner of her mouth.

"Did you see Sheriff Clay?"

Mazy laid her half sandwich on the linen napkin she had spread on the desk. "I did, Sister."

"And?"

"He's dreamy, just dreamy."

"Forevermore, Mazy, you've seen Chanis in church every Lord's Day since the first of summer. Why, you're even in the same Sunday school class."

"But he looked so different today. On Sundays he's just a regular fellow."

"Did you tell him I needed to see him or did you stand on the sidewalk blinded by the light?"

"I told him, and I'm not leaving this office until he comes by."

"It's the uniform."

"And the star on his chest." Mazy fanned her face. "Did you see stars when you first met Tern?"

"Well, not literally," Lilly laughed. "I was only eleven. I was more interested in the beagle dog he had with him than I was in Tern."

"But eventually you saw stars, right?"

Lilly twisted the gold band on her left ring finger. Just mentioning Tern spread warmth from her toes to the top of her head. "Yes, indeed I did. But if you want my advice, don't let the stars sway you."

Mazy shook her head, making her honey-colored curls jounce like bedsprings. "I'm not marrying him, Lilly. I just want to look at him." Her eyes widened and she clapped her hand over her mouth. "Speaking of the devil," she whispered.

Chanis Clay stood just beyond the partially open door. The screen squeaked when Lilly motioned him in.

"Ma'am," he said, removing his hat and tucking it under his arm. "You needed to see me?"

He stood by her desk at full attention as if he were a soldier in a dress parade. The crease in his khaki pants was so sharp it was a wonder he didn't cut himself pulling them on. His calf-high boots were polished to a high shine; the dark-brown leather matched his gun belt and the holster on his right hip. His dark, brilliantined hair was swept back from his brow and parted in the middle. The only thing marring his perfection was a small shaving nick on his chin.

"Yes, thank you, Sheriff. Mazy, perhaps you'd like to finish your lunch on the front porch?"

Mazy wrapped what was left of her sandwich in her napkin and stood. With two fingers she snagged the potato chip bag and tucked it under her chin so that she would have a hand to carry her sweet tea.

"Let me help," Sheriff Clay said. Reaching to take the chips, his hand brushed Mazy's cheek.

Mazy's face pinked like apple blossoms. Her sandwich dropped, still wrapped, to the desktop. "I'm so clumsy," she said.

Somehow, the sheriff wound up with Mazy's sandwich and her chips, while Mazy carried her drink. Lilly heard the front door open and close before Chanis Clay backed into her office. He stood staring down the hallway for several seconds before he turned around.

Lilly thought she could detect a trace of sorrow in his clear blue eyes as he took the seat Mazy had vacated. It hadn't been that long since his father was killed—shot in the chest by an intruder at the mine office. Chanis's father, the first Sheriff Clay, had been forty-eight, a good and honorable man by all accounts. He left his wife and thirteen children; as the oldest at twenty-one, Chanis had big boots to fill.

"Something beyond strange has occurred," Lilly said, leaning forward in her chair. "I seem to have acquired an abandoned baby."

"Yes, ma'am," the sheriff said, retrieving a small spiral-bound notebook from his breast pocket. "You seem to, or you did?"

Lilly took her time relaying all that had happened since Monday evening when Armina had become ill. Chanis listened intently, taking notes with the stub of a yellow pencil.

Every now and then he'd stick the pencil in his mouth to moisten the lead.

"Do you reckon it fell off a hay wagon?" he asked when she had finished.

"A hay wagon?" Lilly said, puzzled.

"Sorry," he said with the trace of a grin. "My daddy used to tease that there were so many young'uns in our family, some of us must have fell off the back of a hay wagon and rolled up in his yard."

Lilly smiled, glad to see some humor in such a serious young man. "I thought the mother would come looking for the baby by now. I'm very concerned that something untoward has happened to her."

"The baby is defective, you say?"

"She has anomalies, yes."

"Most likely somebody pitched the poor little thing."

Lilly put her hand to her heart. "I wouldn't like to think so, but I've heard of such cases. Usually, though, the mother leaves the baby on someone's porch or in a church where it can be easily found."

"We don't know but what Miz Armina found it in some such place. She can't remember, you say?"

"Not yet, but I haven't pushed it. I have to think of her health too."

The sheriff stood, his holster creaking like saddle leather, and put the pad and pencil back in his pocket. "I'll keep an eye out, Doc."

"One more thing: a patient came in yesterday with stab

wounds. He said he injured himself while cleaning fish. I found that highly unlikely."

"Probably a brawl of some sort. I'll bet he's laying low until he can sneak out of town. I see too many drifters just hanging around the mines, hoping to get a week or two of work before they blow away. My opinion, they cause more trouble than they're worth."

Lilly stood and shook his hand. "Thank you, Chanis. I'll keep you posted on the baby."

"You're right to keep it quiet for the time being. Something will shake out—it always does." He started for the back door, then stopped. "Say, you mind if I go out through the front?"

CHAPTER 8

Armina lay in her bed, feeling as stunned as a foundered cow. Her mind swirled with blurry half-formed images, but she couldn't seem to pull them together.

"Concentrate," she told herself. "Concentrate."

The bed was hard. The room was small. There was one window. Craning her neck, she could make out a sliver of light sneaking in through a gap in the tightly closed curtains. So—it was daytime.

She held her hand in front of her face. It felt as heavy as a rock. Best she could tell, she had four fingers and a thumb. That seemed right. One finger wore a slim gold band. She was married. Strange—shouldn't she remember that?

It must be suppertime. She had to get up. There were hungry mouths to feed: Aunt Orie and the kids—her niece and nephew—and evidently a husband, though she couldn't picture him.

Summoning her will, she rose up on her elbows. The room whirled like the carousel ride at the fair Ned had taken her to last summer.

Ned. There. That was something solid to hold on to. Maybe your mind worked better if you didn't think so hard. She fell back against the pillow and closed her eyes. The carousel slowed, then stopped. Always the gentleman, Ned helped her down from the white horse with the yellow mane.

The hot, syrupy smell of melting sugar filled the air. Cotton candy. She wanted a cone of that cotton candy. Ned laughed when some of the airy pink confection stuck to her nose. She was aggravated when he pulled her behind a barker's stand and kissed it off. She wasn't much given to displays of affection.

Ned. Her husband. He'd brought her down from the mountain and married her at the church in Skip Rock. She could never figure why. She was plain as pig tracks with a figure like a sled runner. But her husband acted like she was spun gold—like he could never get enough of her. The way she couldn't get enough of that cotton candy once she'd tasted it.

At first she thought it was because he was marred, that he picked her because nobody would pick him. He had no lack of looks or personality but he was missing a leg. It had taken her some time to get over that particular thing. But she got over it quicker when she saw two girls flirting with him at a fish fry. That was before they'd even started going out, but still it got her dander up.

Her own rusty bark of a laugh in the hushed room startled her. There was no looking back once she'd set her heart on him. But where was he? Where was Ned? Ah, she should get up—go and search for her one-legged man—but this thinking was wearying her. Just for a minute she'd close her eyes.

Something baleful snuck into her carousel of memory—the dark horse she would never choose to ride. Aunt Orie was dead. Oh, oh. Did she have to grieve that all over again?

She'd met Doc Lilly because of Aunt Orie. They'd tried everything to save her aunt—all that modern medicine had to offer. But in the end, she'd died anyway. You couldn't deny death, that cold reaper, his due for any length of time. She lifted her hand to cover her eyes. That was done. Dead and buried, she didn't have to go there again. So . . . if that was past, and the carousel was past, where was she now?

"You're awake," a woman said. "Do you want to try a bite of supper? I've made milk toast."

The woman set a bowl and spoon on the bedside table. Before Armina could think how to answer, the woman hauled her up and stuffed pillows behind her back. Did she have no say-so in the matter?

"Who're you?" Armina asked.

"I'm Hannah, your nurse," she said like she had a right to be hauling Armina around, like she did this all the time.

Nurse? So she was in the old folks' home. Or purgatory—they were both the same. How old was she anyway? She held her hand up again, this time checking for liver spots. The nurse slipped a spoon into it.

Armina flung the spoon across the room. She wasn't eating milk toast. She ran her tongue around the inside of her mouth. She had teeth, so she wasn't that old. She wanted corn bread and maybe some fried chicken and then blackberry cobbler.

Her mind snatched her backward to a dark place—dark and green and whirling, like the sky before a bad storm. Blackberry fronds snagged her legs and trapped her arms in a thorny vise. Rabbits, as big as hound dogs, hopped among the briars. "Run," one said, its mouth twitching fearfully. "Run, rabbit, run."

Her struggle was to no avail as the vines tightened around her ankles and wrists. She was trapped.

"Armina, dear," the biggest rabbit crooned in a familiar voice. "Lie still."

A clink of metal against her teeth and the rabbit said, "Here, this will make you feel better."

Bitter-tasting medicine flowed from a spoon. Armina turned her head. The rabbit pinched her nose. She had to swallow.

Tension flowed from her body like bathwater down a drain. The rabbits munched blossoms of white clover. The blackberry vines offered up their fruit. Her sycamore walking stick felt good and sturdy in her hand. Down by the bridge, two women talked quietly.

"Loose the bonds in fifteen minutes," one said. "She'll be placid for a while."

"I will. I'm sorry, Doctor. There's milk toast everywhere. I thought she was better."

"I'll help you clean up."

"No, please. I'll get it. You have better things to do."

Better things to do—better things to do. Armina had better things to do. With fitful blasts of tinny calliope music, the carousel jerked to life behind her. In a rush she mounted the white horse with the yellow mane. Her steed rose and fell gracefully. Pink cotton candy melted on her tongue. This was a good place. She'd stay here for a while.

Supper was on the kitchen table when Lilly crossed the road from Armina's house. Sandwiches, thick with cheddar cheese and ham on Tillie Tippen's sourdough bread, graced white ironstone plates.

"There are bread-and-butter pickles to go with," Mazy said, popping one of the treats into her mouth. "Crunchy and sweet. Yum."

Kip sat expectantly in Lilly's chair. He hadn't dared to breach her plate, though a thin bit of drool trickled down his chin.

Lilly snapped her fingers, then pointed to the floor. "Kipper!"

The little terrier turned mournful eyes on her before he

jumped down. Lilly took a saucer from a stack reserved for Kip, cut a corner from her sandwich, and put it on the floor.

"We should get Kip a high chair," Mazy said when they had finished saying grace.

"And some bibs," Lilly replied. "He could definitely use some of those."

Mazy rolled her eyes. "I draw the line at diapers."

"Remember my dog Steady? Remember how after she got old and deaf, if you asked her to do something she didn't want to do, she'd just turn her eyes away? Like if she couldn't see you, she didn't have to mind."

"I remember you spent a whole summer teaching her sign language. I was what—six or seven?" With busy fingers, Mazy signed *sit* and *stay*. "I still remember most of it."

A terrible jangling sound made Kip's fur stand on end. Abandoning his saucer, he ran to the door, barking furiously.

"What in the world?" Mazy said.

"Goodness, it's the telephone." Lilly rushed to the wooden box installed on the wall by the door. "Kip. Shush!" She lifted the receiver and shouted into the mouthpiece, "Hello!"

Mazy held Kip to quiet him. They stood in a tight bunch. Kip licked first Lilly's face and then Mazy's. "Hello," Lilly said again.

"How's my sweet wife?" came like a miracle through the wires along with a fair amount of background noise.

"Tern?" Lilly sagged against the wall. Her knees felt like jelly. Thoughtfully, Mazy took Kip outside, closing the door behind her.

"It's me, angel. I've got some news."

"Are you okay?" She couldn't help but pose the question every miner's wife dreaded having to ask. "Are you hurt?"

"No, honey, no. Please don't worry about me. You know I'm careful as can be. But listen, Lilly; I'm not coming home next week like we'd planned—"

"Oh, Tern, you've been gone for weeks."

"I know, but there's been an explosion and a cave-in at a mine in Canada. A dozen men are trapped miles underground. Washington offered our help. I'm on the way there now. I'm calling from the train station."

Her eyes filled with hot tears. What exquisite torture, hearing his dear voice but not being in his presence, not being able to feel his arms around her, not hearing the beat of his strong heart against her cheek. She stifled a sob.

"I love you, honey. You're not crying, are you? Please don't cry. I'll be home soon enough."

Lilly dug her thumbnail into her index finger to redirect the pain in her heart. No sense making this more difficult for him. "I love you too, dearest. Just be careful. Promise?"

"This is the best, hearing your voice. I'm glad this thing works."

"Yes, me too. Tern? I've got something to tell you also."

"I'm all ears."

She took a breath and forced a broad smile—she wanted to savor the moment she gave her husband such wonderful news, and her voice would be lighter with a smile. "Are you ready to be a father?" she teased.

A blast of static followed by dead silence rewarded her question. She tapped the receiver against the wall as if that would clear the line. It was still dead as could be. Frustrated, she replaced the earpiece, cranked the phone, and picked up the receiver again.

"Operator—number, please," eked out in a feminine voice.

"I was speaking with my husband. We've been disconnected."

"Number, please." The woman drew out her words. It sounded to Lilly like she was forcing a smile too.

"I don't have a number."

"Please hold."

Inside Lilly's ear, the phone rang distantly. "Directory assistance. What city, please?"

"I don't know what city."

"Hold, please."

The telephone clicked and hissed. "Number, please."

"I was disconnected—"

The buzzing of a dozen bees replaced the operator's voice. Lilly hung up. Her ear throbbed from being pressed so tightly to the receiver. "Stupid thing," she said to the telephone, which offered no reply. She was of a good mind to jerk the whole shebang off the wall and pitch it through the kitchen window. Progress! Who needed it?

After refilling her tea glass and Mazy's, she stepped outside to join her sister at the small picnic table under the apple tree in the side yard. Tiny green apples had replaced the pretty white blossoms that graced the tree during the spring. Kip jumped up to sit in her lap.

"Oh, Sister," Mazy said. "That was so exciting. It defies logic, capturing a person's voice and flinging it down the road that way. Did he sound the same?"

"He did. Of course, we've talked on a telephone before." Lilly let a bit of ice from her drink melt on her tongue. Her mouth felt numb from unsaid words.

"Isn't God good, Lilly, to let us have such a thing?"

Lilly let the warm night air wash over her. Her yard was newly mown, the grass releasing the lush, fertile scent evocative of summer. She stroked Kip's back. His fur was silky smooth beneath her fingers. And inside her womb, her baby grew safe and sound, no less real for being unspoken. "Yes, Mazy, God is very good."

"You know what else would be a miracle?"

"No, what else would be a miracle?" Lilly asked.

Mazy twisted a curl around her finger. "Me having someone to talk to on that thing."

From across the table, Lilly squeezed her sister's shoulder. "That will happen soon enough. Come inside and I'll give you a lesson on phone etiquette. You can be in charge of answering the clinic phone."

"Wait, wait. I have to practice." She lowered her voice. "Hello. Hello. Does that sound businessy? Or should I be friendlier? Hellooo. *Hellooo.*"

"Your regular voice is just fine, Mazy. I'm sure you'll sound like a person in charge when you connect."

"Really?" Mazy stood and retrieved their glasses. "I've always wanted to be in charge of something." She looked surprised. "We have a visitor."

Chanis Clay tipped his hat as he approached. "Evening, ladies. I just stopped by to . . . well . . . I needed to ask . . ." His eyes lit on Kip. "Maybe the dog needs walking or something."

Mazy's eyes pleaded, *Say yes, Lilly. Say yes.*

"I'm sure Kip would love a ten-minute walk, but I don't want him chasing after squirrels this late in the day. I'll get his leash."

"I'll get it," Mazy said, setting Lilly's half-full glass on the table. "You finish your tea."

As the screen door slapped shut behind Mazy, Lilly gave Chanis a questioning look.

He dropped his gaze, kicking a pebble around with the toe of his polished boot. "I was hoping you'd let me come calling on your sister."

"Hmm," Lilly said, noting the blush that crept up his neck. "Have you ever called on a young lady before?"

"No, ma'am, there's hardly been the time." He stuck his finger under the collar of his shirt and eased it away from his throat. "Plus, to tell you the truth, I've never been tempted before."

"Tempted?"

His Adam's apple bobbed as the blush rose to cover his cheeks. "I meant to say interested. I've never been so interested. I can't seem to get her off my mind." He swallowed hard, his discomfort palpable. "I don't usually talk so much—you'll think I'm addled."

"Not at all, Chanis. Mazy is a memorable girl."

Kip danced excitedly when Mazy returned and attached the lead to his collar.

Lilly noticed a fresh gloss of color on her sister's lips. Mazy seemed a bit too eager. Lilly would keep a close eye on her—and on Chanis Clay. "Enjoy your walk," she said.

CHAPTER 9

ARMINA WAS UP and eating silver-dollar pancakes when Lilly stopped by the next morning.

"No thank you," Lilly said when Hannah offered breakfast. "I've eaten, but I'll take a cup of tea."

Once the nurse had poured Lilly's tea, she left the room.

Armina leaned in close. "What's that woman doing flipping flapjacks in my kitchen?"

They could hear a window being raised in the bedroom followed by a mighty plumping of pillows.

"Hannah's been staying with you because you've been ill, Armina. I can see you're much better today."

"I'm fine as frog's hair," Armina said, upending the syrup pitcher. "I didn't take her to raise."

"Let's give it a couple more days. You need to gather your strength."

"I won't get no strength from that woman's cooking." She took her fork and stabbed one of the little cakes. "Look at these pitiful things, and this syrup's thin as water."

"I'm sure I saw some sorghum in your pantry."

"I know, but I ain't about to ask, and I didn't feel up to crossing the floor to get it."

"That's exactly why you need someone with you for a little while longer."

The seesawing squeak of a drawer being tugged from its base emanated from the room beyond. "I reckon she don't even know how to candle the bottom of a dresser drawer," Armina said.

"I'm sure you could teach her lots of things. She's really very nice."

Armina poured some of her coffee into her saucer and blew across it. "I could start with this here brew, which is all coffee. I've got dried dandelion root and chicory right in the cupboard there. One part to four parts and a body can stretch a pound of joe for weeks." She looked over the rim of her saucer at Lilly. "Nobody wants to fool with making hard-times coffee anymore. But that's pure wasteful, and wasteful's right next door to sinful."

"Hmm," Lilly said as she absently traced a circle with her index finger on the cherry-printed oilcloth table topper. She needed to proceed with caution. "I can't help but wonder where you were when you fell ill on Monday, Armina."

"You've got your days mixed up, Doc. This here's Monday, and I ain't been out of the house." Armina pointed her fork toward the bedroom door. "I can't go anywheres until that woman goes on home. She'd probably steal me blind. You can't trust nobody no more." She took a long draw of coffee. "Why she wants to clean my house is a mystery to me."

Lilly got up and took the advertising calendar from a nail on the door of the pantry. *Scarboro Beach Clam Chowder: A Reminder of Old New England* was emblazoned in red print across the top of the calendar. At the bottom, under the blocks of days, in black it read: *Real Clam Flavor. Sample Can Postpaid 10 Cents. Booklet Free.* Ned must have brought the calendar back as a souvenir from when he was in Boston receiving follow-up care for his prosthetic limb, a very successful trip. One could hardly tell that Ned once walked on a wooden peg.

She removed Armina's sticky plate and put the calendar on the table. It was time to orient her friend to time and place. Lilly tapped a day block. "This is today, Armina. It's Thursday." She ran her finger back to Monday. "On this day you fell ill. Mazy found you on your parlor floor. This was late on Monday. Mr. Tippen carried you across the street—"

"Hold on a minute," Armina interrupted. "I remember Monday now. Something was amiss on Monday." Her face gathered in a knot of concentration.

Lilly watched Armina closely. If she showed any sign of relapse, Lilly had laudanum available in her kit. She wouldn't let it go so far as to have to put Armina in restraints again. But Armina seemed fine, just puzzled.

"Yep, something was dead wrong with Monday."

Hannah hovered just inside the bedroom door. She raised her brows in question. Lilly barely shook her head as if to say, *"Don't interrupt—we're finally going to get some answers."*

Armina turned her face from one side to the other like a prizefighter releasing tension from strained neck muscles. Her eyes flashed with anger. "Turnip Tippen! Well, that just makes me mad enough to spit. I've got about as much use for Turnip Tippen as a hog has for a sidesaddle."

"You were too weak to walk, remember? Mr. Tippen simply helped us get you to my house. He was very respectful."

She set her face in a grimace. "I'd druther you left me on the porch."

Lilly felt they were making progress. Even though Armina was fixating on the wrong thing, at least she was remembering something. Given time and patience, the rest of what happened on Monday would come into focus. "It was threatening rain or I would have left you right there like a potted plant."

"What kind of potted plant do you reckon I'd be?"

"I suspect Mr. Tippen would say a cactus."

Armina hiccuped a giggle, then laughed out loud. "I'd like to be a big old spiny cactus like them ones in the desert."

"My cousin has a cactus patch growing on a rocky hillside," Hannah said. "They have the prettiest orange blossoms every summer."

"There you go," Armina said with a coy smile. "I could be prickly and pleasing at the same time."

Hearing her friend's laughter was a balm to Lilly's soul. She was definitely on the mend. The nurse could be dismissed from Armina's care soon, and Ned would be home in a week or so.

"Well, enough thinking out loud," Armina said, wincing as she stood. "I'm going to sweep the porch."

"Let her go," Lilly mouthed to Hannah as they watched Armina steadying herself on various pieces of furniture and then the wall to make her way across the room.

The screen door squeaked open. "It's going to be a hot one. Wonder what's going on in the garden."

"Bless her heart," Hannah said when the door closed. "She packs a grudge like a ten-dollar mule. I don't believe she even knew Ned when his accident happened."

Lilly listened to Armina's broom swoosh across the porch floor. She was not one to encourage idle talk, but she'd always wondered why Armina disliked Mr. Tippen. Her curiosity got the better of her. "What do you mean?"

"Years back when Ned Tippen lost his leg in a cave-in, story was that his uncle Turnip ran for his life, leaving him behind. Now that's the way I heard it. Ned doesn't seem to bear any ill will toward his uncle, though."

"A mine accident is a scary thing. One never knows what one would do in such a circumstance."

"You do, Dr. Still. I've heard tell that you run in instead of out."

Lilly pushed back from the table and carried her teacup and saucer to the sink. "That's my job, Hannah. I'm here in Skip Rock because of the mines."

"I don't know another woman who'd do what you do, Doc. I'm right proud to know you."

"Speaking of what I do, I'd best get to the clinic," Lilly said while rinsing out her cup. "Keep an eye on Armina. Don't let her wander too far."

"If she does, I'll wander with her. How about that?"

"I should have thought of this before: you can use the telephone in my house to call the clinic if you need me. That would be the best way to handle an emergency. The number to my office is posted on the wall right over the telephone."

"Oh, Doc, I couldn't. I don't hardly believe in them things. My pastor says they're the work of the devil. Pastor says soon enough folks will have ears big as elephants' from pressing up against those machines. I'll send somebody after you if need be."

Lilly straightened her jacket and walked to the door. She'd keep her thoughts about the pastor's teaching to herself. "Right now Armina's sitting in the rocker. Could be she's decided she isn't as strong as she thought she was."

"I'll take some yarn out there and sit with her. Maybe she'd like to do something with her hands to pass the time."

CHAPTER 10

LILLY LOVED her early morning walks to work when everything seemed fresh and new. A smoky haze obscured the mountain ridges in undulating ribbons of blue and gray. The fine mist bathed her face and titillated her nose with the scent of clear mountain streams, unturned loam, bedrock so solid it supported the world, and hidden dark seams of black diamond coal. It was a smell as familiar to her as her own breath.

It was good to have a few moments of quiet time before she started work. As she rounded the corner, she could tell it would be a busy day. A line of folks waited outside the clinic although the cardboard sign in the window said Closed. The nurse must not be here yet, nor Mazy. It was still early. Lilly was glad to be able to slip in the back door.

Mazy followed closely behind. She was dressed in an embroidered, hand-tucked, sheer-lawn shirtwaist over a heliotrope slip. Her skirt was black lightweight wool. Lilly recognized the ensemble because it came from her closet. She'd tried the skirt on just this morning and laid it aside when she couldn't get it to snap.

"You might have asked before going into my closet, Mazy."

"But, Sister, you weren't home, and besides, I knew you'd say yes." She danced through the office, letting the skirt twirl around her ankles. "We're the exact same size except for shoes. Your feet are too big."

"Thank goodness for small favors," Lilly said.

Mazy leaned over the desk and kissed Lilly's cheek. "I look so mature in your clothes. Don't you think?"

Lilly didn't want to burst Mazy's bubble, but with those Goldilocks curls framing her face, Mazy looked exactly her age, and that was a good thing. "You look very professional, Mazy."

"Can I flip the sign now?" she asked. "I love flipping that sign. Nurse let me do that yesterday when we closed at noon."

It was nearly time for lunch. Lilly was removing tar from the scalp of a three-year-old boy. Last evening, his mother had noticed an outbreak of scald head, and using an old-time remedy, she'd boiled a quart of urine along with half a cup of lard and a lump of tar before smearing the concoction all along the child's hairline. Thank goodness she'd let it cool first. Lilly had seen third-degree burns from some such treatments.

The mother relayed that the child had cried most of the night. His bony chest shuddered with hiccups as Lilly worked the tar loose with mild castile soap and water. When she finished, she applied rose ointment and gave the rest of the small tub of cream to the mother. "Use this mornings and evenings on the pustules," she said.

The mother eyed the just-used soap.

Lilly folded the wrapper around it. "And take this, too."

"Thank ye kindly," the mother said, inhaling the scent of the soap bar. "It smells so pretty."

Lilly had just handed the boy a gingersnap from the cookie jar on her desk when four long blasts of a train whistle caught their attention. The whistle was followed by a mighty screech of metal against metal. The lad stuffed the cookie into his mouth and then clapped his hands over his ears.

"Sounds like somebody pulled the emergency brake," the mother said, swinging her son up to her hip. "It takes a mighty effort to stop a train."

Lilly opened the door and ushered the family out. "Come back if need be," she said as she watched folks spill out of the commissary across the street and rush toward the railroad tracks. Even her waiting room was emptying. She'd see if any emergent cases had stayed and then head that way.

The crow-fly way to where the train was stopped was through a farmer's field. As Lilly maneuvered between horseweeds and cowpats, she saw a gang of boys running pell-mell in her direction. Timmy Blair was in the lead. The lad's face was slick with sweat and pale as Cream of Wheat. He stopped on a dime when he saw her, the other boys packing up behind him.

"Doc! Doc!" Timmy gasped. "The sheriff sent me to fetch you! We saw the whole thing. It's the . . . It's the . . ."

"Timmy, take a breath."

"It's the gandy dancer," one of the bigger boys shouted out.

Timmy turned on him. "I was telling her. I seen it first. I got dibs."

"Timmy?"

"See, Doc, me and the fellows was just going over to check out Mr. Griggs's watermelon patch—"

"Stupid, you ain't supposed to tell that part," a boy said, giving Timmy's head a thump with his middle knuckle.

"You're stupider," Timmy said. "Mommy gave me a nickel to pay."

"The cowcatcher caught the gandy dancer!" the bigger boy said.

"Dibs!" Timmy's eyes blazed. "You broke dibs."

"You can't have dibs on words," the big boy argued.

"Timmy, you may show me the way," Lilly said.

Social order restored, Timmy conceded. He grabbed Lilly's hand and tugged her forward. "Come on, fellows. Time's a-wasting."

They walked alongside the stalled train. The air was thick

with the smell of hot ash and grease. Cinders flew about like lightning bugs. Lilly shielded her eyes.

"Look," Timmy said, pointing to a rimmed metal wheel lying amid some broken boards in the weeds beside the tracks. "There should be three more."

"They might be t'other side," the big boy said.

"Yeah, right," Timmy said. "I wonder, did the gandy dancer live?"

Up ahead, Lilly could see the sheriff motioning gawkers to back away. Several men in striped coveralls milled around. A woman was lying on the ground a few feet from the front of the engine, with a man kneeling beside her. Lilly started toward them.

"Leave her," Chanis Clay said. "She only fainted. Her husband's tending to her." He motioned toward a sheet-covered mound on the other side of the tracks. "You'll want to pronounce him."

"Send the boys away," Lilly said.

"They've already seen," Chanis said. "This'll make men of them." The sheriff took her elbow. "Careful; the tracks are slippery."

She knelt beside the still form and raised a corner of the sheet. The railroad men removed their soft-billed caps. "Does anyone recognize him?" she asked.

"It's Dewey Clover," a man replied hoarsely. "He was a section crewman checking the tracks from the hand truck. I don't know why he got caught out here. Surely he knew the train was coming."

"Strange things happen," another said. "You get so used to the noise and the hubbub."

Lilly lifted the watch that was attached to her blouse by a fob and noted the time. "It's 12:15 p.m.," she said.

"What'd you boys see?" Chanis asked, taking his notepad from his pocket.

"He come a-flying up from yonder way," the big boy said, pointing up the track. "He was pumping the handle of the handcart for all it was worth. That can of axle grease on the cart—it fell off and crude splattered everywhere. Good thing it weren't turpentine. We'd all be blowed to kingdom come."

"There weren't nothing to be done," Timmy said. "We all commenced jumping and screaming and waving our arms when we saw the train a-coming round the bend. He looked back when the first whistle sounded, but it was too late."

"The cowcatcher caught him from behind," the big boy said.

Timmy blinked back tears and ground a grubby fist into his eyes. "Dewey Clover won't never dance the tracks no more."

Lilly made sure all the children walked back to town with her. They had seen quite enough.

The boys fell silent until they were nearly to the clinic. "I don't know why God would let the railroad man die that-away," one finally said. "It makes me sore at Him."

Lilly searched her mind for the right words to say. The child needed reassurance.

"It ain't God's fault he was on the tracks," Timmy said,

picking at the sling on his arm. "My daddy says a body will pay a high price for being foolhardy. I reckon God would have liked for the gandy dancer to jump free and leave the handcart to fend for itself."

"That cart was first-rate, though."

"Yeah," Timmy said.

"I've got a bellyache," the smallest boy said.

"You boys go over to the commissary," Lilly said, wiping a smear of grease from Timmy's cheek with her thumb. "Tell the clerk to give you each an iced root beer soda. Timmy, tell her to put them on my tab."

"Should I bring you one, Doc? I can pay," Timmy said, holding forth the aforementioned nickel.

"No, but come by later and I'll put a clean sling on your arm."

"Did I tell you how I broke this here arm?" Timmy asked as the boys headed off.

"That ain't nothing," the big boy scoffed. "I once fell out of the hayloft. I almost wound up like the gandy dancer."

"Did not," Timmy said.

"Did too!"

"Last one in's a rotten egg," Timmy shouted, starting a stampede of barefooted boys.

Lilly watched them go. She had a bellyache herself that soda pop wouldn't help. She'd borne witness to sudden deaths, lingering deaths, accidental deaths, and once death by a person's own hand. By now, you'd think she would be used to it, but she wasn't. When she'd uncovered the section worker's body, she'd fought an urge to gather him in her arms and sing him into that long sleep with a lullaby. But of course, she didn't. He was already gone, and besides, doctors didn't do such things. What she needed was a moment alone with her Bible.

Last winter, she had attended to a young girl who'd suffered terrible burns. According to the parents, the child had been wearing a too-long, hand-me-down nightdress. It was a bitter cold night. Sleet tapped at the windows with icy fingers like a witch demanding entrance. The girl's father held a long-handled, wire-mesh corn popper over the fireplace coals. The girl danced with delight when the first kernel popped. The mother mixed cocoa and sugar together. A pan of milk steamed on a burner of the cookstove. All of this the family remembered and repeated over and over again like a mantra of recrimination.

Lilly remembered the charred smell of the child's flesh mingling with the scorched milk forgotten on the stove. The girl lingered through the night and into the next morning. Lilly plied her with morphine and salve of aloe. The morphine took the edge off her pain. The aloe cooled her skin and gave hope to her mother.

Finally, despite the icy roads, the preacher came. He was a burly man with an air of authority, dressed all in black and carrying a large black Bible. The Bible's leather cover was worn and cracked with use. Lilly was never so glad to see anyone. He bore solace more powerful than all the medicines in her doctor's kit.

The preacher spoke to the parents each in turn and heard the oft-repeated sequence of events. By now there were others present in the room: worried grandparents, stunned neighbors, a few children shocked into silence. He offered up no false reassurance, no self-indulgent words of understanding.

The preacher went to the bed on which the child lay and spoke to her with great tenderness. "Gillian, remember last summer when I baptized you into the Lord?" With the pad of his thumb, he stroked the only part of the child not burned, her sweet right hand. "You're going to that selfsame place tonight. First you'll go down into the deep—remember the dark water? Remember you were afraid? But just like on your baptismal day, you'll come up again into the light and it will be more beauteous than anything you've ever seen. The Lord Jesus has gone before you. He has prepared a place for you."

He had the parents kneel, one on either side of the bed, and joined their hands, making a bridge across the girl with their arms. Then the preacher lifted his big black Bible. He didn't have to search for the Scripture he wanted. He just palmed the open book and held it aloft.

"Hear the truth of the Word as it is spoken in Isaiah," he said. "'The Lord shall give thee rest from thy sorrow, and from thy fear, and from the hard bondage wherein thou wast made to serve.'"

The preacher closed his Bible and spoke directly to the girl. "Godspeed, child of God."

That very day, Lilly had marked Isaiah 14:3 in her own Bible. It never failed to give comfort.

Now, she turned to the task at hand, though there was probably no one sitting in the waiting room. Even her nurse had been at the site of the accident. It was understandable. Here in Skip Rock, folks were either kin or close as kin. She knew the gandy dancer's family would not grieve alone. That was a comfort in itself.

Mazy was busily chatting into the telephone as Lilly stepped into the office. She held up one finger in a wait-a-minute sign. Lilly was surprised and pleased to see how quickly her sister had acclimated to the new device. They'd had a freestanding phone put in this room. It had a long enough cord to provide privacy if needed.

"Thank you very much," Mazy said, replacing the receiver. "Can you believe I'm up to the *J*s? Jessup, Ronald, to be exact. See? The last name of the person you're calling is printed first and the first name last."

"Why were you calling Ronald Jessup?"

"I'm on a mission to place a call to every letter in the alphabet, namewise and countywise. Mr. Jessup from Jessamine

County wasn't home, but his wife answered." She checked off the name. "That should count, don't you think?"

Mazy took three yellow pencils from a blue mug, stuck one into the metal sharpener fixed to the desk, and turned the handle. "The most fun one was David Doolittle from Daviess County." She gave the detachable shavings retainer a quick rap against the inside of the trash can. Curls of brown and yellow spilled out along with the rich smell of wood. "I would never have imagined a person has a name such as Doolittle. He was nice, though."

Lilly rubbed her forehead against the beginning of a headache. "Mazy. There's a long-distance charge for calling any number outside the county. Besides, this is a business phone. It's not for entertaining yourself."

Mazy laid the directory precisely in the middle of the waiting room desk, then smoothed its cover with both hands. "Well," she said with a pout, "you don't have to be so mean about it. I was all alone after everybody ran off. I didn't have anything else to do."

Lilly found she had not one bit of patience left. If she said anything now, it would be more pointed than she meant. "We'll discuss this later. In the meantime . . ."

"I know, I know—no fun allowed." Mazy twirled the desk chair around until her back was to Lilly. "I don't think I like this job anymore."

Lilly went straight to her private lavatory and filled a glass with water. She didn't like to take anything, but this day called for an aspirin—or two. The death of the gandy dancer was enough to spark a migraine and then to find Mazy wasting time and money . . . Well, no wonder her head began to throb in earnest. She caught the reflection of her down-turned mouth and knit brow in the mirror. Leaning closer, she pushed her lips into a smile with her index fingers. "Don't be such a grump," she chided, adding a second aspirin to the dose.

A sudden wave of nausea took her to her knees. She hated to vomit worse than anything—she'd rather have shingles. But she leaned over the pristine toilet bowl and lost her long-ago breakfast.

"Sister," Mazy said, pushing through the door. "What's wrong? Are you sick?"

"Just a little headache—sometimes this helps, for whatever reason." Shaken, Lilly sat with her back against the wall. She reached up to pull the chain that would empty the water closet.

Mazy ran water into the sink. She dampened a washcloth, folded it in thirds, and placed it on Lilly's forehead. "This is what Mama would do."

A sob escaped Lilly's lips as tears sprang to her eyes and flowed down her cheeks. How she missed her mama.

Mazy sank down beside her and wrapped Lilly in a hug. "I'm sorry, Lilly. Really I am. I'll do better, I promise."

"Sweetheart, it's not you. I just get out of sorts sometimes."

"I know. I know you do." Mazy patted Lilly's back in a soothing fashion. "I forgive you."

Lilly rested her head in the crook of Mazy's shoulder. "I'm glad Mama sent you to help me, Mazy."

"Good gravy, it smells of throw up in here," Mazy said, pinching her nose. "Where's that candle you keep for moments such as this?"

Lilly waved her hand in the general direction of the linen cupboard.

"Oops," Mazy said, "I remember now. I took it and a box of matches to the privy. I thought it would give a welcoming ambience to the outhouse. Isn't that a lovely word? *Ambience?* It means the mood of a place or something like that. I looked it up in your pocket dictionary. I'm committed to learning one new word a day—or maybe one a week. Depends on how busy I am."

Mazy offered her hands to pull Lilly up, but Lilly couldn't move. She was trying so hard not to laugh that her belly hurt for a different reason. But just the thought of someone setting the wooden privy on fire with the ambience candle was too much. "Mazy," she said. "Mazy, Mazy, Mazy. You are too precious for words."

"I hope that is a compliment," Mazy said as she hauled Lilly off the floor.

Lilly splashed cold water on her face and rinsed her mouth. "I've an idea. Let's close the office for an hour. You and I could use a walk."

"Good idea, as long as the walk is to the diner. I'm famished."

"So what happened with the train?" Mazy asked after finishing her half of a pimento cheese sandwich.

"A man was hit and killed."

Mazy gasped. "Oh, how awful. How could such a thing happen?"

"It was an accident." Lilly hoped Mazy didn't ask for details. "Finish your chips, Mazy."

Mazy covered her plate with her napkin. "I couldn't eat another bite. Think of his poor family. I'll bet his mother is crying her eyes out."

"I expect you're right."

Mazy picked at a loose thread on the napkin. "You didn't have to look at him—did you?"

"Only for a minute; it's part of my job."

"Well, good thing I decided I didn't want to be a doctor. I don't like dead bodies. Or an undertaker—I don't want to be an undertaker, either. Can you even imagine what they do all day? Gives me the willies."

She turned her gaze to the long window beside their booth. "Look, Lilly, there's a duck on the porch. He's probably looking for a cheese sandwich. Do you think I could take him the rest of my chips?"

"I don't see why not. Just don't make a mess."

Mazy laughed. "Sister, that's up to the duck. That's why Daddy wouldn't let us keep one. Or a goose—they're way messier than ducks."

Lilly sat a minute and watched her sister through the window. Mazy stooped down and opened the palm of her hand. The duck backed up. Mazy put one chip on the porch floor right in front of her feet. In no time, the duck was eating from her hand.

That is so like Mazy, Lilly thought. Her sweet demeanor drew everyone and, obviously, every*thing* in. Maybe her sister was flighty, but she was charming. And Mama said she was sensitive like her brother, Lilly and Mazy's uncle Daniel. He was an artist who owned a gallery in Philadelphia. He had paintings in galleries and museums all over, even in Europe.

Speaking of being drawn in—Chanis Clay was now on the porch with Mazy and her duck friend. Mazy looked up from her crouched position and gave him a smile of pure sunshine. Lilly laid a dime tip beside her plate and picked up her check. She'd better get out there before the *sheriff* was eating from Mazy's hand.

Mazy was coming in as Lilly was going out. "The sheriff wants to speak with you," she said. "I'm going to run in and borrow a napkin. My hands are all greasy from the potato chips. Yuck."

Lilly found Chanis in the yard wiping the sole of his boot on a patch of grass. "Doggone duck," he said. "Good thing it wasn't a goose. Say, we took the body over to Cox's Shady Lawn. I'll walk back to the clinic with you if you like. I can pick up the death certificate and take it over to Mr. Cox. Save you a trip."

"Thank you, Chanis. That would be nice."

"Have you seen that fellow that stabbed himself again?"

"Not yet. He should have come in to have his wound packing changed."

110

"I asked around, but nobody recalls a man of that description, nor was there any report of bar fights or such. Everything's been quiet around here until Dewey got himself run over by a train."

"So you've heard nothing about a missing baby, either?"

He hooked his thumbs on the edges of his pants pockets. "Nary a word. Are you making any progress with Miz Armina?"

"Some, yes. She's recalling bits and pieces."

"It would help a right smart if you could find out the general vicinity of where she was on Monday. I've been up just about every holler you can speak of asking around. Somebody said there was a new family moved in up Tattler's Branch Road, but I haven't had the chance to get up there yet."

Lilly shaded her eyes against the glare of the sun. "At least the baby's getting good care. I can't help worrying about the mother, though. How could she not even come looking for her daughter?"

"You can't figure people, Doc."

Lilly watched his face light up when Mazy came their way holding a small brown-paper sack.

"I bought a piece of chocolate cake to share three ways," she said, swinging her skirts like a schoolgirl. "Don't you just love chocolate, Sheriff?"

"I'll leave the cake to you ladies—sweets to the sweetest."

Mazy batted her eyelashes. "Oh, Sheriff. You flatter a girl."

Lilly was taken aback. It was a little too soon for Mazy to

be so forward, and as for Chanis, she wouldn't have thought he had a flirtatious bone in his body. It wasn't that she didn't approve of them enjoying each other's company, but she expected decorum to be demonstrated.

"Sheriff Clay, perhaps you can stop later in the day to attend to the matter we discussed?"

Chanis tore his gaze from Mazy. Lilly was rewarded to see his face flush with embarrassment. "Yes, ma'am, Dr. Still. Sorry, I forgot my manners there for a minute."

Mazy, on the other hand, didn't have a clue. "Sure you don't want this cake?" she said, flashing her dimples.

"I'd best get back to work," he said with a tip of his hat. "Dr. Still, Miss Pelfrey. It was good to see you."

"Shoot," Mazy said as he walked away. "I didn't buy this cake for myself."

"Mazy Pelfrey, I'm not at all pleased with your behavior just now."

"What did I do wrong?"

Lilly looked around to make sure no one could overhear. "When you are in the company of a young man, you act like a lady. You don't bat your eyes and you don't swing your skirts. What would Mama say?"

Mazy looked as guileless as Kip would just before he stole somebody's supper. "It's not as if I've had any practice! Daddy wouldn't let me or Molly off the porch. Why, I had to sneak out after dark to . . ."

"See T. M.?" Lilly asked, remembering the initialed heart on the bathroom mirror.

"It was only once, Lilly, and I only went as far as the apple tree. We didn't hold hands or anything." Mazy tossed her head. "I don't like him anymore anyway. He is just a boy."

"And Chanis Clay is?"

"A man," she said, as serious as if Lilly had asked a test question. "Don't worry, though. I'm just trying him out."

"I can see why Daddy kept you on the porch."

Mazy sighed dramatically. "Goodness gracious, Lilly. I think you are out of sorts again." With that she flounced up the road toward the clinic. The little brown sack flounced with her.

Lilly saw that she would need to take a different tack with Mazy. Maybe she had been too harsh. It wasn't as if Chanis Clay would take advantage. On the other hand, Chanis was not the only man in Skip Rock. A girl like Mazy could attract the wrong sort of fellow. Lilly had seen too many young women ruined and abandoned after being swayed by the romance of the moment. It was hard to stop a train once it left the station. She wondered if Mama had had *the talk* with Mazy.

She remembered with a smile when Mama had first talked to her about the birds and the bees. Lilly had been as presumptuous as Mazy, if in a different way, saying, "I know all about it already, Mama. There's a whole chapter about procreation in your obstetrical book." After bedtime that night, she'd heard her mama and daddy sharing a laugh over her pronouncement that she knew it all already. Of course she hadn't known it all. And truthfully, she wasn't interested in anything outside the pages of a book until she was courted by Tern. Their marriage license was signed, sealed, and delivered before she chanced to learn what waited outside the facts. Perhaps that's why she was having such difficulty relating to Mazy.

As Lilly walked, drumbeats of pain pulsed in her temples. Maybe she'd just chain Mazy to the bed or, better yet, send her back to Troublesome Creek.

If her head didn't hurt, she'd laugh at herself. If her mother and daddy could handle her leaving home at seventeen to attend college in the big city, she supposed she could handle Mazy's mild flirtation.

The office was swamped. The nurse said all the folks who'd left earlier had returned, which backed up the scheduled afternoon patients. Lilly took her seat behind her desk. A little brown sack sat waiting for her.

"Give me a minute before you start sending them in," she said to the nurse as she silently blessed Mazy's heart. Chocolate was good for headaches.

CHAPTER 12

THE HOG UNDER ANNE'S PORCH grunted a greeting when Lilly climbed the steps on Friday morning. She fought an urge to cover her nose. Besides being unsanitary, the sty didn't give off the most pleasant odor. She wondered why Anne's husband hadn't put the pig out behind the barn as most farmers would.

Before she could raise her hand to knock, the door swung open.

"Mumph," a tall, skinny man grunted before upending a bucket of slop over the side of the porch. The hog squealed with delight.

The man set the blue granite bucket down and left without another word. A long-legged red hound dog sniffed Lilly's ankles before following him across the yard.

"Cletus, I wish you'd rinse the bucket before you set it down," Anne yelled to his back as she stepped outside and pounded the porch floor with the handle of a broom. "Settle down, Sassy. Go on in, Doc. The baby's under the table." She picked up the bucket. "I'm just going to the well and wash this out. Otherwise it'll stink up the house."

Amy was in a high chair pushed up to the table. She flashed a grin at Lilly and held out her spoon. "Eat?"

Lilly pretended to eat oatmeal from Amy's spoon. Amy chortled and fed herself.

"Where's Glory? Where's the baby?"

Amy leaned over the side of the chair and pointed with her spoon. "Baba dere."

Glory was sleeping on her belly in the Moses basket. Lilly was pleased to see her face was turned to the side. Given her poor muscle tone, she might not be able to free herself if her nose got pressed into the pillow that served as a mattress. A fragile tracery of veins was visible under her patchy blonde hair. The baby didn't wake up when Lilly bent to slide the bell of the stethoscope to her tiny chest.

From the chair, Amy tapped the back of Lilly's head with her spoon. When Lilly stood, the child pulled her own undershirt up.

"This one's sharp as a tack," Lilly said, placing the bell over Amy's heart as Anne returned.

"Ain't she, though?" Anne replied. She parted the feed-sack curtains tacked to a makeshift washstand and slid the slop bucket out of sight. "So how do you find the wee one?"

Lilly put the stethoscope in her bag and snapped it shut. "Do you mind if I wake her?"

"Watch this." Anne wiped Amy's hands and face with a wet rag and lifted her from the high chair.

Amy went right for the basket and knelt. With one chubby hand, she gently patted the baby's back. "Moring, sunsine, uppy uppy."

"Morning, sunshine," Anne interpreted. "Up, up."

The baby stirred under Amy's hand. Amy flashed a toothy grin. "Baba up."

Lilly did a cursory exam before taking a portable infant scale from her linen carryall. Amy watched intently as she assembled it atop the kitchen table.

Anne stripped the baby and positioned her in the sturdy cotton sling. The needle swung back and forth before settling on six pounds, three ounces. "Oh, look, she's gained four ounces since we weighed her Wednesday morning."

"A result of your good care, Anne. I wish we knew her birth weight."

Anne reapplied the diaper and tucked the infant's floppy arms into her long cotton sleeper. Amy tugged the sleeper down over Glory's legs. "Dere," she said, a proud little mama.

"So you're saying she's getting better?"

"Her heart's the same, but the weight gain is a good sign." Lilly held the baby's tongue down with a wooden depressor and looked for white patches on the mucous membranes. "Any sign of thrush?"

"No, Amy never had it, either. I keep everything real clean."

Lilly slid the depressor out. "There's no doubt in my mind about that, Anne."

Amy grabbed for the depressor. Lilly gave her a clean one. Just then, the pig set to squealing.

Anne threw back her head and laughed. "Just because I keep a pig under the porch . . ."

"Ah," Lilly said, joining the laughter. "I expect that pig gets a bath every Saturday night."

"I would if I had me a big enough pan." Anne dabbed tears of mirth from the corners of her eyes. "Seriously, Doc Still. If you were to say something to Cletus, I bet he'd move Sassy's sty."

"Might I ask why he put the pen there?"

"He said it'd be the easier, seeing as all he had to do was nail some two-by-fours to the porch posts. And I really wanted that pig, so I agreed. You know when it comes to men, you've got to give a little to get a little."

Lilly nodded. That was so true.

"Now, I ain't speaking ill of my husband. To my mind, the only thing uglier than a woman ragging on her man is one dipping snuff. But I will admit that Cletus is somewhat work brittle." Anne fidgeted with her apron and looked away from Lilly. "Which reminds me, Doc, did you happen to bring my wages? It being Friday and all."

"Oh, where's my mind?" Lilly said. She laid Glory back in the basket and took an envelope containing a few bills from her bag. "I'm sorry you had to remind me."

Anne opened the warming oven atop the cookstove and tucked the envelope inside. "What Cletus don't know won't hurt him," she said. "Or me."

"Gracious, Anne, aren't you afraid you'll forget and burn it up?"

"I've got a hidey-hole in the barn. I'll put it in there when he ain't about."

Amy had settled beside Glory in the basket. Her feet hung over the edge. Anne covered the girls with a lightweight flannel baby blanket. "They'll take a good nap," she said.

Lilly disassembled the baby scale while Anne poured sassafras tea into cups. Lilly had to restrain herself from looking at her watch. The morning was slipping away, but it seemed that Anne needed to talk.

"Sweetening?" Anne asked, offering a bowl of brown sugar.

Lilly stirred half a teaspoon into her licorice-scented tea and took a sip. "Mmm, my mother used to make this for me."

"Cletus found a sassafras tree up on the ridge and dug up a root. He's always bringing in something extra. Yesterday it was mushrooms—reminds me to give you some to take home—and greens for a poke salad." She shook her head. "I didn't mean to make him sound worthless. It's just he . . . Well, if he has a penny, he'll try to turn it into two. In a coal mining town there's always a game going on, if you catch my drift." Her spoon went round and round in her cup. The tea swirled like a tiny copper-colored whirlpool.

"How do you manage, Anne? Who watches your daughter when you work nights?"

"If Cletus ain't out roaming, he does. He's never let me down as far as Amy goes. He's real good with her. If he's gone, I take Amy over to my sister's. A couple of times, she's slept at the clinic in the supply closet." She put her hands up in a what-can-you-do gesture.

Anne seemed to have forgotten to whom she was speaking. This was a bit of information best not shared with Lilly. A hospital, even a small one, couldn't have babies sleeping on the premises. When Anne returned to work, Lilly would have to address the issue. Not to mention, Lilly hadn't thought about what would happen in her own situation. Who would look after her baby when she was off to work and Tern was who knows where? The art of being a woman presented a myriad of problems not faced by men, and for a workingwoman, it seemed the complexity of life increased a hundredfold. Why was everything on the woman's shoulders?

While Anne sliced fresh-baked gingerbread, Lilly thought of her own mother. As the only midwife on Troublesome Creek, she was often called out in the middle of the night and sometimes she would be gone for days, yet Lilly couldn't recall ever feeling abandoned or less than completely cherished. Oh, she needed to talk to her mother. Mama would help her figure everything out.

Anne offered her a fork. The cake was rich and moist, just the way Lilly liked it. She'd better be careful. Chocolate cake yesterday and gingerbread today—she'd soon be letting out her skirts for more reasons than one.

It was eventide before Lilly had a chance to pen a letter to her mother. She'd thought of calling the Troublesome Creek post office, which contained the area's one telephone, and asking the postmaster to get a message to Mama asking her to call Lilly back. But she thought better of it. Receiving a telephone message was much like receiving a telegram: too often a portent of bad news to come.

She carried her portable writing desk to the dining room, where she could sit in a chair beside the open window. Outside, the pink and white peony bushes were in full bloom, nearly past their prime, and their lush scent drifted in like a sweet benediction. She kicked off her slippers and rested the soles of her feet against the cool hardwood floor. By the end of the day her feet often hurt. If her husband were home, he would massage them with scented lotion. Where was a man when you needed one?

Mazy was out for a walk with Chanis Clay. Lilly had had a word with him and she trusted he would be respectful. She had yet to talk seriously with Mazy, but the time would come. They had taken Kip, so she should be able to write without interruption.

The inside of her desk had various-size compartments: one for business envelopes, one for personal correspondence, one for stationery, one for clean blotters. There was even a small drawer for miscellaneous items like stamps and nibs.

She chose two sheets of lavender-scented stationery and a matching envelope.

Lilly loved the art of writing. She liked the mechanics of unscrewing the metal lid from the small pot of navy-blue ink and relished the piercing scent of ferrous sulfate released like a fluid genie from the bottle. It mattered to her that the ink pot fit perfectly into the inkwell atop the desk, and she enjoyed the heft of her favorite tortoiseshell pen when she dipped its nib into the dark liquid, spreading tiny ripples across the surface. She was particular about her ink. Too thin and it dripped off the nib in ugly splotches, ruining the pristine page; too thick and it left dregs of goopy snail's tracks.

The ink flowed perfectly in lovely swirls as she began:

My dearest Mama,

I trust this letter finds you, as well as Daddy and Molly and the boys, enjoying these long midsummer days. My mind wanders with you through the garden and along the creek, perhaps to the bench under the willow tree, where we could sit and talk for a while in the cool of the evening.

Mazy is well—perhaps too well. She is quite taken with a fellow. Chanis Clay is the sheriff here in Skip Rock and a fine young man. But you know, Mama, Mazy follows her heart and never her head, and so I watch her carefully. I am allowing them to take short walks together, always with Kip to chaperone. (I send a smile along with the last sentence.) I hope you don't disapprove, as I'm sure Daddy does, but she will soon be eighteen.

You and Daddy both will be pleased to learn that Mazy started helping out in the clinic this week. She catches on quickly and does good work when it is in her interest. It is really quite nice to have her here, especially now that it seems Tern might be gone for the rest of the summer. Tell Daddy there was a major accident at a mine in Canada that begged Tern's attention. He might be able to read about it in the Lexington Herald *newspaper. A patient told me he saw the story coming over the wire when he went to town to place a telegraph message. It will be old news but still news when the postman delivers it to your mailbox.*

My practice is busy, Mama, and sometimes difficult. You will be distressed to learn that a baby appears to have been abandoned in our community. The little thing is quite compromised physically and more than likely intellectually. For the by-and-by, she is in the care of a local nurse. No one seems to be looking for the baby. At first, I was in fear for her mother, but the sheriff thinks the baby was just thrown out with the bathwater and I tend to agree. As if that weren't tragedy enough, yesterday a local man was killed when he was hit by a train on a nearby track. Of course, I'm thankful for my training and for being of assistance, but still, one's heart aches at times. Just as I've watched you do in moments of travail, I cling to Scripture for solace.

"He maketh me to lie down in green pastures: he leadeth me beside the still waters." Is there another verse as lovely, as comforting, as these words from King David?

Lilly dipped her pen and drew a fanciful vine with leaves and flowers across the page to separate the busy news from the delicate and private words that were for her mother alone.

My dearest Mama, I have news that I am sure you long to hear. My heart is so full with it that I'm holding back tears that threaten to spill over onto the page. I'm twelve weeks with new life. A tiny heart beats beneath my own. How to explain the joy mixed with trepidation this presents to me?

Did this happen when you became expectant with me, Mama? Did you know before you even missed, as I did? From the very first moment, I was aware. I left my husband's embrace with the surety that life had quickened from our time together. And with awareness, strange fears and odd superstitions beset me. I watch for signs—if a wren swoops in through an open door, a loss is coming. If the robin builds her nest in the apple tree, then my nest is secure. Both have happened, so what does it mean? Because my trust is in the Lord, I know these things have no import, but I seem to no longer be in charge of my mental faculties. (Another smile here.)

I've told no one, although I attempted to tell Tern via telephone, for who knows when I will see him next?

It was unsettling to have the words carefully formed for expression only to have them abruptly denied by something as impersonal as a telephone line.

You would laugh to see me already stretching the waistbands of my skirts. It seems I am showing very early. Oh, Mama, surely this doesn't mean twins! Twins like Molly and Mazy! I hadn't thought of the possibility until this moment. Now I suppose I will have true signs to watch for, like two heartbeats instead of one. I will be so relieved when enough time has passed that I can hear my little one's life force through the bell of my stethoscope or feel him kick against my belly. Him? We'll see, but I feel sure.

I so wish I could see your face when you read these words. I miss you more than I can express. Thank you again for allowing Mazy to come for the summer. I pray you can somehow find a way to visit soon. I forgot to say I now have a telephone in the house—the number is 32—and one in the office, number 33. Please call; I long to hear your voice.

I must close now. Mazy has not returned from her walk, so I must go out and call her in. Perhaps I'll cut a switch. I'm sure Mazy is quaking in her shoes from fear of stirring up my wrath.

Oh, Mama, just writing to you lightens my mood. I send you all my love.

With fond regards,
Your daughter Lilly

Lilly laid the pages aside to let the ink dry. The envelope was already addressed.

A sudden warm breeze sent one sheet flipping across the table. She moved them to the sideboard, then leaned on her hands and looked out the window. There might be rain tonight. If so, the last of the peonies would be blighted.

Grabbing her shears and a vase from the kitchen, she went out the door and around to the bed. The luscious flowers bent double, nearly sweeping the ground with their heavy heads. She should have taken the time to stake them. After cutting a few long stalks, she stripped the lower leaves and put them in the vase.

Running the V of her fingers up underneath one plump blossom, she let the weight of it rest in her cupped palm. The pink petals were delicate as silk and fragrant with perfume. This one would be nice on her nightstand. She tugged gently, but the bloom disintegrated, showering her feet with disappointment.

Last year, in this same season, she'd lost her first pregnancy. She'd been so shocked that morning as she dressed for her day to feel the one tugging pain and then the tiny bit of tissue loosing its hold in her womb just as quickly as the peony loosed its petals. The loss felt immeasurable.

She'd cried for days, holding the pain so tightly to her heart that she could barely catch her breath. She should have told Tern; it was his loss too. But in the pattern familiar to them, he'd been somewhere else. By the time he was home again, she'd stored the words away like flowers drying stiffly in an attic.

To this day Lilly blamed herself. She supposed that's why she hadn't told Tern or even her mother. The day before her miscarriage, some bow hunters had carried another man into the clinic. He'd been shot through the chest from behind. The arrow rose and fell with each of his shuddering breaths.

"I thought he was a bear," one man kept repeating. "I mistook him for a bear."

Lilly hadn't felt at all well that morning, but she'd still come in. Who would do her job if she wasn't there? The man presented an interesting case. What if the arrow had pierced his aorta and was now serving as a tamponade to arrest bleeding? Would he hemorrhage and go into shock when the weapon was removed?

His hunting companions struggled to hold him upright on the surgical table while Lilly worked to sever the sharp tip from the wooden shank with her small bone saw. The man was corpulent. Fat jiggled with each back-and-forth movement of her saw. Rivers of sweat coursed down his chest, making the operative site slick as grease. Lilly struggled to keep the saw steady. Her fingers cramped with the effort. Her own perspiration stung her eyes. Finally free, the chiseled flint clattered when she dropped it into a waiting metal basin.

Moving to the man's back, Lilly grasped the wooden rod just above the feathered end. Her patient rested his chin on a buddy's shoulder. The other fellow kept a steadying hand on his arm. Lilly pulled. It was harder to do than she thought it would be. The rod resisted removal. It made an odd sucking sound when she pulled harder, and the man groaned.

It all went bad at once. The man with the steadying hand turned white as a sheet and fell backward, hitting the floor like a felled tree. As Lilly pulled the arrow, her patient came with it and so did his companion. In no time they were all in a heap behind the surgical table. Lilly was on the bottom, clutching the bloody arrow to her chest.

With great good fortune, it wasn't the disaster it could have been. The men crawled out from behind the table. The fainter recovered. They picked Lilly up and dusted her off. The arrowed man didn't hemorrhage, unless a person could hemorrhage embarrassment. Lilly dressed his wound and sent them all on their way. They promised deer meat in season as well as squirrel and wild turkey for Thanksgiving.

Everything had turned out okay, or so it seemed, until the next morning when Lilly lost her baby. She had been so foolish to think she could carry on as if being pregnant didn't change anything—as if she could manage the same way she always had. As if pluck and determination alone would carry her baby to term. Of course she blamed herself—who else was there?

And now here she was, a scant year later, still doing the very same thing. There was a lesson to be learned, but obviously she was reluctant to learn it. It all came down to responsibility, and she was responsible to many. If she could just hold on until Ned came home, everything would be all right. He would take much of the day-to-day burden from her.

The breeze teased the petals just out of reach when she

bent to pick them up. They danced across the yard and out of sight. Lilly lifted the vase and studied the peonies. They wouldn't last long either, but they were no less lovely, no less significant, for the briefness of their time. She would enjoy them while she could.

CHAPTER 13

ARMINA STOPPED chopping weeds long enough to pluck a grasshopper from an ear of corn. The insect glowed oddly in the pinky-lavender twilight. He cocked his tiny head and looked at her straight on as if to say, *"What? Is there not enough for both of us?"* She didn't have the heart to twist his head off. Instead she flicked him through the air. To spite her, he left a spew of brown sap on the heel of her hand.

Though the ear of corn was still tiny with unformed kernels, she shucked it, slicked off the tender silks, and tasted of what would soon be summer's bounty. A body had to be quick to get corn for the table—one day it'd be plump and juicy, fine for roasting ears and corn pudding, and next it would turn tough and chewy, the milk dried up and the meat sticking between your teeth. And past that, in the fall, the corn would be rich as gold and ready to harvest. Even her small crop would yield enough to supplement her chickens' feed all winter. For her own use, she'd grind some into cornmeal and boil some with lye to make hominy.

Later on, when the weather turned bitter, she'd pass the time weaving chair bottoms from dried shucks. She had two busted-out chairs of her own, and one of Doc's, sitting in the shed, waiting to be rescued. And just you wait, as soon as word got around that she was weaving, a neighbor or two would drop by with their own worn-out seats. That was okay. It made a body feel useful and kept idleness at bay—devil's workshop and all that.

Armina parted two cornstalks and looked to see where Hannah might be. There she was, plucking pole beans from a tepee and dropping them into her gathered-up apron. The silly thing had tried to turn Armina's mind away from the garden. She wanted to sit on the porch and fiddle around with the embroidery they'd started that morning—colorful flowers and birds on the hems of pillow slips. To Armina's mind that was foul-weather work, like weaving with husks. Who would choose to fritter away a fine evening like this on fancywork? Especially when weeds were getting the jump on the garden. From the looks of things, Armina had lain idle a little too long.

Armina hated worse than anything to admit, even to herself, that the nurse was right, but she had used up all her strength. Her legs were weak as day-old kittens, and here she'd barely scratched the ground with her hoe. She wished she'd brought a milk pail so she could upend it and take a seat. If she could rest for a minute, her head would clear up.

When she first started feeling poorly, around the time she'd planted the corn seed in the spring, she'd carried a milk stool from end of row to end of row. She'd push herself down the furrows, even when she thought her body would plumb give out, by promising a rest on that stool. She could have just sat on the ground, except if she got that low down, she had a dickens of a time getting up. She'd have to turn over into a crawl and heave herself to her knees and then to a crouch and finally straight. She'd be mortified if somebody caught her in such a humiliating position, looking like an oversize baby.

"Ha," she shouted in glee. There was the stool poking out from the weeds at the end of the row just ahead.

"Miz Tippen?" she heard Hannah call. "You okay? You ready to head in?"

"A few more minutes," she said. "It ain't dark yet."

"You need me, you holler."

"Sure thing," Armina said, wishing the woman would keep still. Gabbing back and forth was using up all her lung reserves.

The T-shaped milk stool felt good and solid beneath her weight, and from where she sat, she could see Turnip Tippen's cow pasture and his herd of a dozen fawn-colored Jerseys. Jerseys were her favorite kind of cow; their milk made the best butter bar none. Guernseys were okay too, but she didn't much care for the splotchy black-and-white Holsteins with their high rumps and long legs. She liked a cow a little closer to the ground.

The round-bellied Jerseys were on the other side of the fence, all bunched up under a tree, murmuring low to each other. The lead cow shifted from foot to foot, jarring the bell around her neck. Armina had always taken pleasure in cow talk, but you'd think if cows had sense enough to converse, they'd be smart enough to stay out from under trees. One pop-up storm, one bolt out of the blue, and the whole bunch would be hamburger meat.

As the cows stirred, insects shot out from the pasture grass and weeds. A brown-headed cowbird darted around the herd plucking bugs from the air. Armina fairly hated those pirates of the sky for stealing the nests of smaller birds, the finches, warblers, and wrens. The songbirds hunted and gathered from daylight to dark just to have their nests taken over by such trash. The cowbirds were clever, though; she'd give them that. Generally they'd lay just one egg in as many as five borrowed nests, spreading their brood over half an acre. Then they were off scot-free while songbirds hatched and fed their wayward, aggressive young, often to the detriment of their own nestlings. She'd climbed many a tree in her time plucking the oversize eggs from among the valid ones and pitching them to the ground.

A warm zephyr, shepherding in a hint of rain, stirred the air around Armina's feet and waltzed through the treetops.

Leaves sighed in pleasure. The cowbell tolled dully, its sound muted by a dozen thickset bodies. One cow mooed softly and another replied.

Oh, but for lack of vigor, Armina would climb the fence and go stand among the cows. As soon as Ned got back, she'd tell him she wanted a cow of her own. He'd say, "But Uncle Turnip gives us plenty of milk." Which would be true enough, but she'd never liked being beholden to his family. Besides which, there was more benefit to keeping a cow than milk. A cow got you up in the morning and called you in of an evening. They had straightforward needs and when those needs were met, they gave straightforward reward.

Besides, by the time Turnip got around to their house with his leftover bucket, it was no longer fresh. Armina liked her milk still warm and swirled with yellow. Turnip skimmed the cream from the top and sold it at the cream station over on Market Street. She just knew it. You couldn't churn the stuff long enough to make the butter rise.

Why was her brainpan circling in on itself to dredge up thoughts of Turnip Tippen? Here she was on a fine summer evening with her piece of the world spread out before her like a picnic supper, but instead of offering psalms, she was entertaining herself with bits of aged aggravation.

A couple walking down the road distracted her. She could see them clearly from where she sat. It was Mazy and a fellow—that young lawman. What was his name? She screwed up her face and concentrated. It started with a *C*— didn't it? Canny or Cholly, something unusual-like.

Mazy giggled and he responded, his deep-throated laugh an undercurrent to Mazy's light one. When they came to the red metal gate that led to the pasture, Mazy tucked Kip under her arm and stepped up on the bottom rung. Her companion unlatched the gate and swung it back and forth. Mazy shrieked with delight like she was on a carnival ride. The cows stirred but did not leave the comfort of the tree.

Armina supposed she needn't worry about the livestock. Surely a man with a badge on his chest wouldn't forget to close the gate. Nor should she worry about Mazy; they were just playing the fool like all courting couples did, as she and Ned had done not so long ago. No way would Doc Lilly let her sister step out with Chanis Clay until she'd given him the once-over twice.

How about that? She'd remembered the fellow's name: Chanis Clay. Her brainpan was cranking again. Maybe she'd been trying too hard. Speaking of hard—Chanis had him a hard act to follow. His daddy had been a stand-up guy and tough as groundhog leather. One time, on a Sunday afternoon, she and Ned had come upon a couple of swags slugging it out on the church lawn, fighting over a quart of whiskey. The church lawn! On Sunday! Who would have thought of such? Then came the sheriff, busting out of a deacons' meeting, grabbing a collar of each of the bums, and tossing them over the graveyard fence—and not gently, either. He made those old boys stay in the graveyard all night—told them if they stepped one foot out, it would be three days in the hoosegow. Come the next Sunday, those two boys had been in the first row.

Poor Chanis. Everybody expected him to be his daddy all over again. And now he had all his brothers and sisters and his sickly ma to take care of. Armina wondered if Chanis even wanted to be a lawman. He seemed a bit tender for the job.

Mazy hopped off the gate and put Kip down in a tangled heap. Chanis stooped to free Kip's leash. The dog held up each foot in order like he knew exactly what needed done. When Chanis straightened, he brushed against Mazy. Armina held her breath. Surely Mazy would move away. But she didn't. It was just a brushing of his lips against her cheek until Mazy turned the other cheek. Armina was sure she could see sparks, but no, it was just a thousand lightning bugs rising languidly from the pasture grass, testing out their tiny lanterns.

Well! If Chanis Clay had a hard job now, just wait and see what would happen if he took Mazy Pelfrey into the mix. Mazy was pretty as a speckled pup tied to a red wagon, but she needed a lot of attention. And what if his mother's health continued to decline? Mazy would break like a dry limb in a windstorm under that kind of pressure. Armina was not sure if the girl could boil water without scorching it.

Ah, she was getting ahead of herself. It wasn't even a real kiss. They hadn't jumped the broom. Every little thing would work out if it was meant to be. Just look at her and Ned.

Night was creeping down the mountain like a thief stealing light as he went. She might as well go in while she could still see the way. From a high exposed perch, a female cowbird let loose with a harsh, rattling *glug-glug-gl*ee. Armina shook her fist, wishing for a rock to toss at the noisy thing—sounding brass, tinkling cymbal—no care in its heart for its fellow creatures.

The milk stool wobbled beneath her. Without a thought, she reached down for her walking stick to steady her rising. Her fingers skimmed the weeds she'd left drying in the row and scrabbled through clods of dirt but felt no familiar trusted aid. What had she done with her sycamore stick? And furthermore, how would she ever get up from her own exposed perch? Oh, to have the wings of a bird.

As if she could read Armina's mind, Hannah appeared and offered a supportive hand. Armina had no choice but to submit. She felt like a useless old codger as she clung to the nurse's arm.

"Should I bring in the seat?" Hannah asked.

"Leave it. I'll need it again." With a kick of her foot, Armina moved the small wooden stool back up under a row. "Ha, the old gal's got some kick left."

Hannah patted her arm. "You're far from old, Miz Tippen. You did real good today. We'll soon get you set right again."

Armina was in no position to chide Hannah for her patronizing way. They shuffled down the row, scrunching their shoulders tight to escape the green pointed blades. It would sting like a hundred paper cuts if you got sliced by one.

"Say, isn't that Mazy with Chanis Clay?" Hannah asked as they came out of the garden.

"Mazy," they could hear a voice calling through the dusk. "Mazy Pelfrey!"

"Yep," Armina said, "and that's Doc Lilly calling her in."

"They make a cute couple," Hannah said.

Armina nodded. She'd keep the kiss to herself. "Yep."

Hannah patted the bundle of beans tied up in her apron. "We'll have a good dinner tomorrow. I'll scratch up some new potatoes to go with."

Armina let go of Hannah's arm. The woman's constant attention had just about wooled her to death. She might bust a gut, but she'd walk the rest of the way home on her own. And when she got there, she'd find her sycamore walking stick.

CHAPTER 14

SHADE HARMON crossed his arms, leaned one shoulder against the side of the building, and waited. From where he stood in the alley between the Market Street Commissary and the cream station, he could easily watch the doctor's office. It was Saturday night. You could tell even if you didn't already know by the faint sounds of rowdy music from a couple streets over. You'd think the office would be closed on a Saturday night, but the light still shone in the window.

An hour later, he was still watching. Although the shade at the window was pulled to the sill, he could see a flicker of shadow—the manifestation of the doctor, he was sure. He could tell it was her by the way she carried herself, like she was in charge of something important. Even in shadow, she appeared sure of herself. It was different to see a woman that way. Tuesday, when she'd treated him for his wounds, she'd looked him straight in the eye without as much as a blink, and her hands had been strong and steady when she worked. And whoa, Nellie, she was a looker with that dark hair and those gray eyes. What impressed him most, though, was that she didn't ask his name—like she didn't give a hoot if he was the governor or Jack Sprat.

He liked to study people. Some might think he was too quiet, even standoffish—like he cared what anybody else thought—but the truth was, he was taking their measure. Like a snake hiding under a riffle, he was waiting to strike.

Working one finger between the buttons of his blue chambray shirt, he rubbed around one of his wounds. They itched worse than a mosquito bite, but he was afraid to scratch them. Scratching might start up the bleeding again.

The stench of sulfur in the alley bothered him. Coffee grounds, eggshells, and apple cores littered the area around an overflowing garbage bin. Unbound newspapers were piled on top of the bin—just waiting for a storm to blow them all over town. People were so lazy. To his mind there was no excuse for being slovenly—he liked things clean and orderly.

Shade reached into his shirt pocket for his tobacco pouch and a rolling paper. Tapping the pouch, he filled the paper with cut leaf, licked the edge, then rolled it in a tight spool. He cupped his hand to block the flare of the match he struck against the building. Tar-paper shingles made a perfect strike plate.

Maybe he should go make another call on the good doctor. Hadn't she told him to come back? He could claim he was still worried about gangrene. That would be a sad, lingering way to die, but when he'd pulled the packing, it didn't stink. Surely gangrene would smell as bad as a lye-free outhouse.

He narrowed his eyes with the first deep draw on the cigarette. A smoke would take the edge off, and he needed something to do that. The edge on him was sharp as a whetted knife. Booze wouldn't work. He had to keep alert.

Man, he was that surprised when he'd walked into the office and seen a lady—and a pretty one at that. Since when did women become doctors? He leaned and spit in the dirt. She didn't yammer on, either—bossing him around like his wife did. No, *had done*. Just like his wife had done.

Bile and tobacco smoke backed up in his throat and he spit again. That was never supposed to happen, but Noreen had finally said one word too many. She'd stoked his anger like cordwood in a cookstove, chunk after chunk after chunk; who could blame him for what had happened? He'd kept his tongue and kept his tongue until finally he broke.

Shade was so tired he could sleep standing up. He hadn't been able to rest since. Every time he closed his eyes, that rock came crashing down again. Why hadn't he just walked away? If he could just turn back time like the poet wished—"Backward, turn backward, O Time, in your flight."

Although if he was going to wish for time to turn backward,

he might as well wish he'd never met Sweet Noreen. He could see the big *T* for trouble stamped on her forehead from across the street that night in Cincinnati. She'd been alone, standing in a puddle of gaslight outside the train station. The hack stand was empty, and it was freezing cold, spitting sleet. So what did he do? Like a white knight drawn to a damsel in distress, he crossed the street.

"Hey, little lady, what are you doing out here all by your lonesome?" he'd said as blustery as the weather.

"I'm minding my own business," she shot back. "Who might you be?"

He swept the hat from his head and bowed. "Shade Harmon, at your service, ma'am. And you are?"

"Sweet Noreen," she said.

"That it?"

"That's enough for you to know, mister." She fished in her handbag and pulled out a small pot of carmine. She rubbed its waxy surface and patted fresh color on her already-shiny red lips, then capped the pot and dropped it back inside her bag. "Say, do you have a smoke?"

He resisted the urge to brush sleet from her hair. She was just about the most intriguing creature he had ever seen, and that was saying a lot.

"I know a place a couple of streets over. We could go there—grab some coffee, get out of the weather."

"All right," she said, "as long as you mind your manners."

"Ah, Sweet Noreen, my mother taught me how to treat a lady."

"Oh, she did, did she?" Noreen flipped the long braid of his hair off his shoulder. "Why didn't your mama teach you not to wear your hair like a girl?"

Suddenly, the night lit up like the Fourth of July. He liked a gal with a little sass. Or so he'd thought, that cold winter's night in Cincinnati.

Yawning, Shade dropped his smoke and ground it under the heel of his boot. He had to stop thinking about Noreen. *What's done is done.*

The shadows were still playing on the window shade across the street. Maybe he'd rest just a minute—take a load off. He took a few sheets of newsprint from atop the trash bin and spread them on the ground. Lowering himself, he crossed his legs at the ankle and let the rough tar-paper wall support his shoulders. If he kept his head turned to the side, he could see the doctor's office just fine.

The next thing he knew, a booted foot was tapping his leg.

"Move along, buddy," someone said. "Go home and sleep it off."

Glancing up, he saw moonlight bouncing off a six-pointed star. Keeping his head down, he scrambled to his feet. He was a real smooth operator, letting the sheriff catch him sleeping on the job. "Sorry," he mumbled, moving away, pretending to stumble over his own feet. Hopefully, to the sheriff, he was just another drunk.

Shade kept walking, swaying ever so slightly so as not to appear too intoxicated. The last thing he wanted was to spend the night on a jail bunk. He could feel the eyes of the law boring into his back—tattooing *murderer* between his shoulder blades.

Two streets over and he was at the only place to buy spirits in the one-horse town. *Sally's Teas and Fine Chocolates*, the sign out front said. It should have read, *Teahouse by day and blind tiger by night*. The sturdy back door of the fine tea emporium sported another small hinged door through which money could be exchanged for whiskey or pure locally distilled moonshine. Like most other alkie-free burgs he'd been in, the law turned a blind eye to such establishments if they turned off the lights before midnight on a Saturday. There'd be no drinking on Sunday.

He wasn't interested in spirits. That wasn't his particular vice. But where you found alcohol, there was sure to be a furtive game going on—another thing the law turned a blind eye to in most mining towns as long as you kept it on the q.t. The men who played craps were mostly burned-out miners looking for a bit of action to stretch thin paychecks. Some of them weren't half-bad at turning a dime into a dollar. Except for that one fellow—he was the unluckiest gambler ever to pitch a die. Shade had never seen him win a single penny, yet he kept pulling money from his pocket, and like a rube, he blew on the dice before they rolled from his hand.

Shade was careful not to seem expert. So far, on the few nights he'd played with this particular group, he placed wins and losses. No one had caught on that he was biding his time, like that snake under the riffle.

Yep, there they were under the light from the bar window: Hoppy, Happy, and Grunt, hunched on the ground like toads waiting for bugs. Shade liked to assign names to people he didn't know, and never hoped to, based on their actions. It was a way to keep people straight in his mind. Hoppy jumped like a gigged frog when he was lucky. Happy kept a grin on win or lose, and Grunt never said a word you could understand without effort. Shade could predict what a person would do by the moniker he gave them. Except, that is, for Sweet Noreen. Her goal in life had been to keep him guessing.

Happy had just won playing a single roll on the hop, so the fellows made room for Shade. He hunched down, calling out bets in turn, his money a short stack of indulgence. Grunt rattled the dice, blew on his babies, then rolled them against the stair stoop they used for a backstop. One die bounced off into the sparse grass ringing the packed-dirt playing field. Short roll—didn't count. Grunt found the die and rattled both again. Hoppy leaped and settled on his haunches when he won.

The game continued. Shade glanced at his pocket watch; it was 11:55, time for one more roll. The heat was on. Bets were placed. Grunt hadn't won a cent all night but he threw down a ten spot. It was like taking honey from a dead bear. Shade called a hard way and won with boxcars just before the light over the window winked out. He raked in his money and stood. No sense saying adios. He'd see them again Monday night unless he hit pay dirt in another way.

He walked down the passway between the bar and the bank. The incongruity was not lost on him. Both took your money and then turned a cold shoulder. He should know. Once he'd been a regular working stiff, putting his earnings into an account bearing interest. He was saving for the house with the white picket fence his first wife yearned for. It took him five years to save that money, but the look on Betsy's face when he turned the key to the front door of that five-room house made it worth every single day he toiled for the Man.

Then the business hit the skids and the Man let him go. He could have found another job easy, but Betsy was sick. There wasn't anybody else but him. Two months was all he was behind, but the bank was hiding under the riffle. They called in the mortgage, and he lost Betsy's white picket fence and her five-room house. She died in one of those rooms as he was packing up their belongings. He couldn't help but believe that her broken heart hastened that sad day.

It wasn't good to think about Betsy, but she'd had these eyes the color of bluebonnets and hair such a pale yellow, it was almost not a color. Her face and eyes and that silky hair refused to fade from his memory.

"Don't forget me, love," she'd pleaded that long last night, her voice fading away to a whisper. With effort, she'd put her frail hand over his too-full chest. "Keep me here. Don't forget."

Toward morning, he'd bathed her with rose-scented water before dressing her in the soft cotton chemise she'd had him buy for just this purpose. He hadn't expected it to be so difficult, maneuvering the lilac-printed nightdress over her lifeless frame. She'd wanted hose, so he wrestled them up over her knees before tucking her feet into the backless slippers he'd given her for Christmas. Last he brushed her pale hair.

Afterward, all the while he walked to the undertaker's, he was sure he could hear the invalid bell that had begged his attention for days that bled into weeks. How could he live without her want, her need?

It was noon when the hearse came. He'd helped lift her into the simple wooden casket, making sure she was exactly like she'd wanted to be, her gown arranged just so, her cream-colored hair loosely gathered with lavender ribbon, streaming over one shoulder, and a sprig of lilac tucked into her folded hands.

There was no funeral, for who was there to mark her passing but him? A minister, called out by the kindly undertaker, he supposed, said a few words at the graveside that very afternoon. And it was done. Shade was free of Betsy's need and Betsy's illness, but what was he to do with that freedom?

The preacher offered a ride home, but Shade walked. He wanted to walk a thousand miles, but it was only three to the big house that Betsy no longer craved. He'd gone straight to the kitchen and pulled out a chair, sitting heavily, relishing unending time without the tiresome tinkling of the bell, without water boiling for tea too weak, without burned toast needing to be scraped, without butter too cold to spread, without honey turned to crystal in the jar.

He tried to think of something he'd done right for her as

death crept into her body a sickly inch at a time. But her ill-ness was a wall he could never scale. Everything about it was a rebuke to him who had promised before God and man to care for her—what was the word that had so easily slid off his tongue? *Cherish*. He had promised to cherish her.

Finally, when it got too dark to see without a lamp, Shade rose from his chair. He'd finish packing—tidy up the place before morning, when the bank would put him and their things out on the street. They'd tack a cardboard Foreclosed sign on the door that was no longer his anyway. Let them have it.

It wasn't as bad as he might have thought. The broom and the dustpan ordered the chaos in a soothing way. He'd finished the kitchen—pans all in a box, dishes wrapped in newsprint, icebox wiped clean—and headed for the bed-room. The bed needed stripping, small amber vials of medi-cines needed pitching, windows needed raising so the room could be aired.

He hadn't stepped a foot across the threshold before he saw it lying there in the gloom of the fading day—one lonely slipper on the throw rug. He hadn't even managed to bury her right. He would have walked on hot coals for her if it would have helped. He hoped she knew that. But all he could do was let the fire of his grief char ashes to ashes and dust to dust.

Now, midway up the alley, Shade stumbled over his own feet and steadied himself with an elbow to the wall. The weight of remorse always took him by surprise. He wished there was a suitcase made to store heartache so you could slide it under the bed and get it out only when you had the need for a moment's penance. Man, he'd have a trunkful.

Coins jingled in his pocket. He pinched his dice from among the coins and folding money and secured them in a small flannel bag. He was sure the players had not seen him switch the dice for his own on that last shot. He had his tricks: a clearing of his throat or a shift in posture would take attention from his hand as he removed the weighted dice from the cuff of his trousers. He didn't consider it cheating because he was good at it. He had studied the craft and lost a lot of lucre in the process. Some men robbed with a six-gun, some with a fountain pen; he used what he had at his disposal. Turnabout, what goes around—all of life was just one fat gamble. It didn't seem that much different to him than a man laying a bet against a roof fall every time he went down in the mines or a banker calling heads-I-win when a body fell behind on his mortgage payments.

Shade adjusted his hat and strode out of the alley. Right now he was betting he could have an easy look-see around the doctor's office. She knew where his daughter was—he'd wager good money on it—and he aimed to find his Betsy Lane no matter what it took.

CHAPTER 15

MONDAY MORNING dawned hot and muggy, and Lilly was off to a late start. She wanted to wear her lightweight linen skirt, but no matter how she tugged at the button on the waistband, it would not fasten. She would have worn the same skirt she wore Friday, but Turnip Tippen had already come by for the laundry. Mrs. Tippen was going to spot clean and press her serge and lightweight woolen skirts today—would they even fit tomorrow?

"Where is that skirt that was too big when the dressmaker sent it? You know, the brown one?" she asked of Kip. In order to be of help, he leaped into the clothes closet and sniffed around. The closet smelled of cedar and made her slightly ill—everything made her slightly ill these days, especially odors.

She sat on the edge of her freshly made bed and surveyed the closet. It was truly a thing of beauty. Most houses didn't even have a press, just pegs on the wall or, worse yet, two-penny nails pounded into a doorframe. But in his thought-ful way, Tern had constructed roomy closets in each of the bedrooms as well as a linen closet in the bathroom and a coat closet by the front door.

"Oh, Kip, how can a person have so many options and not a thing to wear?" She rose and sorted through the wooden hangers once again. This shouldn't be so hard. All her things were neatly and precisely ordered: shirtwaists in the front, skirts next, arranged by color, then dresses: day dresses, business wear, Sunday go-to-meeting, and last the gowns she kept in cloth protectors. Hatboxes were on the top shelf, undergarments and nightgowns folded between sheets of tissue paper in built-in drawers, shoes side by side on the floor. Tern had his own closet on the other wall.

"You know, Kip, I think I put that skirt in a box with some other items and stuck it on the shelf in Tern's closet. He has more room."

The closets had sliding doors, another innovation. She slid Tern's open and looked up at the shelf. There was the pasteboard box. She should go to the pantry and get the folding stepladder, but instead, she pulled the bench from her vanity table over to the closet. She was already behind, and the bench was sturdy.

Even standing on the bench, the shelf was above her head, and the box was big and awkward. She heard the squeak as she slid the box toward the edge. A mouse poked its head out a ragged hole. With a yelp, Lilly lost her balance. Box, clothes, tiny baby mice, and she herself tumbled to the floor. Kip went crazy as the mother mouse darted around the room.

"Kip," Lilly yelled from where she lay on her back. "Leave it! Leave it!"

Gingerly she stood and rested her hand on her abdomen. Thankfully, her back had taken the brunt of her landing and she hadn't fallen hard. Everything seemed fine. What a foolish risk she'd taken. Now she had ruined clothes, a nest of shredded tissue paper, and a host of mice to deal with before she even started her day. Lilly sighed. She was doing nothing but stamping out fires this morning.

She could see the mother mouse's whiskers twitching from underneath her dressing table. Kip nosed one of the babies. "Kip! Sit!" His whole body twitched, but he obeyed. Such a good dog. Now, what to do with the mice?

"Lord, I could use a hand," she prayed sincerely and wondered if there was a Scripture for this particular problem. All she could think of was "A prating fool shall fall." That sounded like Proverbs. Surely she had played the fool by ignoring the sturdy ladder in the kitchen in order to save a minute. She could have hurt her baby.

Before she could berate herself further, she heard the kitchen door push open and a familiar voice calling.

"Doc Lilly? Mommy sent you some eggs and some honey

that Daddy took from a hive. Doc Lilly? Want to see my stings? I got seven."

"Just a minute, Timmy. I'll be right out." There was nothing to do but wear one of her loose-fitting dresses today. Slipping one over her head, she buttoned the dozen buttons. With a quick look in the mirror to straighten her pearls, she went to the kitchen. The good Lord did provide. Of all the people in the world, Timmy was perfect for mouse removal. She'd take Kip to work with her to get him out of the way.

"Hey, Doc," Timmy said. "Say, did you know someone busted out your window last night?"

Lilly looked around the room. "My window?"

"Not here, at the clinic." At the drain board, Timmy arranged the eggs in a pyramid—the better to make a mess with when one fell from the stack with a plop. "Oops."

"Timothy," Lilly said with a sigh, "explain the window."

"Well, Mommy dropped me off at your work so's I could leave you the eggs and show you my stings, but you weren't there, so's I brung them here." He held out one arm dotted with red blotches. "See? Daddy says never stick your arm up a hollow tree before you smoke the bees."

"The window, please, Timmy," Lilly said as she mixed baking soda in water and began to dab the paste on Timmy's wounds.

"Well, the sheriff was there, but he wouldn't tell me nothing. The bust-in I figured out for myself. The windowpanes are smashed to smithereens."

"Did you go in?"

"Nah, the sheriff, he's making everybody stay outside until he finishes his look-see. You got all kinds of people minding your business. Daddy could smoke 'em for you if you want." Timmy laughed at his own joke.

Lilly ruffled the boy's hair. You couldn't tell where one cowlick ended and another began. "I'd best get a move on, then. But first I need to show you something."

Timmy's eyes widened when she cracked the bedroom door. "Boy," he said. "You oughta turn Kip loose in there. He'd make a stack cake with mouse guts."

"Now, don't hurt them. Take them out to the woods and turn them loose. Okay?"

"I could take them down to Miz Tippen's. She's got all them cats."

"That wouldn't be a fair fight, would it, Timmy? The babies are not big enough to run."

"Nah, that'd be like two on one. I'll keep them safe, Doc Lilly, and sweep up the mess they made. Where's your broom?"

Lilly got the broom and dustpan from the back porch and a brown-paper sack from the pantry. "Here are your tools. Do you have time to do this properly before you meet your mother?"

"Yeah, sure, she's going to that reading and Bible study class. You know the one that meets on Friday but got postponed till Monday on account of the teacher got sick? Daddy says, 'It's Monday. When're you going to do the laundry?' and Mommy says, 'Whenever I get around to it, Landis.' Daddy knows whenever Mommy says Landis thataway that he's got on her last nerve. Usually she calls him honey."

Lilly opened her coin purse and handed Timmy a quarter. "I trust you to do a proper job."

Timmy flipped the coin into the air with the nail of his thumb. "Heads!" The coin rolled under the stove. "Oops."

"You can fish it out with the broom, Timmy."

The boy looked up with a crooked smile. "Well, lookee there. Kip's got egg all over his mouth. He's done cleaned up one mess for me."

A deputy stood outside the private entrance to Lilly's office, keeping the gawkers well away. Lilly stepped inside to find Chanis waiting.

"Dr. Still, can you open the pharmacy cabinet? I figure whoever broke in must be looking for drugs. But as you can see, he didn't jimmy the lock."

Since she carefully inventoried the medication cabinet every evening, Lilly could tell there was nothing missing when she surveyed the amber-colored vials and the paper-labeled bottles. "He didn't take anything from here. Have you checked the surgery and the waiting room?"

"I walked through. Nothing seems amiss, except for right around the window."

"Maybe someone threw a rock through it."

"Good thought, Doc, but rocks don't bleed. This guy got a nice cut for his efforts."

"Thankfully there weren't any patients in-house."

"He wouldn't have busted in if anybody was about."

Lilly turned the key in the lock and faced the room. It all looked as tidy as when she had left it except for her paperwork. The metal-bound charts were kitty-corner on the desk. When she'd finished working Saturday night, she had left them as she always did, squared up at her right hand, ready to be filed by Mazy.

Reflexively, she reached to straighten them. "Someone went through my charts."

Chanis caught her hand. "Let me look first."

As if he thought a copperhead might be lurking between the pages, Chanis opened the top chart with a pencil he took from the desk. "Why would he be interested in this medical stuff? There must be something else. Keep any money, any pills or jewelry, in the drawers?"

One by one, Lilly pulled them open. Everything was just as she had left it.

"Doggies," Chanis said, obviously disappointed. "I was wanting to lay this off on a morphine addict or some such fly-by-night." Careful of the glass, he leaned on the windowsill and looked out. "Look here, Doc."

Lilly positioned herself beside him. Kip nosed his way in between.

"See across the road? See how you can look right up the alley between the commissary and the cream station? Saturday night I found a man sleeping there. He acted like he was drunk, but there wasn't a hint of alcohol about him. I didn't think much of it at the time." Chanis rubbed his hand across his chin. "I want to have a talk with that gentleman."

"Why, Chanis? Do you think he had something to do with this?"

"I think he was staking out the office. He'd made himself comfortable like he was going to be there for a while."

Lilly shivered. "I was here until past dark catching up on work Saturday evening." She indicated the two medical tomes on the desktop. "And I was doing some research on mongolism and cleft palate."

"You're speaking a foreign language, Doc."

"Our little foundling has those disorders. I was reading about them so I'll know how to best treat her."

Glass crunched under the sheriff's heel, and Lilly said, "Let me put Kip up before he gets a sliver in his paw."

Kip howled when Lilly shut him in the bathroom. She opened the door and shook her finger. "No whining!"

Then she looked about the office. "Are we safe here, Chanis?"

"Until we get this sorted out, don't stay late, Doc, and never work alone. I'd say he was passing through, looking for something to steal, but you never know." Chanis began to pick up shards of glass and burnt matchsticks, pitching them into a black metal waste can. He looked up from his task, his eyes frowning. "Where's Miss Mazy this morning? I wouldn't want this to frighten her."

"Mazy has the morning off. She had some errands to do."

"Good. Good." He put the waste can out on the porch

and motioned to his deputy. "Let the nurse and Doc's patients into the waiting room; then go see if you can find Turnip Tippen to come fix this window."

The deputy tipped his hat to Lilly. "Why you reckon he broke out the window instead of busting through the door?" he asked of Chanis.

"Easier and less likely to attract attention," Chanis said. "See, he only needed to tap the windowpane to break it, reach in and turn the latch, then slide the window up. Once he was inside, he struck a match and had a look around. Piece of cake."

"Takes all kinds," the deputy said.

"Sure does," Chanis replied, following the deputy out. He leaned in again. "I'll stop back by directly. Don't worry—we're on the job."

Lilly dusted the seat of her chair although she didn't see any bits of glass. A feeling of disquiet unsettled her. She wished she had time to look through the charts remaining on her desk. As improbable as it seemed, there might be a clue there. But the nurse was ushering in her first patient. Later—she'd have time later.

"I ain't staying long enough to sit," Armina said when the nurse pulled out the patient chair for her. She was wearing her best print dress, her wispy brown hair pulled back into a tight bun. She carried a black patent-leather handbag with an imitation gold clasp—a castoff of Lilly's. The faint scent of Cashmere Bouquet powder accompanied her.

"Armina, what are you doing here? Where's Hannah?"

"She's resting her fanny in the waiting room," Armina said. "Ain't I got a right to talk to you in private?"

"Oh, Armina, of course. I'm sorry. I didn't mean to question you. Please, sit down."

At the sound of Armina's voice, Kip began scratching frantically on the other side of the bathroom door.

"Either you got a beaver in here or Kip wants out," Armina said, turning the knob to the lavatory door.

Kip bounded out, barking at the top of his lungs. The hair on his back stood up in a ruff.

"Quiet yourself, Kipper," Armina said, making a stop sign of her right palm. "How'd ye get yourself shut up in there?"

Kip licked Armina's palm. Finally somebody was listening to him. Lilly laughed despite herself.

Armina sat down and patted her knees. Kip sprang into her lap, and Armina settled him up against her purse. Four brown eyes looked accusingly across the desk at Lilly.

"I come for one reason," Armina began, her words as straight as a sourwood sprout. "I don't need a nursemaid a-fetching for me and a-humoring me all the livelong day and half the night. I won't stand for it no more. Ye got no right to make me a prisoner in my own house."

"Do you think that's a fair charge against me? I'm your friend as well as your physician."

Armina dropped her eyes. "I'm a right pain, ain't I?"

"Sometimes you are, but I love you anyway."

"I've been a-thinking. What if I stay days by my lonesome

and stay evenings and nights at your house? I promise not to go off berry picking or any such thing."

Lilly's ears perked. "Have you wanted to go pick berries?"

"I don't rightly know where that thought come from. It's just Friday evening—when I was looking for my sycamore stick—I noticed my berry bucket was gone. You recollect I always keep it hanging on a peg in the storage cupboard. My walking stick's always leaned up beside it, resting against the wall."

Confusion clouded Armina's face, but she didn't lose composure. Lilly took that for a good sign.

"I've got myself off track. I didn't come here about my berry bucket. A lard pail's easy to come by. Fry a few chickens and you've got another one." She fixed Lilly with her eyes again. "Are we square?"

Lilly searched her mind for something to barter with. "Would you be willing to let Mazy stay days with you? You know she won't follow you around—most likely she'll be propped up reading a book. We could all eat supper together; then you could spend the nights at my house."

Armina rubbed a spot between Kip's ears. Her voice fell to a whisper. "Ye think I'm going loony, don't you?"

"I don't think anything of the sort. There's nothing wrong with your mind that time won't heal."

Armina slid Kip from her lap and stood. "Okay, then." She stuck her hand across the desk like she meant to seal the deal.

Lilly moved to Armina's side. She hugged her friend

gently. Maybe Armina didn't want the contact, but Lilly did. "You'll be fine, Armina."

Armina relaxed just the tiniest bit in Lilly's embrace. It made Lilly sad to think her friend kept a wall up against her.

When Armina cracked the outside door, Kip nudged around her and stuck his nose into the opening. "Looks like Kip's a-coming with," she said.

"Don't you want to go out through the waiting room so you can get Hannah?"

"Nope."

"She'll need to collect her things."

"I'll set them on the porch."

Lilly threw her hands up in exasperation. "Armina . . ."

Armina cast a devilish look over her shoulder. "I was only funning you. I got my sea legs back. Me and Kip will walk around and peck on the window. That'll call her out. Mayhaps I'll fix some morels for lunch. Serve her for a change."

Lilly shook her head. "Armina, you really shouldn't be foraging for mushrooms."

"Didn't. There were a brown-paper poke of them spang in the middle of my porch this morning. The bag looked like a big old wilted frog. Somebody didn't want them to go to waste, I expect."

Lilly couldn't resist. "I'll bet Mr. Tippen left them for you."

"Humph. Then I'll pitch them out—paper poke and all."

"Waste not, want not," Lilly preached Armina's favorite sermon.

"If I thought Turnip brung them, I'd take them over to

Anne's and feed them to that fat sow she keeps under the porch. I ain't seen Anne in a coon's age." Armina adjusted the cracked leather purse strap over her shoulder. "I'd like to have me a fat old hog—and a cow. I've a mind to get me a cow," she said as she took her leave.

The frisson of unease that pricked Lilly earlier returned. The berry bucket, Anne—Armina's mind was laying down clues, bits of information it had stored in a deep, dark recess now coming forward, mingling with things Armina had probably overheard. What might happen when her fragile being remembered what had driven her to snatch baby Glory?

A shard of glass glinted on the threshold. Lilly bent to pick it up. She held it to the light as if there were great truth to discern there. A tiny rainbow sparkled atop the research books resting beside the kitty-corner charts on the desktop. When Lilly moved the glass, the rainbow disappeared. Laying the shard on the windowsill, she reached for a chart only to be interrupted once again.

The next patient filled the doorway, truly filled it. Bobby Bumble stumbled in. Lilly could barely see his sparrowlike mother behind him. Even though the chair was extra large, Bobby's egg-shaped body barely fit the space between the armrests. The nurse put his chart in front of Lilly.

With a quick read, Lilly refreshed her memory. "How's that sore throat, Bobby?"

"He cain't hardly eat a bite," Mrs. Bumble interjected, flitting around behind her son, smoothing his hair and straightening his collar. "And see here? He's got this swole place on his neck." She pressed two fingertips below his double chin.

Lilly took two tongue depressors from a jar. "Turn your chair this way, Bobby."

Bobby swiveled the chair on its casters as Lilly pulled up another straight-backed one. She sat down facing Bobby and handed him one of the depressors. "If you'll let me look at your throat, you can take this depressor home." That always worked with him.

"Quinsy again, ain't it?" Bobby's mother said as Lilly probed the depths.

"We've talked about this before, Mrs. Bumble. These tonsils need to come out."

"I cain't do it. I just cain't put him through that."

"Do you need more salicylate of soda? Was he able to gargle with that?"

"We could use some more if it ain't no trouble. You done good this morning, didn't you, Son?" Mrs. Bumble put her hand straight against the side of her mouth, as if Bobby couldn't hear her if she spoke behind a shield. "I made him gargle before I would fix him his breakfast."

Lilly studied Mrs. Bumble. Bobby was well cared for, except for his obesity, but his mother was elderly, already stooped from rheumatism. Who would take him if, God forbid, something happened to his mother? Had she made any provision? "Doesn't his sore throat keep him from eating?"

"Not if I make gravy. Gravy's your favorite thing, ain't it?"

Bobby flipped the tongue depressor against his hand.

"He loves them things," Mrs. Bumble said, motioning for Bobby to stand. "Thank you kindly, Doc Still. Say thank you, Bobby."

He graced Lilly with a lopsided smile. His mother patted a bit of drool from his chin.

"I'll stop by one day if that's all right," Lilly said as she stood and went to the cabinet to get the needed soda. It would be easier to talk about Bobby's future if Mrs. Bumble was in her own home.

"You'd like that, wouldn't you, Son?" Mrs. Bumble put the packet of medicine in her pocket. "Come on, Bobby. Let's go to the store." She shielded her mouth again. "The clerk always gives him lemon drops."

CHAPTER 16

Monday progressed as Mondays do. Lilly saw three more patients before noon: a case of colic, a fractured thumb, and a terrible bout of shingles. Her stomach grumbled. Amid the chaos of the morning, she'd had only an apple and a piece of cheese for breakfast.

Outside the window, Turnip Tippen tapped on the remaining glass. He motioned for Lilly to come.

He had pried a section of the frame loose with a crowbar. "See this here?" The wood was powdery and riddled with holes. "This is all et up by termites. It would pay you to fix the whole shebang now whilst I'm here."

"How long would it take?"

Standing back, he mopped sweat from his brow with a blue bandanna. "Oh, three shakes of a dead sheep's tail and I'll be done with this here project. I'll need to smoke the foundation with brimstone, though, else the bugs will keep munching until all you got's a pile of woodchips. The smoking will take a while longer."

Forevermore, this day was bringing nothing but trouble. "Let me check with my nurse. Maybe I can close up shop for the afternoon—get everybody out of your way."

Mr. Tippen stuffed the bandanna in the back pocket of his overalls. "I'll be back—gotta fetch the rest of my tools and stop over to the lumberyard."

Lilly was glad to turn her key in the lock—very glad for an afternoon off. Her linen bag, full of the unfiled charts and the research books she wanted to peruse, hung heavily from her arm. Heat shimmered like a desert mirage from the ground. Birds sat listlessly in the trees, too hot to sing. Under the shade of a maple tree, an old hound dog raised his heavy eyes to watch her pass by. The taffeta silk dress she wore clung uncomfortably to her back and swished limply around her ankles. Oh, for her usual attire to protect against the noonday sun. Her boxy linen jacket didn't help, but it would be unseemly not to wear it. The whole day had been off. It would be good to get home.

Momentarily she considered swinging by the beauty shop to see if her sister was still there, but she decided against it. Mazy would see the Closed sign in the office window and

know to come on home. Lilly could have a light lunch prepared by then.

She stopped to fetch Kip from Armina's. Could that be
an actual conversation she heard through the open window?
Hannah's carpetbag and a small train case were just outside
the door. Lilly knocked.

Armina insisted on wrapping some of the cornmeal-
battered, deep-fried morels in newspaper for Lilly to take
home. Hannah added a bowl of coleslaw and a round of
red-crusted grainy corn bread to her haul. Suddenly weak
from hunger, Lilly hastened across the road. Kip beat her to
the porch.

As soon as she made it to the kitchen, Lilly tore a piece of
the bread from the round and stuffed it into her mouth like
a savage. *Oh, my word . . .* It was the best she'd ever tasted.
Taking a saucer from Kip's stack, she put a small piece of
bread on the floor, then went to the icebox and poured a glass
of milk from the pressed-glass pitcher on the top shelf. The
butter she wanted for her bread was hard as rock, so she set
it on the drain board to soften. Kip left the saucer rattling on
the floor to follow Lilly to her bedroom.

The clothing from the upended box was folded neatly
on the dresser bench and there was not a mouse in sight.
Timmy had earned his quarter. Lilly pulled her dress over
her head. Between sips of milk, she patted perspiration stains
from the underarms of the garment with a rag dipped in
cold water. Wearing her good dresses to work was simply
not doable. Besides being uncomfortable and unprofessional,

they would be ruined—not to mention, at the rate she was going, quickly stretched out of shape.

Lying back on the bed, she closed her eyes. What was she to do? She couldn't very well go to work in her chemise. The rapid growth of this baby had caught her off guard. She was nearly this far along when she lost her first pregnancy, but she'd remained as flat as an ironing board. It seemed she should have had plenty of time to get her wardrobe ready. You would think a doctor would have more sense than to believe any two pregnancies would progress alike. She was probably right that this was a hefty boy baby.

She smiled to think how Tern would laugh, how delighted he would be. "Lord, thank You for this wondrous blessing," she prayed. "Forgive the foolish risk I took this morning. Help me to keep this little one safe. Help me to nourish and sustain him."

Without rising, Lilly took her Bible from the nightstand and, holding it aloft, flipped through the concordance in the back. Goodness, why was the print so tiny? The word *womb* was followed by several Scriptures.

She turned to the first one listed, Genesis 49:25, and read aloud: "'Even by the God of thy father, who shall help thee; and by the Almighty, who shall bless thee with blessings of heaven above, blessings of the deep that lieth under, blessings of the breasts, and of the womb.'"

Against a sudden spurt of tears, she closed the Bible and laid it on the bedspread, covering her eyes in the crook of her elbow. Scripture often reduced her to tears in this way. As a girl, she'd wondered how God had time amid unending wars and upheaving weather and His million daily tasks to speak to her, an insignificant bug of a girl. The Word, His Word, brought the Lord so near, it frightened her but at the same time delighted her.

She remembered explaining this to her mother, who'd only said, "Hmmm" as she stirred a steaming pot on the stove. Mama had waited until pitch-dark to answer Lilly's questions.

As if it were yesterday, Lilly could feel the dew-soaked grass against her bare feet as Mama led her deep into the meadow beside the barn. She spread a worn quilt atop the tall grass and bade Lilly to lie down beside her.

In her patient way, Mama had waited until the world receded, drawing away like a skim of cream until there was nothing between them and heaven but a trillion shining stars. She took Lilly's hand in her own. "You are not a bug to the Lord, my darling daughter. You are a brilliant star, an integral part of God's holy universe."

"But bugs are important too, right? God made bugs, too."

Mama had laughed and drawn Lilly so close that she could feel the beat of her heart against her cheek. "Girl, someday you're going to ask one too many questions."

"But how do I know, Mama?" Lilly persisted, reaching out to touch a star. "How do I know I'm more important to God than a katydid or a grasshopper?"

"We know because God didn't give His Book to the bugs. Just hush, and let Him reveal Himself to you."

Now, as Lilly rested on her comfortable bed, Kip jumped up beside her, settled down, and laid his head on her chest. Usually when she was lying on her back, he would stand on her chest with front feet on her breastbone and hind feet on her belly, gazing down until she gave in and got up. He was being uncharacteristically gentle. Lilly scratched behind his ears just the way he liked. "So you've already figured it out, Kip. How did you get so smart?"

Kip rolled his eyes as if to say, *"Who do you think you're fooling?"*

The dog had begun snoring and Lilly was drifting into a pleasant dream when the sound of weeping woke her. Disoriented, she sat up. Kip headed out the door. She could hear his nails clicking on the polished wood floor down the hall to Mazy's room. Pulling on a plain princess wrapper, Lilly followed fast behind.

Mazy was a sodden heap in the middle of her unmade bed. A Turkish towel was knotted on her head.

"Mazy? Whatever is the matter?"

"I'm ruined, Lilly, simply ruined." Turning her face into her pillow, she sobbed, "I can never go outside these doors again. I'm going to die a lonely old maid right in this room."

"Sweetheart, it can't be as bad as all that. Let me see."

Mazy swept the towel from her head dramatically. Her hair was indeed different, just as she'd wished, but it didn't lie like shiny silk upon her shoulders. Instead, a frizzy halo of yellowish stubble sprung crazily from her scalp. She looked like an angel gone awry.

Lilly clapped her hand over her mouth. "Oh, Mazy."

"See? I told you," she said, hiccuping amid fresh tears. "Today's word is *disaster*. Now I'm broke and bald both."

"Are you burned? Come in the kitchen, where I can see you better."

Mazy bent over the sink while Lilly poured water mixed with baking soda from the same box she'd used on Timmy over her head. "Your scalp has first-degree burns, Mazy. We'll be lucky if your hair doesn't all fall out."

Mazy wailed, "Why did you let me do this, Lilly?"

"Just be glad Mama isn't here," Lilly said, wrapping her sister's head in a fresh towel. "She'd turn you over her knee."

"Doc Still?"

They both whipped around. Mazy's towel fell to the floor. Forevermore, there stood Chanis Clay in the door Mazy had left wide open.

His hand rested on the butt of his gun. "I heard someone yelling."

It seemed neither of the women could find their voice. What a picture they must make, two soggy sisters in a cloud of soda powder. Poor Chanis. He might as well see what he was getting into if he pursued Miss Mazy Pelfrey.

Mazy lifted her chin. "I've been to the beauty parlor," she said inanely.

Chanis nodded, his face poker blank. "You've cut your hair."

You can tell he has sisters, Lilly thought.

"I can't go out with you again for at least a year," Mazy said.

"Let me go get my sister," he said. "She's studied fixing hair and all that girlie stuff."

Mazy's chin trembled. "This is the ugliest I'll ever be, Chanis."

"Then I'm a lucky guy," he said, turning on his heel.

Mazy kicked at the towel. "It's not fair. Men always get to leave."

Lilly slid the towel around the floor with one foot, mopping up the mess they'd made. "Sometimes it seems that way."

"Why is it, Lilly, that he can look so good doing nothing but standing there, and meanwhile my head looks like a circus clown because I wanted to be pretty?"

Lilly sidestepped Kip, who was busy tracking something through the baking soda dust. "Are you and Chanis getting serious?"

"He makes my heart go wobbly. That must be serious."

Lilly did not want to get into this today—but opportunity had knocked. "Mazy, has Mama talked to you about . . . things?"

"I'm afraid so. It is more than strange to contemplate. I suppose that's why your heart gets wobbly—else it would never happen."

Lilly took her sister's heart-shaped face in her hands. "The wobbly part is what gets girls in trouble. That part's for after you are married."

"Don't worry, Lilly. Daddy talked to me too."

This was bound to be good, Lilly thought.

Mazy giggled. "You won't believe what he did. He took

Molly and me to the fishpond and said he'd pitch us in if we ever brought trouble home."

"You're right. I can't picture our sweet daddy threatening you. What did you and Molly say?"

"Nothing. We just pushed him in the pond and high-tailed it home."

Lilly laughed so hard she nearly got a stitch. "Oh, my goodness, I wish I could have seen that. How did Mama react?"

"She never knew. He came in all covered in mud, carrying a turtle for supper. It was tasty."

Suddenly a darting gray mat of fur trailing a long hairless tail ran over Lilly's foot. "Yeep," she yelled as if she'd never seen a mouse before. Mazy jumped, screaming, onto a chair. Kip barked, pounced, and missed.

Lilly hurried to open the screen door Chanis had closed. Sensing his chance, the mouse raced right through.

Whap! The business end of a broom wielded by Armina dispatched the poor thing to its reward.

Armina narrowed her eyes at the sight of the messy kitchen. "I can see you've been a-needing me."

CHAPTER 17

TILLIE TIPPEN'S HOUSE was only a short distance farther on, once Lilly walked the quarter of a mile into town. Truthfully, she'd been glad for the excuse of collecting the laundry to get away from the hubbub in her kitchen, where Armina fussed with broom and mop, Mazy primped, Chanis's sister heated curling irons, and Kip mourned the one that got away.

At the clinic, smoke billowed from charcoal pots of heated brimstone placed strategically all along the foundation. Mr. Tippen's wagon was gone. Lilly supposed he wanted to fumigate the walls before he put up the new window. Hopefully he wouldn't fumigate himself.

The Tippens' white two-story house was grand considering the leaning shotgun houses of their neighbors. The wide front porch was painted gray and sported two white rocking chairs and a matching swing, suspended by chains from a beam. A banty hen and six half-grown chicks scoured the bountiful flower garden beside the steps for errant ladybugs or hapless wiggle worms. In the side yard, drying laundry fluttered lazily in the sparse hot breeze of the day.

Lilly was too early. She should have waited until evening. She knocked lightly.

"Well, look who's here," Tillie Tippen boomed when she opened the door to Lilly. "Come in and set yourself down. You're looking a little wilted from this heat."

Lilly was surprised anew each time she heard Tillie's loud, gruff voice. She was short, less than five feet, and portly—built like a rain barrel. Half of her had to be lung. Lilly wondered how she managed the high clotheslines. Maybe Mr. Tippen hung the wash and took it in.

Before Lilly could say, "I came to collect the laundry," she was seated in the parlor, a glass of sweet tea in her hand and a dessert plate of Tillie's town-renowned yellow cake with coconut icing resting on her knee. As her eyes adjusted from the glare of the sun to the dim interior of the room, she noticed she wasn't the only visitor. Anne perched on the horsehair sofa directly across from her. Lilly raised her eyebrows in question.

"As I was just telling Tillie, it's good to have a husband like Cletus, who don't mind me taking a minute for myself," Anne said.

"Anne helps me on wash days—but generally Amy comes

along. You should have brung her. You know that child's the best part of Monday for me."

"Maybe next week," Anne said, standing. "I'll just go out and take Doc's linens off the line. They're more than dry by now. Do you want the sheets and pillowcases sprinkled?"

"No, she don't like the bedclothes ironed," Tillie said as if Lilly were a lamp or a chair. "You can put them and the towels and kitchen things, everything that don't get ironed, in that white wicker basket."

"I'm sorry to interrupt your work," Lilly said.

"I love me a bit of company whatever time of day it comes," Tillie said, taking Anne's place on the sofa. "Turnip said somebody broke your window."

"Yes, he's repairing it now. I closed the office for the afternoon."

"Turnip's good at fixing things—unlike some husbands I know," Tillie said, jerking her head toward the window, where they could see Anne taking pegs from a sheet.

"Tillie, this cake is delicious, so light, and the icing is divine," Lilly said, hoping to divert gossip to recipes. "I've never tasted better."

"It's the coconut with a sprinkle of orange zest; makes all the difference."

Tillie straightened the doily on the arm of the sofa. "You know Anne's my sister, don't you? She's sixteen years younger, so I feel more like her mother. She's got that broken-down house to take care of, and little Amy, plus you know she works every hour at the clinic she can get."

Tillie's face gathered in a knot of indignation. "Still yet, she needs the money I give her for helping me on Mondays. Ornery, layabout Cletus Becker—I don't know why she stays. It's the same song the old cow died on over and over again. It's not to be put up with!"

Lilly was at a loss. She took a sip of tea to wash down the sudden lump in her throat. Her silence seemed to egg Tillie on.

"Cletus gambles away every last cent she earns—and her owing back taxes on that ridge rock he calls a farm. Humph! Turnip's going to the bank tomorrow." Tillie kneaded her hands in her lap. "It's not that we don't have the means to help, but how long can we keep it up now that Turnip can't work down the mine? That black coal dust settling in his lungs has just about kilt him."

She put a finger to her lips. "Don't say anything—Anne won't like me asking—but I hoped maybe you could put her back on at the clinic. She ain't worked in what, a week?"

"I'm sure things will pick up soon," Lilly said, thinking about the folded bills she'd seen Anne hiding in the oven. "The hospital beds never stay empty for long."

Lilly regretted having put Anne in such an awkward position—having to pretend to not have work so that she was free to care for the baby. She suspected Tillie minded more of her younger sister's business than she should.

Tillie refilled Lilly's glass. "Now about your skirts. Do you want me to cut out the fronts and bind around the hole, add some ties? Or I could set buttonholes around the waist and sew buttons to match on your blouses. Have you seen that done?"

"Forevermore, Tillie, I just came for the laundry. I haven't told a soul."

Tillie leaned forward and put her hand on Lilly's knee. "I can help you hide it for a short time by adjusting your skirts, but I'd say that pot you got a-cooking won't stay under the lid for long."

Suddenly it all seemed very real and permanent to Lilly. She was almost glad that someone knew—even if that someone was the biggest talebearer in Skip Rock. "I had hoped to tell my husband first."

"Of course you do, honey. But shared joy is a double joy. And what if, God forbid, something goes awry? Shared sorrow is half a sorrow. I can hold my tongue when need be. But folks will guess soon enough. You got that look. It's written all over your face."

The *honey* weakened Lilly. She wished she could put her head on Tillie's shoulder, let Tillie pat her back as her mother would do. "I guess you should get started on those skirts, then, Tillie."

"I'll do one directly and have Turnip bring it by so you'll have it for tomorrow. I'm a good hand with my Singer sewing machine. Come back by one day and we'll look at patterns for your maternity clothes."

After supper, Armina was across the road gathering her night things, Mazy was weeping again, and Lilly was taking the charts from her linen bag when she heard Kip at the back door, barking. *What now?* Lilly wondered as Mrs. Blair rushed Timmy through the door. The boy looked peaked and out of breath.

"First he can catch his breath and then he can't," Mrs. Blair said. "He says he swallowed a dime."

Timmy's eyes were as big as the quarter Lilly had given him earlier. "It's a-resting right here, Doc," he said huskily, pointing to the area on his chest that would be in line with the bifurcation point of the right bronchus. "It's stuck." The effort to speak sent the boy into a fit of sneezing so violent it left him limp in his mother's arms.

"Do something, Doc! He's going to die before my eyes."

The kitchen grew still as death. Armina and Mazy came in, standing back, watching with eyes as big as Timmy's. Even Kip was still. Lilly's mind scrambled backward to a time in medical school when she'd seen a case such as this one. A policeman had come into her mentor's office complaining of swallowing a coin after he tossed it up and caught it in his mouth. He'd accidentally thrown the coin back into the pharynx, where, coming in contact with the posterior nasal orifices, it excited a strong disposition to sneeze. The spasmodic inspiration that followed drew the piece through the windpipe and lodged it at the separation of the bronchus. Sneezing made the coin rise but also made suffocation imminent; thus the man would be forced to let the piece fall back. Fortunately the officer didn't realize how close to death he was before he was induced to vomit, which brought forth the coin.

Lilly grabbed the castor oil and poured a tablespoonful. Timmy grimaced and clamped his mouth tight, as any child would, as soon as he smelled the vile oily liquid.

"Timothy Blair, open your mouth and swallow," Mrs. Blair said.

Tears squirting out the corners of his eyes, Timmy opened and swallowed, soon retching and coughing violently until the dime flew out and hit the far wall. The retching was followed by copious vomiting that Lilly nearly caught in the dishpan. Nearly.

"Did you learn your lesson, Son?" Mrs. Blair asked when Timmy had recovered.

"Yes, ma'am. I should not have bought chocolate bars with that quarter. I should have saved it for Sunday school."

In the middle of the muddle, Turnip Tippen came by with Lilly's altered outfit. "You got a nice new window and lots of dead termites," he said proudly. "Say, Armina, how'd you find them morels I brung you?"

"A-sitting on the porch."

"I meant, was they good?"

"They fried up tasty. Thank ye. Now I got work to do."

Turnip took his leave, and Armina and Mrs. Blair scuffled lightly over the mop. Armina won and began to clean the floor once again. She was back to her force-of-nature self, physically anyway.

"Come by tomorrow, Timmy, so that I can listen to your chest and take another look at your arm," Lilly said.

"Good, this here sling is slowing me down."

"Oh, Doc Still," Timmy's mother replied, "maybe you'd best just leave it on."

"Nobody even noticed my hair," Mazy said later, fiddling with her tight blonde curls.

"You look quite modern," Lilly said.

"I guess I'll have to wear hats for a while." Mazy turned her head this way and that at Lilly's dresser. "Can I borrow yours?"

"They're in the closet. We'll get the boxes down tomorrow. But listen, Mazy; I need a favor."

Mazy's shoulders slumped. "I've got a feeling this means more work."

"Not more, just different. Armina dismissed Hannah today, but I'm not comfortable leaving her alone yet. Would you . . . ?"

"Watch out for Armina? Yes, I will. I'm not ready to show my face at the office." Leaving the bench seat, she gave Lilly a kiss on the cheek. "I'm going to pray that God will restore my hair, but I don't think that will work. I think maybe He wants me to learn a lesson like Timmy did." She dabbed at the corner of one eye with a fancy hankie. "Oh, Sister, life is so hard."

Lilly slept fitfully. She had never found a private minute to look at the charts, and now they beckoned, interrupting her rest like a dripping faucet. Kip didn't stir as she padded from the room. The coal-oil lamp that Chanis's sister had used to heat the curling irons was still on the kitchen table. Dreading the harsh glare of the electric light, Lilly lit the lamp instead, put the teakettle on the stove to heat, and opened the first chart.

Nothing in the pages but progress notes on elderly Mrs. Clark's battle with scrofula. The last inscription noted that the mix of sulfur, cream of tartar, licorice, and one-quarter part nitrite all mushed in honey, taken in a regimen of three days on and three days off, was helping. The next time she came in, Lilly would need to lower the dose, else the poor thing's bowels would get too loose. Scrofula was a nasty, multiform disease. No wonder the old-timers called it the king's evil.

The kettle whistled. She spooned black oolong leaves into a tea ball and selected a mug. Three charts later, her cup was nearly empty, and she had discovered nothing.

Weary, Lilly crossed her arms and rested her chin on her stacked wrists. She'd been so sure she'd find a clue to the break-in in the charts. Why else had they been disturbed? With the clarity of afterthought, she doubted her instincts. It made no sense that someone would be interested in another person's medical history. Like a blind coonhound, she was barking up the wrong tree.

Idly she pulled the textbooks closer. On Saturday night, she'd begun to research the malady that plagued baby Glory. The unfortunate infant was beset with three distinct medical issues—two of which, mongolism and heart murmur, often went hand in hand. Cleft palate, while not unusual, was not a marker. Because of the mongolism, the baby would certainly be slowed in her intellectual and physical development. But because of the heart condition, she mightn't live long enough for that to matter. The cleft palate was simply a complicating factor.

She flipped through the pages of the first book. The thumb card she was sure she'd left to mark her place was gone . . . and so was the page.

Startled, Lilly jarred the teacup with her elbow. The remaining tea sloshed over the side and dripped to the floor. She jumped up to grab a dish towel. With one hand, she wiped tea from the table as with the other, she turned pages in the textbook. One page—just one—had been ripped from the spine, leaving jagged margins but no script. A smear of red stained the page next in turn, creating a marker of another sort.

An eerie feeling inched up her spine, one bony knob at a time. This was too, too strange. The only page missing was the one she'd studied Saturday night, the one with images of mongoloid children and text clarifying their unique condition.

Lilly took a deep, steadying breath, but still her hands shook with nerves as she poured more tea into her cup. The room was closing in. Carrying her teacup, Lilly inched open the kitchen door and gingerly pushed against the screen. Despite her precaution, it screeched its screen door warning, alerting Kip that something was amiss. She heard him thump from the bed to the floor. He followed her outside and took off lickety-split for the lilac bush.

Gathering her robe around her, she took a seat on the top porch step.

How was she to interpret the broken window, the missing page? Why wouldn't the baby's mother just come to her and ask after her daughter? For surely it was the mother, regardless of Chanis's supposition of a drifter breaking in.

A sad and lonely sound stirred Lilly's emotions—a cow bawling from the lot next to Armina's, where Mr. Tippen kept his herd. The bawl sent goose bumps parading up Lilly's arms. It was a sound straight from her farm-girl childhood—one she hated. It meant the cow was separated from her calf for weaning purposes. Just as, for reasons Lilly couldn't begin to fathom, Glory's missing mother had been separated from her baby. Perhaps she was very young—perhaps she'd hidden the pregnancy from her family out of shame and guilt, and fear of the farm pond, and then, once the baby was born, she put her in a safe place where someone like Armina was sure to find her.

Lilly sipped her tea, now grown cold. The moon was waning. The distant hills played peekaboo through a thick gray mist that swirled around her feet, wetting the hem of her robe. Kip hopped up on the porch and Lilly pulled him close, glad for the solid comfort his little body provided, and wondered what this day would bring. She'd find Chanis and they'd walk up to Anne's. All together, they'd decide what to do about Glory.

CHAPTER 18

SHADE HARMON staggered under the weight of the paper in his pocket. He'd been lost in misery since early Sunday morning, when he'd broken into the doctor's office. It had taken the light from only three matches to hit upon the reason the doctor had been working so late on a Saturday night. Match number four had burned to ash as he stared at the picture on the marked page of her medical book. Stared but didn't comprehend.

He'd taken the folded paper from his pocket twice since, but he hadn't been able to study it. Single words leaped like rabid dogs from the page, tearing his flesh worse than broken glass ever could: *Idiot. Degenerate. Asylum.*

He knocked the back of his head hard against the rough trunk of the tree he was sitting under. Then he hit it again and saw stars. Fingers, stiff with pain and cracked with dried blood, scrabbled in his shirt pocket—searching for what, he didn't want to know but had to learn all the same. Smoothing the page against his bent knee, he forced himself to look. Once again the picture of a sweet-faced infant looked back at him. The baby could have been his own Betsy Lane.

Letters swam in and out of focus until his brain corralled them—forced them into words, lined them up in sentences. He knew what *mongoloid* meant—that wasn't bad, was it? Weren't they fierce warriors? Able to survive the harshest of winters and the bleakest of times?

But it wasn't for the Mongolians' fierceness that their name was commandeered, he learned; rather it was for the oddity of eyes that slanted upward and outward. For that little bit of difference, his daughter was set apart.

He turned the paper over and continued. So that small, round head that fit perfectly in the palm of his hand, the tiny flat nose, the odd little low-set ears meant she was in some ways lesser than? Who would have known? Who would have guessed that such a thing could happen—and happen so much that somebody captured it in the pages of a book?

The words continued, harsh as lye soap. *Public perception,* the article relayed in stark black-and-white, *holds that children born with retardation . . .*

Whoa, Nellie. Hold on a minute. Shade closed his eyes tight. He felt sick—like he was on the verge of some kind of lingering illness. He huffed out a ragged breath. *Retarded.* It meant stupid, slow, ignorant. Who had the right to pigeon-hole Betsy Lane that way? Didn't she smile a crooked smile sometimes and make nice bubbling noises when he chucked her gently under the chin? And when he held her in the crook of his arm, didn't she stare at him with gray-blue eyes that seemed to know his every secret?

He looked out upon a world no longer familiar; even the trees in his backyard seemed unsolid, untrustworthy. Finding his place, he continued to read: *Public perception holds that children born with retardation are a result of the parents' overall degenerate ways.*

Wait. He'd surely missed something. Was this fellow, whoever wrote the book, pretentious knower and relater of all things, saying that what Betsy had was something dirty? Something nasty passed down to offspring from parents? Why did this guy, learned though he might be, get to decide that whatever Betsy had was bad?

Shade tried to muster up a few tears, but he was too dry to spit. His heart would just have to hurt without benefit of release. How long had he been leaning against this tree? And what had possessed him to come back to this haunted place?

The muscles of his legs seized in protest as he stood. He staggered around stiff-legged until the charley horses released their fearsome hold. Clutching the paper to his chest, he stood in front of his house, willing himself to go in. Maybe Sweet Noreen would be standing in the kitchen, ready to berate him for going off without saying a word. Maybe Betsy

Lane would be in the high chair he'd made from hickory wood. Maybe she'd be fat and happy, and maybe her eyes would look just like his.

The door stood open as if in welcome. He stepped hesitantly into the kitchen. It looked normal: same chairs at the table, same cookstove in the corner, same red-checked curtains at the window. But on the table, pastry folded over a rolling pin was shrunken and cracked. Blackberries moldered in a Blue Willow bowl. A brown beetle lay upended in a tin pie plate. Leaves, dry as dust, gathered in the corners—blown in through the open door.

The room smelled faintly of decay and of fires gone cold. Shade opened the door to the cookstove and used the stoker to shake down the ashes. He scooped the discards into the coal bucket with the small fireplace shovel. There was wood cut to length in the wood box beside the stove. That proved he'd been a good provider. Didn't it?

When the wood caught, he filled a cauldron with water and set it across two burners atop the stove. He put a pot of coffee on another. He'd soak his sore hand, have a bath and a shave, wash his dirty clothes, and start over clean.

Tasks completed, he took his wet garments outside to the clothesline in the side yard. A single dingy cotton diaper lay forlornly on the ground. Shade took it, returned to the pot in the kitchen, and scrubbed it gently with Fels-Naptha. When the wash was hung, he felt well enough to fry some bacon and scramble some eggs. After dishing up the eggs, he picked mold from a piece of bread and fried it in the bacon grease.

Coffee steamed from his cup. He scooped eggs onto his fork. He'd forgotten the pepper. It was right in the cupboard where it should be. Everything felt so normal, like the baby was sleeping in the bedroom and Noreen was—what? Run off. Sweet Noreen had run off, back to Cincinnati. It was his lucky day.

Scooting the high chair up to the table, he tore tiny bits from his toast and put them on the tray, practicing for when Betsy Lane came home. How old did a baby have to be before she could sit upright in a chair? Could a baby even eat toast? He dipped a crust into his coffee and let it soak before putting it back on the tray. That should work. And egg—seemed like any age could eat egg. Once she got her teeth, he'd let her try some bacon.

You'd think he'd know these things. He was an only child, but he'd been raised around his cousins. There was always a baby in the family. He still had lots of kin in Missouri, although he hadn't kept up with them. Sweet Noreen had been one of nine, though he'd never met any of the Ohio Potters. He knew she had a sister named Joy Irene, but Noreen never paid a visit, and he was of no mind to spend time with folks who'd saddle their daughter with a name like Sweet Noreen Potter. No wonder she was nuts. And she was—nuts. Maybe because of him or maybe because she was always searching for something she could never find.

Before they married, she'd been a hairdresser. Mostly she went to the homes of society matrons, fixing them up for parties, family portraits, and weddings—that sort of thing.

Putting whitewash on an old fence, she called it. He'd been attracted to her independence and her glamour. She wasn't a beauty, but she did a lot with what she had.

Noreen was happy when they first came here—glad to shake the Cincinnati dust from her feet. She dolled up the house—made the checked curtains herself and helped him lay linoleum in all the rooms. Together they planted a garden and tilled ground for a pear orchard. They'd work side by side until evening, when he'd go out to ply his trade, leaving her alone. It had to be that way. How'd she think he was able to pay cash money for this place? He thought she'd get used to it. A couple more years of the same and, with luck, they'd be set for life. A man did what a man had to do.

The room was so still Shade could hear himself chewing. His throat made a gulping sound when he forced food down with too-hot coffee.

One night he'd come in late—of course it was late; furtive games called for the cover of darkness. He'd come in late, carrying his shoes in his hand—Noreen didn't like to be wakened once she was asleep—and found her carving big *X*s in the new linoleum with a butcher knife. And once he'd found her in the well house, dangling her feet into the well shaft and it dark as pitch. He never was able to retrieve the water bucket. She'd cut the rope with that same butcher knife just to hear the splash. They went two towns over to buy a new bucket and another length of rope, her sitting beside him in the carriage as if nothing untoward had happened.

Things took a good turn when Noreen was carrying the

baby. He could kind of see why her folks had named her Sweet. She loved all that laying by of stores, stacks of folded diapers, and scores of tiny gowns and little undershirts. She'd take skeins of floss and a small round hoop out to the porch on sunny days and sit embroidering all sorts of baby animals on the gowns and bibs. She grew round and gratified, plump as a watermelon on the vine.

Noreen had gone into labor during one of his nightly forays. Shade hadn't given it a thought; the birth wasn't supposed to happen for two more weeks. Maybe that was why the whole thing wasn't so difficult. He'd made it home just in time to deliver the baby himself, cutting the cord with Noreen's sewing scissors.

They'd been like two kids at Christmas dickering over the same toy. Neither of them could get enough of the tiny new being. For two days they'd argued over the naming. Noreen didn't catch on why he insisted on naming their daughter Betsy—he'd told her his first wife's name was Diane—but she thought it was too cutesy. She didn't mind Lane, his mother's maiden name, but she wanted the baby called after her own mother too. The mother she didn't ever visit or write. He stood his ground. Maybe that started the whole dark slide. Why hadn't he left it alone?

But the thing was, the baby looked like a Betsy—tiny and adorable and helpless as a kitten. He would have carried her around in his pocket if he could have. He stayed home nights, though Noreen had recovered quickly, on her feet just hours after giving birth. And milk—she had plenty of milk.

It was probably a week before either of them noticed that Betsy wasn't doing so well. Mostly she slept. That's what babies were supposed to do—but they were supposed to eat, too. And that was the difficult part. Betsy took hours to nurse, and her cry, when she mustered up the energy, was not a joyful, lusty newborn cry, but a thin fret that set Noreen's nerves on edge.

The next day, after they'd tried everything else, they'd set off for the same town where he'd bought the new well bucket. He'd thought the trip would cheer Noreen up. She liked the big overstocked general store there. Maybe she'd buy some new face cream or a bauble for the baby. But when they arrived, she wouldn't get out of the buggy. When he'd tried to cajole her, she gathered the baby closer and turned her taciturn face away. He hated when she got that way; it made him want to punch a hole in something. Instead he hurried into the store, sure his purchase would solve everything.

If he could take back only one thing he'd ever done in his entire life, it would be what he'd said to Noreen a few days later, the thing that had started that last terrible fight.

The chair scraped against linoleum as Shade stood to stack his dishes and pour another cup of coffee. Once settled, he laid the stolen page on the table, determined to study it like a scholar would, interested, instead of like a loser spoiling for a fight. He read the article probably a dozen times, underlining each word with his index finger, not allowing himself to skip past what might upset him. If you left out the ugly, condemning words, it described his daughter to a tee: slow to feed, hard to nourish, floppy limbs, weak cry.

His anger didn't dissipate with knowledge but simmered like a kettle on the stove. He forced the rest of his food down and drank the coffeepot dry. At the very least, he knew Betsy Lane was somewhere alive, not carried off through the open window by some hungry animal or traveling gypsy.

On the peg beside the door hung the peeled sycamore walking stick and the red gallon bucket he'd found after he discovered the baby missing. His wild search had taken him down to Tattler's Branch, where he came upon the spilled blackberries and the cane. That stick had been a divining rod; finding it had helped him settle on Skip Rock as the place where Betsy had been taken. It was logical that whoever had been helping themselves to the berries from his property had walked from somewhere nearby; the town was the best bet. It was clear as the water in the creek that that person had taken his daughter. What didn't make sense was why the law hadn't been nosing around. Maybe the sheriff was too green to put two and two together. Or maybe whoever had taken Betsy didn't see what he had done. Maybe they just wanted a baby.

Absently he rubbed circles around the healing sores on his chest. Maybe the law had come with a warrant and a set of leg irons. But he didn't think so. The house was too much like it had been on the night he'd fled, not even bothering to close the door, figuring he'd never be back, figuring his amazing luck would give him one more chance. He'd been halfway to Tennessee when Betsy Lane's need had called him back. He'd take his chances with the law, but his heart couldn't leave his little girl behind. How would he know she got proper care unless he gave it himself?

He'd rented a room at the boardinghouse in the town with the big general store and journeyed from there to Skip Rock. He figured the best place to start was at the doctor's office. His wounds gave him the perfect excuse to pay a visit. Intuition, a sixth sense honed by years of speculating, served him well that day in the fancy lady's office. His gut told him he had hit the nail on the head. The paper he was pleating into perfect folds confirmed it.

Outside the open door, a dry, hot wind kicked up. Swirling bits of leaves and twigs danced across the threshold, caught up the errant page, and flung it away. It stuck against the wall as if held by an unseen hand. He should get up and close the door before the kitchen was full of grit, but he sat there too dejected to move.

Man, he was wrecked. He needed a plan. He needed to find his daughter so they could get on the road. He needed a gun.

CHAPTER 19

CHANIS CLAY was coming up the road as Lilly was coming down. He hailed her with a big wave.

"How's Miss Mazy this morning?"

"Still sleeping. She's keeping an eye on Armina today."

"Miz Armina doing better?"

"Much. I won't be surprised if the whole story comes spilling out soon," Lilly said, putting a hand on his sleeve. "Chanis, we need to talk. I've a theory about the break-in."

They matched steps as Lilly relayed what she'd found inside the book. "I believe the baby's mother is searching for her. Maybe she was hiding and watching that first night when I carried Glory to my office. She might have thought she'd find information in my charts, and instead she stumbled onto the book. It must have been quite a shock to her."

Chanis listened politely, stroking the line of his jaw with his thumb and index finger. "She'd be a mighty big woman," he said as they reached the clinic. "Come and look."

Outside the office door, the air smelled of fresh-cut lumber. Chanis pointed at a mishmash of tracks outlined in the brimstone dust. "See here how the dust revealed the prints of the culprit's boots? We couldn't see them before Turnip fumigated out here. I wish I'd thought of such."

"Goodness, Chanis, all I see is a mess."

He hunkered down, picked up a stick, and indicated one set. "These here are mine. Back-and-forth ones I figure to be Turnip's—see how they go off toward where he would have parked the wagon? These littler ones are Timmy Blair's. They're what I noticed first—so obviously different." He stood and went to a perfect pair planted beneath the new frame. "He would have stood just so, squaring his stance to leverage the window." Chanis took hold of the unlocked sash and raised the window halfway up.

"I took the liberty of looking around," he said, using his passkey to unlock the door. "Inside tells an even better story."

Lilly was appalled. Gray grime covered every surface, including the floor. She'd have to get someone to mop and clean before she could see patients. "What a mess."

"Turnip didn't spare the fire and brimstone; that's for sure," Chanis said. "These prints could be used in court if there was a way to preserve them."

He was right. It was amazing. The fine dust worked the same way it had outside, collecting around shoeprints. "It seems more likely that these would be made after the dusting, not before," Lilly said.

"I thought the same at first. It took me a minute to figure out that something from the bottom of our shoes repelled the dust. See, you can see yours also."

He was right. There she was in heels and toes. "How odd."

"I checked my soles. Are you wearing the same shoes you were last Thursday?"

Balancing on the edge of the desk, Lilly bent her knee, lifting her foot. "Yes, but I don't see a thing."

"Run your hand across it."

Lilly took her handkerchief from her pocket and ran it over the sole. "It looks greasy." She folded the hankie dirty side in and put it back in her pocket.

"That's it. Just as I thought. Remember at the accident, the axle grease that was all over the tracks? We all—you, me, Timmy, Turnip—were there. I suspect we've tracked it all over town."

"Makes me glad I leave my shoes at the door when I get home," Lilly said. "But if that is so, how do you explain the culprit's prints?"

"He was there among us. Sure as shooting. There were a lot of folks milling around the site." He ran a finger through the dust. "This stuff is great. I might start using it all the time to turn up clues."

Lilly sneezed. "You might ruin your lungs in the process, Chanis."

"Yeah, well . . ." His voice trailed off as he indicated where the man who broke in had walked. A few steps in—a few steps back out.

Lilly leaned against the desk. She would not sit in her chair until it was thoroughly cleaned. She tapped her index finger against her chin. "He must be the baby's father, else why be snooping around my office? This whole thing is so bizarre."

Chanis whisked his hands together. Dust motes danced in the early rays of sunlight streaming in through the clear windowpanes.

Lilly sneezed again. "Chanis."

"Sorry," he said, tucking his hands in his pockets and rocking back on his heels. "There's something we haven't considered."

Lilly raised her eyebrows, giving him a look.

"Maybe Miz Armina stole the baby. Maybe her parents didn't abandon her at all."

"Armina wouldn't do such a thing," Lilly huffed.

"You said yourself she's been acting mighty fey."

"Not fey enough to abduct a baby!" Lilly put one finger underneath her nose in an effort to stifle another sneeze.

Chanis pulled a perfectly ironed handkerchief from his back pocket and handed it to Lilly.

"Thank you." She *ka-sh*ooed, eyes watering. "If the baby was taken, why wouldn't the father's first stop be your office?"

"Some folks would rather fall in a pit of vipers as to have the law come calling. Maybe they're making moonshine up a holler somewhere, or maybe somebody in the family's got a warrant on their head."

They could hear the front door open. "Hannah's working a day shift today," Lilly said. "Give me a moment, and then we should go to the Beckers' and check on the baby. Is it all right to get this mess cleaned up?"

"Um, yeah," he said, already busy with his pencil and pad of paper. "I'll just make a few more notes." He moistened the tip of the pencil. "What size shoe do you wear?"

They took the back way to the Beckers' place. It was a little longer but a more pleasant walk.

The morning air, still light and fresh, carried the scent of the honeysuckle that tumbled riotously over a fencerow. Unfolding the blade of his pocketknife, Chanis cut two long sprigs, handing one to her.

"Did your daddy ever tell you that honeysuckle vines draw snakes?" he asked, the flower stalk bobbing in his mouth.

Lilly made a show of stepping around him, putting his body between her and whatever might slither out from under the vines. "Yes, that's why I keep my distance."

"Tastes sweet," he said, dropping the frayed stem to the ground. "That could be fixed up." He indicated a neglected-looking house behind the fence. "It'd make a good home for somebody. Wonder if it's on the market."

"Houses look sad when they're boarded up like that," Lilly said, sipping nectar from a fragile yellow trumpet. "Mmm, it tastes like it smells." She shortened the stem and tucked the flower into the sturdy gold chain that held her watch fob. They walked on. "Tell me about your father, Chanis."

"Well, for starters, he was a big man. Tall with broad shoulders—I thought he carried the world on his back. He was that strong. He was good to us kids and to my mother, and he smiled all the time." Chanis took a breath. "There was this tune he hummed. I don't know what it was—wish I could get it right, but it won't come to me. And he whistled; we could hear him coming from far up the road whenever it was suppertime."

A bumpy-skinned toad hopped halfway across the path, then stopped to stare at them from alert jade-green eyes. Suddenly the toad's long tongue darted out, snaring a hapless dragonfly, which, except for one papery wing, disappeared into the toad's wide mouth. Daintily the toad used its front feet to stuff the leftover wing into its mouth.

The toad struggled, emitting birdlike chirps, when Chanis plucked it from the dusty path. He held it out for Lilly to see.

"Ah, Bufo," she said, stroking the creature gently between its eyes. As if in bliss, the toad leaned its head toward her. "I loved playing with toads when I was a girl."

"Me too, and I never once got a wart. I bet Mazy never touched one," Chanis said.

Lilly smiled. "I expect you're right. One time we watched as a full-grown toad ate its skin—you know how they do when they shed? Mazy cried for hours. She thought it was hurting itself. It took me forever to convince her that the toad was only doing what comes naturally."

"She's sweet that way," Chanis said, freeing the warty creature.

"Yes, she is."

"Say, since we're on the subject . . ."

"Well," Lilly teased, "I do know a bit more about *Bufo americanus*. Shakespeare wrote about the beauty of a toad's eyes."

"Now, Doc Still," Chanis said, turning serious, "I was talking about Mazy. There's not one thing pretty about a hop toad. But Mazy—that's a whole different story."

"She's young yet, Chanis. You must give it time."

Chanis kicked a pebble. It hopped up the rutted washboard road like the toad had done, leaving little puffs of red clay dust in its wake. "I'm willing to wait. How long do you reckon? A year?"

Lilly could see heartache coming around the bend. "Mazy may not be here past the summer. She only came for a visit."

"Yeah, she said as much, but there's always the mail, and she really likes the telephone. Do your folks have a telephone?"

"Not yet. Soon, perhaps."

"I can hardly look at Mazy without my heart swells up like an ole full-throated bullfrog. I just wanted to tell you that."

A bridge made of stone crossed a meandering stream so blue that it might have captured the sky. Flecks of early morning sun breached the leaves of overhanging trees, dappling the water with golden fingers. A heron fished the banks on long sticklike legs.

"Stop right here, Chanis, and tell me which way you'd look to study this creek."

"Upstream," he said without pausing to think. "Upstream

fills you with possibility, the way the water rushes toward you like time out of mind, forever and enduring. Downstream everything is already past."

Hands on the built-up railing of stone, they leaned over the bridge, listening to the hypnotic gurgle of water flowing over moss-covered rock. Catching their presence, a muskrat scurried off into the thick weeds, leaving its stockpile of cattails behind for the moment.

"This quiets your soul, doesn't it?" Chanis said.

"The salvation of living water," Lilly replied. She was glad for this walk, this opportunity to get to know Chanis Clay in a deeper way. If Mazy so chose, he would be good for her, but Mazy was flighty and immature.

As if Lilly should judge. Her mother would say Lilly was born an old soul, yet she'd nearly married a man who could never have fulfilled her. Her aunt Alice was already picking out her wedding dress and drawing up the guest list when true love intervened. It was as if God had plucked her up and set her feet on the true path when she found Tern.

Under cover of her linen jacket, she patted the growing mound of her belly and sent a silent prayer heavenward. *Thank You, Lord, for sending Tern to me, and please be with Mazy and with Chanis.*

They walked on between dangling fronds of creek-side willows. "It's so peaceful here," Lilly said.

"Until now, that is. Sounds like somebody's hog is setting up a fuss," Chanis said as they angled up a twisting trail to a high and bony ridge.

"Must be Sassy." Lilly folded her skirts around her, trying to dodge the sticker weeds. She'd always hated sticker weeds.

"Reckon Cletus could have found a more awkward place to live if he'd tried?" Chanis said, offering Lilly a hand across the shifting shale.

In the valley below, they saw the house sitting in a swirl of fog. It could have been a ship on the open sea.

Cletus was attempting to drag Sassy out from under the porch. "I'm a-taking her to market," they heard him yell over the clamoring of the hog.

"Cletus, don't," Anne pleaded from the porch, where little Amy buried her face against her mother's legs. "I'm sorry. I'm sorry I said anything." She unpeeled Amy from her knees and set the child inside the doorway.

Cletus tugged on the hog's big, floppy ears. Sassy bucked like a frightened horse and backed up, dragging Cletus right into the sty. Soon they couldn't tell the pig's squeals from the man's.

Anne lumbered down the steps, shrieking and praying. "Cletus! Cletus! Oh, Lord, help us."

Chanis took off in a run, down the rocky slope and across the yard to the pen, rolling his sleeves as he went. Lilly hurried after him, careful of her footing. By the time she got to the porch, Anne had collapsed against the stair rail. Cletus was lying in the yard, where Chanis had dragged him, covered with stink, one shoe missing, and heaving for breath. Sassy was rooting a red-rimmed watermelon rind around in the muck of her stall.

Cletus raised his head from the ground and looked at Anne. "I'm a no-good so-and-so."

"The next time, Cletus Becker, I'll let Sassy eat you!"

"Mama, no," Amy whimpered from the doorway. "Mama, no."

"Just shuck my hide and call me bacon," Cletus said, letting his head fall back.

Anne fanned her face with the skirt of her apron. Lilly could see she was on the verge of tears.

"Come on, dear." Lilly took her arm and helped her up. "Let's go inside."

"See to Cletus first," Anne said. "I'll heat up the coffee."

Once Lilly had treated Cletus's minor scrapes, using much more stinging iodine than was necessary, she went inside, wishing she had a potion for misery.

"You'll think I'm lazy, seeing breakfast still on the table at all of eight o'clock in the morning," Anne said, filling two chipped mugs with steaming coffee. "Just let me take this out to the menfolk."

Lilly dipped hot water from the fifteen-gallon reservoir on the wood cookstove in the corner, filling a granite wash pan nearly to the brim. She scrubbed her arms up to the elbows with lye soap and dried them thoroughly. Wishing she had some spot remover, she dipped a corner of the feedsack towel in the wash water and blotted a skim of slop from the hem of her skirt. Refreshed, she played peekaboo with Amy until the child was more like her sunny self again. Life could be so hard on children.

"Want to help me with baby Glory?" Lilly said, lifting the infant from her Moses basket and laying her on a pallet she made on the table.

"Me hep," Amy said, trying to lift Lilly's kit from the floor.

Lilly followed her usual routine, beginning with the heart and finishing with a check of the mouth for the white patches that signaled digestive upset. Thrush was so common in infants and children that Lilly gifted a solution of borax and glycerin, along with a camel's-hair brush for application, to all her young charges' mothers. She also showed the mothers how to cleanse their infants' mouths with a clean flannel cloth and warm water. Since she'd instigated those simple practices, she'd seen not one case of ulceration or gangrenous inflammation caused by thrush.

Because of her cleft, Glory was at an even higher risk for mouth ulcers than most children. Lilly was pleased to see the baby's mucous membranes were pink and healthy. Glory squirmed but did not cry. She was a placid baby.

Darling little Amy stood at Lilly's knee, her mouth stretched wide open, mimicking Lilly's examination of Glory.

"Close your mouth, baby bird, or you'll likely catch a worm," Lilly said, standing with the baby. "Let's go check on your mama."

Amy stood just behind Lilly, sucking on two fingers. She wasn't totally over the distress of the morning yet.

The yard was empty, but they could hear sawing and hammering from across the weedy lot. Anne came out of the yawning darkness of the barn, carrying the empty cups. Her face was red as a just-boiled beet. "They're fixing a pen for Sassy in one of the empty stalls. If Cletus would have done what I asked him to in the first place . . . Men!"

Amy stomped her foot. "Men!" she said.

Back in the house, Anne fussed around like a broody hen after a grasshopper, scraping plates, splashing water, wiping the table. Lilly held the baby and let Anne go. Sometimes a body just had to wind down.

Finally Anne stopped and put her hands on her hips. "It's past my understanding why this keeps happening," she said, pouring remains from a skillet into a grease keeper. "It seems like he cain't abide having a penny extra." She blew a strand of hair out of her eyes and neatened it behind her ear. "If he drank like he throws money around, he'd be a sot."

Tears shone in Anne's eyes. "My mother had a saying: 'When hard times come in the front door, love goes out the back window.' Good thing I ain't got a back window." She blotted her tears with the tail of her apron. "He found that coffee can of folding money I had salted away," she said. "I found it empty when I went to gather eggs for breakfast. He didn't even bother to pitch it—just left it laying there for me to find, like my feelings didn't matter a whit."

She shifted her head in small movements—more a tremble than a shake. Her face crumpled. "That hurt more than the money, him willing to hurt me thataway. I think he loves that old hound dog better than he does me." She wiped another tear. "When I reminded him we got taxes to pay, he got all het up and flung his coffee outen the door.

Said he'd take Sassy to market—like that would solve every-thing. Blowhard! That's pure selfish. What would we eat on this winter?"

"Men," Amy said.

Anne rubbed her hand over Amy's head. She looked at Lilly's untouched coffee. "Would you druther have tea, Doc Still?"

"I wouldn't want to be a bother," Lilly said, using her mountain manners. Making tea would allow Anne time to pull herself together. Serving Lilly's need would help her to save face.

When the tea was poured and served with biscuits and honey, Anne took the chair across from Lilly. Amy left Lilly's side, where she'd been stroking the ribbon binding on Glory's blanket, and climbed up in her mother's lap.

"Well," Anne said, "I know in reason you didn't bring the sheriff by this morning to witness mine and Cletus's cater-wauling. Is there some news about Glory?"

A screeching sound like nails being pried loose from boards interrupted them.

"They're fixing to move Sassy." Anne picked up a biscuit dripping with butter and long sweetening. "I'd best go help."

Lilly and Amy took a seat in the doorway to watch the fes-tivities. Snuggled in her blanket, Glory slept in Lilly's arms.

Chanis stood partway between the porch and the barn, brandishing a stout stick. Anne chanted, "Soowee—soowee—soowee," while walking backward with the biscuit held just out of reach of Sassy's searching mouth. Cletus brought up the rear, one hand resting on Sassy's broad rump, tiny pink piglets in each of his pockets and one under the bib of his overalls.

Amy clapped her hands in delight. "Me one, Dada. Me one."

Cletus removed one piglet. He wouldn't meet Lilly's eyes when he placed the squirming bundle in Amy's lap. "This un's yours, baby girl," he said.

CHAPTER 20

THE MORNING WAS FADING AWAY. Lilly and Chanis took the short way back to Skip Rock—in spite of passing the household full of measles.

"It was good of you to help Cletus move Sassy to the barn," Lilly said.

"It needed doing," Chanis said. "It got Cletus talking, anyway."

"Have you known him a long time?"

"Yeah, his folks lived just a whoop and a holler up the road from mine. They was poor as garter snakes. Cletus come up hard—and you know he can't half hear. His daddy slapped him upside the head one day for taking an extra piece of corn bread. It busted his eardrum."

"Was he treated?"

"For the ear? Nah, he just learned to duck."

"Are his folks still around?"

"Influenza took his ma and pa—probably six, seven years ago. Cletus dug their graves himself, wouldn't let a soul help. He keeps their family plot clean as a whistle."

Lilly waved when they passed the Coopers' place. Along one side of the house a line of sunflowers turned their faces toward the sun. Two of the girls played jacks on the porch. They waved back.

"Have you had the measles, Chanis?"

"There's not much I haven't had. My mom and her sister had 'catching parties' whenever any one of us came down with something. They believed in kids getting things early on—thought it would protect us somehow when we grew up. Is there any truth to that?"

"Some, yes. Eventually scientists will discover ways to protect against most communicable diseases. It's only a matter of time."

The sun bore down. Lilly felt wilted, and the heel of her foot ached—probably a stone bruise from walking the ridge. She was glad to reach the clinic. Chanis looked as fresh as when they'd started out this morning.

"Do you think we were right to leave Glory with the Beckers?" Lilly asked.

"What else could be done? Lock her up in the jail? I'd have to take Anne in as well—and her little girl. Then Cletus would be hanging around waiting for Anne to set up housekeeping." He nodded as if he were pondering the situation. "And Sassy would need a sty."

Lilly laughed with delight at the picture Chanis was painting. It was good to lighten the moment.

Chanis handed her the satchel he'd carried for her. "Don't fret. Nobody followed us up there, and when we left out, Cletus was drilling a hole in the barn so's he could keep a watch on the house—like he couldn't just look out the door. At the very least this'll keep him out of the doghouse for a while."

"Or the pigpen, as the case may be," Lilly said.

"I got a feeling this whole thing is getting ready to bust wide open," Chanis said, turning the knob to the clinic door.

"I fear you're right." Lilly stepped into her now-spotless office, bidding Chanis good-bye. She could hear murmurs coming from the waiting room. It was half past ten o'clock. She was late, but she needed a minute to herself before the fray began.

At the lavatory sink she ran cold water over a facecloth, then pressed it to her cheeks, her forehead, and the back of her neck. She sponged the hem of her skirt again and another spot near her waist. She was so much more comfortable in her altered garment. Tillie had stitched buttonholes at intervals on the blouse's hem and sewn buttons to match on the let-out waistband of her skirt. When it was done up, the buttons were cleverly hidden.

Sitting on the closed lid of the commode, Lilly pulled off her shoe and stocking and examined her foot. Just as she'd expected, a purple bruise bloomed painfully on her heel. Funny how things hurt worse once you'd actually seen them. She hopped on one foot to the linen closet, where she kept a tin of salve, and smoothed the greasy ointment on. There was nothing known to be more healing than the fragrant yellow resin from the buds of the balm of Gilead mashed and stewed in melted lard. She never made the salve without snippets of Scripture running through her mind. So powerful, the words from Jeremiah: *"When I would comfort myself against sorrow, my heart is faint in me. . . . Is not the Lord in Zion? . . . Is there no balm in Gilead; is there no physician there?"*

It was a tribute to her mother and to her Sunday school teachers that Lilly had committed so many verses to memory. Every Sunday there'd been a new verse to learn before the next class, and every Saturday evening her mother listened to her recitation. No memory verse—no supper. Lilly learned easily. She never went to bed hungry.

A smile played about her lips as she massaged her foot. Her mother was not overly strict. Lilly, as well as her brothers and sisters, had gotten by with more than they should have, unless Daddy John was home. But when it came to honoring the Scripture, Mama was a stickler. Lilly was thankful for a mother who loved and lived the Word.

She wrapped her heel in gauze before putting her stocking and shoe back on, then washed her hands again and tidied up her hair. She didn't look any worse for the morning's wear. Tillie Tippen was right. Her face had that expectant-mother glow.

Oh, she wished Tern would get home. She didn't want to be busting out all over before she saw him next. She should go by the post office; often the postmaster had information beyond the confines of Skip Rock. Maybe there'd be some news about the mining disaster in Canada. If the men had been rescued, Tern could be on his way home. She prayed so.

Lilly worked through lunch. Timmy came by for a post-coin-swallowing check. He was fit as a fiddle and left the office sporting a clean sling and with instructions for gentle—Lilly emphasized *gentle*—exercising of his arm and hand to prevent joint stiffness. "Five more weeks and we can leave the splints off," she said in answer to a posited question. He bounced out the door, coins jingling in his pocket, on his way to the commissary to pick up a newspaper for her. Maybe the *Herald* would have an update, save her a trip to the post office.

Hannah brought her a lunch tray. "You need to eat, Doc Still. I'll keep the natives at bay for a few minutes." She dragged a side chair close to Lilly. "I noticed you were limping. Why not put your feet up while you eat?"

Lilly did just that, resting her feet and relishing the mellow taste of creamy yellow cheese on lightly buttered wheat bread, the sunny taste of sugar-dusted blueberries, and the full aroma of the steaming tea. Often she didn't realize how hungry or how tired she was until she forced herself to rest. Caring for her patients always seemed more urgent than caring for her own needs. That would have to change now that there was a baby on the way. If she could just hold on until Ned finished his training, her workload would halve.

She rounded her shoulders and let them drop, releasing tension. "Physician, heal thyself," she said, popping a blueberry into her mouth.

Timmy jumped over the doorsill. "Here's your paper, Doc, and your change and an oatmeal cookie the lady at the register sent you. It's got raisins."

"Open your mouth, Timmy; let me see if there's a dime hiding in there."

Timmy dropped his head. "I ain't likely to pull that stunt again, Doc. I learnt my lesson good."

"I was teasing you." She handed him a nickel from the change. "Thank you for the paper." Taking the wax-paper wrap from the still-warm cookie, Lilly broke it in half. "Help me eat this while I look at the news."

Timmy looked over her shoulder as she turned the pages. His piece of cookie disappeared in three bites. "Anything interesting in there, Doc?"

"Not much."

"You need anything else?"

"No, not for now."

Timmy licked crumbs from the cookie wrapper. "Say, Doc, you know that man who was here that time?"

Lilly folded the paper and put it aside. Timmy had a crumbly oatmeal mustache. "What man?"

"'Member the one that wore his hair like an Indian, but he wasn't? 'Member he had his hair pulled back in a braid?"

"I do remember him. Why?"

"I seen him again this morning. It was way early—don't tell Mommy, okay? I was supposed to be taking the cream to the station and coming straight back. You know they open up way early so's they get the cream straight from the cow. Mommy said, 'No dillydallying, young man.' But I sort of wanted to see if Mr. Tippen had got your window fixed."

Lilly's neck tingled. "Where was he, Timmy?"

"I can show you."

Lilly stepped outside with Timmy. The boy raised his uninjured arm and pointed straight across the street to the alley between the commissary and the cream station, just as Chanis had done.

"He was crouched down in the alley there. When he seen me looking, he acted like he was picking something up off the ground—like maybe a coin or something. When he went to straighten up, he caught the brim of his hat on that window ledge there. I seen that long snake of his hair spill out." Timmy twisted side to side. "It made me feel funny—like a goose was walking on my grave."

Back inside, Lilly offered the rest of the cookie to him.

"Anyways," he said between bites, "I just wanted to tell you that."

"I think Sheriff Clay would like to hear about what you saw, Timmy."

"Really? I want to be him when I grow up." He crumpled the cookie wrapper and tossed it toward the waste can. "Daddy says he'd like to see me on the right side of the law."

"If you see that man again, don't talk to him."

"Is he a bad guy? Did he break your window?" He picked up the wad of wax paper from the floor and dropped it in the can. "Do you go to jail if you break a window?"

"No, a person doesn't go to jail just for breaking a window."

"That's good, else half my buddies would be in the hoosegow."

"Hold still," Lilly said, wiping crumbs from his face.

He squirmed away. "At least you didn't spit on your finger like Mommy does. Reckon I'll just mosey on over to the jail. Maybe Sheriff Clay will let me look through the bars."

As Lilly settled in to finish the afternoon with more patient cares and thus more charts, she fought the urge to pull the window blind. If someone was watching, he'd have to come closer than the alley to be a threat. Tomorrow she'd bring Kip to work. He was the very best watchman.

Home was a welcome sight when it finally came into view. Lilly had almost given in to her sore foot and asked Mr. Tippen for a ride. He'd stopped his wagon on the road as she passed by to ask if she'd seen any termites about. She could have laughed at the thought after the way he bombed the clinic. "Not a one," she said.

"Good," he'd said. "I'm off, then. Got to see to the cows before supper."

Lilly purposely hid her limp on the walk home. She didn't want folks fussing over her. All she wanted in the world was for Tern to come home and rub the soreness from her feet.

Silly vanity—wishing niceties to come her way when there was so much sorrow all around.

She thought of Anne. Would her husband's gambling cause them to lose their place? She'd had to bite her tongue to keep from offering to pay their back taxes herself. It might be a poor excuse of a farm, but it was theirs.

She wondered why Anne put up with Cletus—why she stayed. But she knew the answer, of course. Staying was what women did. Partly to save face—mountain women were so very proud—and partly because there were no other options.

As she walked, her mind wandered to the poorest place she'd ever seen. She'd been in Skip Rock for only a short time when, one overcast day, she was called out to deliver a baby. The man of the house had pulled her up behind him, and the horse took off in a trot. She'd clung to the man's back all the way up and across the ridge dubbed Devil's Shoestring, scared within an inch of her life at the steep drop-off on either side of the narrow crest. One misstep and the horse would plunge them all to sudden death.

"Hold tight as a tick," Mr. Dweezil Pratt had said. "It's about to get a tad rough."

Lilly found that was a severe understatement when the horse locked knees and slid them all the way to the bottom of the hill, shale cracking under its hooves like ice on a mud puddle. After that, things got a "tad" easier as their sure-footed mount picked his way upstream in a mostly dry creek bed. She was glad they weren't making the trip in a rainy season.

Lilly thought she was looking at a corncrib when at last they reached the rough-hewn cabin surrounded by a dense forest of trees. Mr. Pratt handed her down to a broad-shouldered, barefoot boy who swung her to her feet, then, without so much as a word, began to wipe foamy lather from the horse's withers.

Four skimpily dressed children with wildly unkempt hair spilled out of the door. There were no windows, but with cracks in the walls big enough to pitch a cat through, one could easily see in or out.

The stoop was a large, rectangular limestone slab creating a high step to the doorsill. The main house was one square room with a loft and a packed dirt floor. A chink-rock fireplace took up the wall across from the door. A double bed was pushed up against another wall. A few broken-down chairs and an oak pedestal table were the only other furnishings. Some limp clothing hung from pegs on the walls.

A dogtrot led to the kitchen, where there was a stove, a wash bench, and an open cupboard holding plates and cups and a few jars of canned vegetables, mostly green beans and tomatoes. One shelf sported a pasteboard box cut in half. The box held bars of lye soap. A basket of long-eyed, withered potatoes was pushed under the lowest shelf alongside a blue twenty-five-gallon bucket of lard. Lilly shuddered to think of the effort required to haul that lard can across the back of Devil's Shoestring.

Three shotguns and a rifle made a tepee in the corner. The hides of various animals were tacked, curing, along one wall. Lilly recognized the skins of a beaver and a mink. It seemed early in the year for trapping. Maybe these animals had natural deaths or maybe Mr. Pratt had shot them. She knew one thing: they were decidedly unsanitary. And she knew another: they would cure better out of doors. Her poor Daddy John had to dry his hides on the back side of the barn out of sight of his girls. Even her mother couldn't bear to see his handiwork. Hides done right brought good money, though.

That day in a stranger's kitchen, Lilly suddenly realized she was the only person in the house. Where had all the children gone, and where was the expectant mother? Back through the narrow dogtrot and with a little leap down to the stoop, she saw the children gathering around their father. He was doling out penny candy, one stick at a time. The littlest one sat astride a sister's hip, making give-me motions with her fingers smacking her palms. A smile stretched ear to ear on the little one's face when Mr. Pratt broke a stick in half and stuck it in her greedy paw. So it appeared there were five children counting the older boy.

"Mr. Pratt," she called out from the stoop, "where is Mrs. Pratt?"

"My, my," he said. "I near forgot all about her. Geraldine! Where you at? I brung the doc."

Lilly was becoming decidedly uneasy. She should have asked more questions before she agreed to come along to this place six miles from nowhere. This should be Mrs. Pratt's sixth delivery. Unless she was severely run-down or ill, her labor probably wouldn't last long—why wasn't she already abed? Short, rapid deliveries could be as dangerous to the baby as overlong ones.

As Lilly watched, a young, stout-looking woman emerged from a scraggly garden bordered by a broken-down fence. She carried a heavy-bladed, short-handled, one-eyed hoe.

"Don't bust a gut, Dweezil," she said, continuing across the yard. "It'll be a time yet."

The children, except for the biggest boy, followed her across the yard like ducklings after a hen. "You'uns wait out here for a spell," she said to the children. "I need to visit with the lady."

She followed Lilly into the house, the hoe still resting on her shoulder.

"I'm Dr. Corbett," Lilly said. "I'll be taking care of you."

"A doctor, you say," the woman said. "I thought you were kindly dressed up for a granny woman."

"Can we sit?" Lilly asked. "I have a few questions."

"Land sakes," the woman said, setting the tool down with a thunk. A clod of dirt broke apart on the floor. She didn't pay it any mind. "I didn't plan to bring this into the house. I'm kindly nervous about this whole undertaking, but I reckon it's time to play the fiddle or pay the fiddler or how-some-ever that goes." She stepped back to the open door. "Dweezil—come and take this here mattock. I seen a copperhead long as a man's arm out there among them dried-up cucumber vines."

She turned her big, velvet-brown eyes on Lilly. "Dweezil Pratt—wouldn't it make you poor to pack a name like that?"

The balding Mr. Pratt reached up from the low stoop and took the hoe. "I'll get that snake for you, sweet thing."

"Thank you, darlin'," she said, drawing the words out slow as molasses from a spoon.

They watched the kids take off toward the garden in their father's wake. The least one bobbed like an apple on her sister's skinny hip.

Geraldine laughed low in her throat. "There weren't really a snake, but this'll give us a minute."

The young woman had a handsome, if not pretty, face with a square chin and high cheekbones that would age well. The light was beginning to dawn on Lilly. Geraldine was decidedly not the first Mrs. Pratt.

The chair Geraldine offered her was possibly the best one in the room. It listed to the right on two short legs, keeping Lilly slightly off-balance.

"Have your pains set in yet?"

Geraldine rubbed her stomach. "Ow-wee, yes. I was trying to walk them off in the yard there. Dweezil was gone half the day. The baby catcher don't live that far away. I was praying for all I was worth that Dwib didn't have to birth this young'un. The girls, they're all too young to be much help." Her face twisted in a grimace. "Excuse my poor manners. I'm talking like you been formally introduced and all. Dwib's Dweezil's eldest and his only boy. I got high hopes for this'un here." She crossed her fingers and held them aloft, then said, "Ow-wee" again, this time stretching it out into a moan. "It didn't hurt near this bad until I set eyes on you."

"Is this your first, Geraldine?"

"Ooh-ahhh," she said. "First and last."

If Lilly had a nickel for every time she'd heard that, she'd have a jar full of nickels. She helped Geraldine into a night-dress and had her keep walking as she prepared the bed with the stack of newsprint the family had been saving since early winter. There were no extra linens. There was really not much of anything at hand.

Mr. Pratt came back and forth with buckets of water to fill a kettle and a big cook pot on the kitchen stove. He tied two strong knots in the corners of a sheet and draped it around the bedposts. Obviously he had been through this before.

Geraldine was soon in active labor. "I wisht I'd never met you, Dweezil Pratt," she panted, tugging on the knots.

"You don't mean that, sweet thing," Mr. Pratt said as he stroked the hair from Geraldine's forehead. "Do you want me to leave, sugarplum?"

"I want you to go far, far 'way," Geraldine said through gritted teeth. "I don't ever want to see your ugly mug again."

"I hate to leave her," he said to Lilly, "but this part is always hard for me."

"We'll be fine," Lilly said. "Maybe you could draw some more water and fill the washtub."

"Me and Dwib will put it by the back door. I'm ever so grateful you was willing to come. You were my last hope after I found out the baby catcher was busy having a baby of her own." He wiped his forehead on the sleeve of his shirt. "Whew, what a day."

Geraldine planted a foot in the middle of her husband's chest and shoved him off the bed. "Shut up, Dweezil. I'm the one's doing all the work here."

He scrambled up and indicated one of the wild-haired children milling around the open door. There was no screen. "I'll leave Suzy a-setting on the porch. She'll come to the barn and fetch me you need anything. The rest of you young'uns come with me."

Lilly could tell he was glad to show them his back as his wife groaned and pulled on the knotted sheet.

Less than two hours later, with one last mighty push, Geraldine's healthy baby boy was born. Her youth and muscular build had made easy work of the delivery. Crying out, she reached for the infant, snuggling him against her chest, following mothering instincts ages old.

Lilly worked quickly to cut the cord, deliver the afterbirth, stem the bleeding, and clean up both mother and baby. She wished all births were so uncomplicated.

Geraldine praised the Lord and asked for Dweezil.

"I thought you never wanted to see him again," Lilly joked.

"I reckon I didn't there for a minute," she said, her countenance turning serious. "He ain't a bad man to be tied to. He's not mean or nothing." She shifted the baby in her arms, letting his tiny searching mouth find purchase. "Poor Dweezil. His wife up and died on him, and I weren't doing nothing but taking up space at my daddy's table—just withering on the stem. My folks had about given up on me ever having a place to set up housekeeping." She tossed her thick auburn hair over one shoulder. "It's not like I'm a beauty."

Lilly undid the knots in the corners of the last clean sheet and expertly exchanged it with the soiled one on the occupied bed. She wadded the newsprint, stuffed it in the fireplace, and struck a match, listening to the whoosh before turning away from the sudden metallic reek of blood and printer's ink. After washing her hands for the umpteenth time, she sat on the edge of the bed, watching the baby nurse.

"Geraldine, you just did an amazing thing. You are precious in God's sight." She put her hand on the young mother's knee. "I've never attended a better birth."

Maybe it was the slant of the sun coming in through a crack in the wall or maybe it was from within, but Geraldine glowed. "Really?" she asked. "The best?"

"The best bar none," Lilly said, giving her knee a light pat. "Do you want me to call your husband now?"

"He'll be so proud," Geraldine said, cupping the baby's chin in one hand, burping him with the other. "Dweezil Jr. will bind the whole family together—make it all worth it."

She ducked her head, suddenly shy. "At least I hope it does so—it ain't like I have much choice."

Lilly often thought of Geraldine and sometimes wondered why she'd never been called back to that hardscrabble cabin hidden deep in the shadow of Devil's Shoestring. Now, as she limped through the door of her own house, she thought again of Geraldine's words. *It ain't like I have much choice.*

Perhaps Geraldine didn't feel she had a choice, but Anne

Becker did. Because of her training, she could support herself and her daughter if she so chose. Lilly hoped Anne had the strength to do the right thing, whatever that might be. It was not for Lilly to say.

CHAPTER 21

THE SCREEN DOOR SQUEAKED its familiar welcome as Lilly pushed it open. The scent of supper tickled her nose. Oh, if Armina had made chicken and dumplings, Lilly would be in heaven. She leaned against the wall just inside the door and kicked off the shoe that was so offending her stone bruise. "Kip," she said as he bounded up, "go fetch my slippers."

Of course, all Kip heard was *fetch*. Whining, he leaped hopefully against the door she had just come through. Lilly hobbled back outside and found a short stick to cast about the yard for Kip. He ran and fetched, ran and fetched until finally he wound down and sat panting at her feet. When she tried to take the stick, he growled his mock growl and tugged against the pull.

"Oh, Kip, let me sit a minute." She scooped him up and he rode her hip to the lawn chair under the shade of a maple tree. Once they were seated, he dropped his stick onto the wide wooden arm of the chair. He sat in his usual stance, back to her, rump pushed up against her belly, ears perked, eyes alert and tracking. She stroked his head and ran her fingernails up and down his back in the scratching motion he loved. The repetitive action calmed them both.

Lilly couldn't imagine life without Kip. He was not the first dog her husband had given her, but he was the best.

Many years ago, when she was just a girl, Tern had helped her rescue a beagle and her one remaining pup. The other puppies had been drowned in a pond—cast there in a gunnysack tied at the neck with baling twine. Though the mother dog belonged to Tern's family, he let Lilly keep her as well as the pup. Steady had lived a long and fruitful life. Lilly still missed her, but sweet, energetic Kip eased the sore spot in her heart.

Kip came about in a different way. When Lilly and Tern had been married for only a short time, he was called to a mining accident in Pennsylvania. As he polished his shoes and packed his duffel in preparation, Lilly had become weepy—nearly distraught with an overwhelming high-lonesome feeling.

"Honey," Tern had said, taken aback by her distress, "I'll be back before you know it. You're so busy at the clinic, you'll not have time to miss me."

"I know," she'd said, mopping the tears that would not

stop no matter how hard she dug her nails into the palm of her hand. She didn't want her husband to think of her as weak—a weeping sob sister. She didn't understand why she was carrying on so, but just the thought of him boarding a train—hurtling off into who knew what dark danger— unnerved her. She paced about their bedroom, folding his shirts just the way he liked before wrapping them in tissue paper to prevent wrinkling. At the last moment, she tucked a length of her blue hair ribbon into the front pocket of the first shirt in the stack, where he would find it unexpectedly. It would remind him of how lonely she would be without him.

At the train station, she'd turned into a puddle of tears again, clinging to the lapels of his coat, biting back the words that would beg him not to go. He'd found a private place a few steps away from the hectic platform, enveloping her with his strong arms, kissing away the tears from her cheeks.

"Sweet girl," he'd murmured in her ear. "What's all this about? Where's my feisty, independent woman?"

Lilly turned in his arms, leaning into the strength ema- nating from him, hoping to absorb it, hoping to pull herself together. "I don't know, Tern," she said shakily. "I feel like you're going off to war or something."

Draping his arms over her shoulders, he pulled her close, resting his hands lightly at her waist. She covered them with her own and bowed her head. "I never expected to be this despondent over you."

"But I'm not even gone yet."

"You were gone to me the minute you got that telegram

from Washington. You were gone when you got your duffel bag down from the shelf."

"I'll be back," he said gruffly, resting his chin on her shoulder. "You know that, right? I've promised you I'll always come back."

With a great screeching of brakes and belching of smoke, the train pulled into the station. Tern disengaged her gently and kissed her softly. "I have to go."

"Wait, Tern. We didn't pick a Scripture to bless your journey."

"Lilly, we don't have time now. My Bible's clear down in the bottom of my bag," he said. "We should have done this last night."

Lilly stood beside him, holding his hand tightly. She took a deep breath and cleared her mind, waiting for the proper verse for such a moment as this. "I don't remember exactly where this is, but I know it's from Isaiah. Mama gave me this one when I left for school: 'Fear not: for I have redeemed thee, I have called thee by thy name; thou art mine.' . . . Oh, I can't recall the rest. It's about keeping you safe." She gave him a wobbly smile and straightened his lapels. "Look it up when you get there—promise?"

He put his knuckle under her chin and lifted her face to kiss her swollen eyelids and tenderly caress her lips. "I promise. Now you have to let me go so I can get ready to come back."

"I'm sorry to carry on so, Tern."

"It's a little thing called love, baby; may it ever be so." He lifted her off her feet, twirling her around, not caring who saw. He didn't set her down on the platform until she was laughing aloud.

People were staring. One woman frowned. "Well, I never," she said through prim lips.

"Go," Lilly said, playfully shoving his shoulder. "Go before you get us arrested."

"I know the law. You can't put a guy in the slammer for being in love." He doffed his hat to the frowning woman. "Begging your pardon, ma'am. Didn't mean to cause offense, but my girlfriend here's a little tipsy. I was trying to straighten her out."

The lady gave Lilly a stern look. Lilly shook her head, hiding a smile behind her gloved hand, praying she didn't see that woman in the office anytime soon.

Tern walked away backward, locking eyes with Lilly until the porter took his duffel and called out, "All aboard!"

Kip came two days later, brought by a huckster. In broken English the man relayed how he had found the tiny puppy left to die in the weeds by the side of the road. It had been run over. The huckster had docked its fractured tail and clipped its dewclaws on the spot. He'd sold the pup to a "beeg" man outside the depot in Jackson. The man paid him "much lira to deliver it to the preety lady doctor in Skeep Rock."

"He's leg, it is broken," the huckster said. "The beeg man say you can fix."

The peddler unhitched the long-eared mule from his

traveling grocery store and stayed for supper. His own dog, a black-and-white shepherd with a beautiful full ruff, never strayed from his feet. Lilly put his bowl and water dish under the huckster's chair.

"Blackie, we go now," he said as soon as he had finished sopping up the last bit of gravy with his biscuit. With one finger he flipped the puppy's ear. "I think is terrier. You think?"

Lilly took in the almond-shaped, dark-rimmed eyes; the V-shaped, forward-carrying drop ears; the black nose; the long, sloping shoulders. The puppy's coat was all over white with one ginger ear and a gingered spot around his left eye. Her mentor in college had such a dog. As she remembered, it had been a challenging, busy, strong-willed animal.

"I think you're right. He's definitely a Jack Russell. I believe you've brought me a bit of trouble."

Bundled in an old, thin towel and held in Lilly's arms, the puppy chose that moment to kiss her chin with one light lick of his pink tongue. The bargain was sealed.

"Jack is good," the huckster said.

"Is very good," Lilly replied.

That evening, she carried the puppy to her surgery. After giving him a small portion of pain medication, she set the crooked leg, making splints from tongue depressors. The animal lay quietly, as if he knew she meant to help, and only whimpered a little when she carried him back home.

She named him in honor of the only other Jack Russell she'd ever known, and because she liked the way the word felt when it left her mouth—the little puff of air at the end.

Kip. A dog needed a strong name to call him back in from his wanderings.

She'd prayed this one would live long enough to wander, for Kip wouldn't take nourishment, not even water. She put the water dish up under his mouth, but he turned his head like it was too much effort to drink. Lilly had despaired until she thought of the leftover chicken noodle soup in the icebox. She heated half a cup and poured it in a saucer. Kip turned his head again. Sitting on the floor, she lifted him to her lap. Swirling her finger in the soup, she laid it against the puppy's mouth. His pink tongue darted out and he licked her finger clean. Over and over the puppy nursed until finally she spooned a bit of the broth into her cupped palm and let him drink until he was sated.

Tummy full, Kip slept on her chest that night like a newborn baby comforted by the *lub-dub* sound of its mother's heartbeat. It was the only way she could get a bit of rest, for he whined piteously every time she left his side.

For three days he slept in a basket under her desk at the office and by her side at night. Lilly knew she was starting a very bad habit, but she didn't care. They were good for each other. On the fourth morning he woke up in a sunny mood, chasing sunbeams across the kitchen floor on three legs and a splint. He'd been sunny ever since.

"Sister," Mazy called from behind a window screen, breaking her reverie. "I've been looking all over for you. Come in. There's a surprise."

Armina bustled about the dining room, folding napkins,

dishing up delicious-smelling chicken and dumplings and filling water glasses, nearly her old self again. In Lilly's chair was a package wrapped in brown paper and tied with white string. The return address simply said, *Tern Still*. The postmark read, *Lexington, Ky.*

Mazy clapped her hands. "I thought you'd never get home. I almost opened it myself."

Armina pointed a serving spoon toward Mazy. "Eat first. I ain't heating this up again."

"Wonder what it is," Mazy said, cutting a piece of stewed chicken with knife and fork. "It's something romantic, I'm sure."

"I don't know," Lilly said, looking at the package, which Mazy had placed in the center of the table. "It looks like a couple of shoe boxes."

"Maybe it's a hatbox!" Mazy said, plumping her short, tight curls. "I surely hope it's a hatbox."

Lilly savored the moment, trying her best to leave the worries of the day—Anne and her distress, the innocent baby Glory, the menacing stranger—alone for the moment. There was always trouble of some sort—it was the nature of her business. But for now her supper was tasty, refueling her body, and a good part of her family was present, refueling her spirit.

Mazy removed the dirty dishes and refilled the glasses. She pushed the waiting package in front of Lilly. "Open this before I explode."

"We should have dessert first," Armina teased. "We bought oatmeal cookies at the store today."

"I thought you were never leaving the house again, Mazy," Lilly said.

"Oh, Lilly, we wore hats. Didn't we, Armina? We had fun trying them on."

"Let me see," Lilly said, all smiles. "I've never seen you in a hat, Armina."

They disappeared into Lilly's room and came back sporting two of her frilliest chapeaus. Armina's was a black beret with red drooping feathers. "I look like a rooster," she said, tilting back her head. "Cock-a-doodle-doo."

Mazy looked positively fetching in the gray felt cloche with cascading yellow ribbon Lilly had purchased in Chicago while on an excursion with Tern. She put a straw skimmer atop Lilly's head. "Now," she said, "it's officially a party." She handed Lilly a pair of scissors. "Sister, open your package."

The paper fell away to reveal two shoe boxes. Mazy's face fell, then brightened. She clasped her hands to her heart. "I'll bet they're opera pumps—probably kid high heels. If so, I'm stuffing tissue in the toes and wearing them to church."

Lilly lifted the first lid and took out a pair of lady's high-topped shoes, size six. They were two-toned brown with laces—decidedly fashionable. An advertising brochure sported a picture of the shoes and boasted: *The burning and aching caused by stiff soles are entirely prevented by the RED CROSS SHOE, for it bends with the foot. RED CROSS SHOES are made of pinch-free, flexible, noiseless leather. Try them—you'll like them. We guarantee.*

Lilly sighed. She could feel Tern's presence as strongly as if he were sitting in the chair across from her. He was the most thoughtful man.

Armina rubbed the smooth leather toe of one shoe. "How nice," she said.

"Try the other box," Mazy said.

"Forevermore," Lilly said as she unearthed a pair of low-cut canvas shoes. She examined the thick rubber soles. "I think these are plimsolls—deck shoes for boating."

"Well," Mazy said, "won't they be handy the next time it rains?"

Lilly slipped the canvas shoes on her feet and clomped around the room. They were decidedly unattractive, but they felt as relaxing as house slippers. "Oh, my goodness, these are wonderful."

"You look like a duck," Mazy said.

Armina set about unlacing the leather high-tops and pulling wads of paper out. "More like a goose the way you're high-stepping."

"They feel so good," Lilly said, her stone bruise easing already. "I'm sure I'll get used to the looks."

Mazy sat at the table, resting her chin in her hands. "I was so hoping for a hat."

"There's something in the toe of this'n here," Armina said, giving the shoe a mighty shake.

Silk scarves flowed smooth as melted butter from the throat of the boot. One of Tern's calling cards followed. The note on the back said, *To my love—both comfort and beauty. See you soon. Your loving husband.*

Mazy pounced. "There are three," she said, raking a long rectangular cloth from the pile. "I claim this one." She removed her hat and wrapped the shiny white fabric, shot through with threads of gold, over her tightly wound curls, tying the tails under her chin. "Do I look like Cleopatra?"

"Perish the thought," Lilly said. She selected the red-and-black batik print and draped it around Armina's thin shoulders. "This one is definitely for you, Armina. It matches your hat." That left the sky-blue scarf for her. Tern loved to see her in blue.

Armina stroked the silky fabric of her gift. "I never felt anything so soft in my livelong life. It's like a baby's . . . like a baby . . . a baby." She faltered, stricken; her eyes searched the room wildly before landing on Lilly. "Where's the baby?"

CHAPTER 22

SHADE HARMON had had just about enough. He had stayed too long at this particular dance.

Yesterday he'd spent a good part of the morning darting from shadow to shadow trying to figure out where the doctor was. Then she popped up with the sheriff, them walking and laughing together like their heads were strung with gold, like there wasn't a care in their particular world. And who gave a whit about his? Man, he was sick of this game.

He pulled a straight-back chair out onto his porch to clean and oil the revolver he'd won in a craps game last night. The gun was small and short-barreled but had substantial heft. It also, somehow, had a feminine air—menacing as a spurned woman. He supposed it was the pearly-pink handle that made it seem girlie. He bet Jesse James would never put a fancy bit like this in his holster.

Shade stretched out his long legs, keeping his back to the pear orchard. He held the pistol loosely against his knee. That would have been the life, wouldn't it? Running the back roads with the James gang, taking no guff, robbing from banks instead of being robbed by one.

A blue jay landed just in front of him, cracking open a sunflower seed against the wooden porch railing. When Shade shifted in his seat, the bird called a raucous warning and flew away. Its wings shone like sapphire in the early morning sunlight.

Shade and Jesse had something in common besides their disdain of banks: both lost their fathers at a young age, and both their fathers had been Baptist ministers as well as farmers. Shade's father raised tobacco, and Jesse's grew hemp. Before she died, Shade's mother used to tell of the time both men preached during the same brush arbor meeting. She said the tent was full every night and that two dozen men were baptized following the revival.

"Poor Zerelda," Shade's mother would lament whenever Jesse's latest escapade blazed from the newspaper headlines in bold black print. "She loved her blue-eyed boy, but she raised him hard."

"Poor Zerelda indeed," Shade said to the returning jay. "She got her arm blowed off because of her wayward boy. Not to mention, the outlaw Jesse James got shot in the back of the head whilst dusting a picture frame. What an inglorious end. I wonder if the portrait was of his mother."

Seed hulls flew from the bird's mouth. The blue jay cocked its head and stared at Shade with black, piercing eyes. He fancied the bird could peer into the darkness of his soul. "It's good my mother didn't see how I turned out."

Disdainfully the bird turned its back and winged away again. Shade twirled the oiled pistol on his index finger. The butt banged square against his kneecap before falling to the floor with a dull thud. He hopped across the porch on one leg, swearing in pain.

He sat back down, resting his head in his hands. The gun lay in shadow where he had dropped it. Some bandit he would be. Lucky he didn't shoot himself in the foot. Did he actually think he could shoot a man in cold blood like Jesse James had done? Agony clutched his heart with an icy hand. Had Jesse ever killed a woman?

A wild hot wind rustled through the pear orchard like a cry. Like a call from the grave—like the voice of Sweet Noreen. The incessant droning insects in the drying grass and weeds chanted a funeral dirge.

Shade tugged his hair with both hands and cried out, "Lord! Lord! Is it too late for me?"

There was no answer—not from God, not from his mother or father dead these many years, and not from Sweet Noreen. He was on his own. But only for a little while, only until he found Betsy Lane—his last chance to do something good with his life.

He swore to himself that he would raise her right, try to fix whatever might be wrong with her. But if it proved impossible to change, he'd love her anyway. He was all she had.

Picking up the rag, he recommenced polishing the gun, stopping every so often to sight down the barrel. The blue jay mocked him from the limb of a sugar maple. Maybe the bird would be his first target; he could take it out in a blaze of guts and feathers. Except he wouldn't, of course; instead he went in the house and came back out with a fistful of bread crumbs. He flung them over the rail. The jay dived for one before it even hit the ground.

He didn't intend to shoot anyone. The firearm was for show in case whoever had Betsy Lane didn't want to hand her over. The very thought made him mad all over again.

Twirling the gun, he drew on his own shadow.

"Blam!" he said before ramming the loaded firearm in the pocket of his pants and drawing again. "Blam! Blam! Blam!" He could get good at this. The gun made him feel powerful—like everything was even for a change.

He made to draw one more time, but the hammer caught on his pocket, cocking the gun. Impatient, he grabbed the pistol and tugged hard. With a mighty blast, the gun discharged.

Shouting, Shade fell back against the floor, sure his time had come. His ears rang and his heart pounded. He was alive, but he dared not move. He didn't want to know where the bullet had lodged.

From the corner of his eye, he watched the jay sidestep

over to some crumbs. The bird pecked and ate while keeping one eye trained on him. *"Life goes on,"* he fancied it would say if caws were words. *"Your loss is my gain."*

With an effort, he raised his hand and let it flop. The bird didn't even flinch, just kept pecking, cleaning up the bread one tidy piece at a time. The repetitive striking of the bird's beak no doubt masked the sound of his blood dripping through the floorboards. Tears leaked from his eyes and pooled in his ears. He sighed mournfully. Soon the buzzards would come.

A fulminating anxiety bloomed in his chest like mold on overripe fruit. How had his life come to this? What had he ever done to bring himself to such a dark and desperate place? Someone once said life is about choices. . . . Well, could be, but what about other people's choices? What about how they had affected him?

Yeah, what about growing up without a father? What about having to be the man of the house at eight years old? What about his nervous, clingy mother who couldn't or wouldn't support herself? What about her spending the better part of every day rocking and staring out the window while her mind slipped away like a shadow in the night? What about the Missouri Home for Indigents where he'd been forced to place her? What about it taking ten long years for her to die alone?

One dark thought bumped up against another—like his brain was a chain-smoker bent on self-destruction.

The only peace he'd ever had was during the early years

of his marriage to Betsy. She'd been a loving presence in his life—stabilizing, even. It seemed to him she was his reward after years of strife. She made him want to get up in the morning. And then she got sick. What about that? What about how someone else's illness could suck the life right out of you? Did he really ever have a chance?

His father had preached that all of life was preordained. There was an answer for you. Some folks were destined to stumble in shadow and others to dance in the light.

The one thing he'd cop to was Sweet Noreen. He'd waltzed right into that with eyes wide open. She'd had the opposite effect on him than Betsy. Where Betsy calmed him down, Noreen revved him up. She was the whirlwind to Betsy's calm zephyr. Once they'd met, they stayed on the go—living in six towns in two years. It was the perfect life to ply his trade, and Noreen thrived on change.

Of course it had to end. Everything did eventually. And that was fine. He'd been ready to settle down. The way they were living was taking a toll. They made plans. He'd get a daytime job. She'd take care of the house, cook and clean, be a regular wife. Problem was, settling down unsettled Sweet Noreen. She wasn't wired for the mundane life.

The porch floor was getting hard. Shade's back seized in protest. The blue jay spared him no sympathy. With one easy hop, it landed on his chest and went to work on a shiny metal button. Gathering his energy, he brushed the bird away, then cautiously patted his chest. The only wounds he found were the old healing ones. He sat up, then stood. The bullet had splintered the place in the floor directly under his feet. Maybe he wasn't so unlucky after all.

He shook his head, his shoulders, his arms—letting the problems fall where they would like so many dry leaves on a windy day. Then, back inside, he cooked a hearty breakfast, adding fried potatoes to his usual bacon and eggs. After pitching the coffee grounds, he set about his tasks. It was time to put his plan in motion.

Last night he'd tossed and turned, discarding first one strategy and then another. Finally, about 5 a.m., he rose and put on a pot of coffee. It seemed every plan he came up with had a kink. He wasn't concerned with the actual taking of Betsy Lane—one look at his gun should convince the doctor that he meant for her to lead him to his daughter. No, the problem was how he could get the baby on a train without stirring interest. He'd traveled east to west and back again more than once, but he'd never seen a man on a train alone with an infant.

Then he'd hit on what might be the solution. His old Army duffel would make the perfect little nest for Betsy Lane. He wouldn't close it fully so she could have plenty of air. Once aboard, he'd retire with the baby to a sleeper car. He only needed to make it as far as Cincinnati. It would be easy enough to disappear in the big city.

He prepared the house for leaving. First he boiled all the baby's bottles and the rubber nipples, putting them in a paper sack when they dried. He washed Noreen's delicate pink-and-green dishes and mopped the kitchen floor with sudsy bleach water. His clothes were in the duffel from his aborted trip to Tennessee. He took out some things—pants and jackets of rough material—and put them in a separate bag, leaving only soft things like shirts and underwear and socks. Atop these he put the few diapers he had left and some little drawstring gowns. They'd make a good bed for the baby. There was plenty of stuff in plenty of stores in Cincinnati, and he had plenty of money.

Whoa, Nellie. He'd just about forgotten about the baby's head. Noreen never took Betsy Lane outdoors without a hat. She said it would prevent earaches. She said nobody wanted to be around a baby with the earache.

He searched the house over before he found the knit cap tangled up in his own bedcovers. A yearning, lonesome feeling washed through him as he held the tiny piece of fluff. He fingered the pink ribbon ties attached to the bonnet with delicate pink rosettes. Betsy Lane looked like a doll baby when she had that ribbon tied in a bow under her sweet chin. At first he'd fretted because she didn't seem to have a neck—her wobbly head set square on her shoulders. But Noreen said babies didn't have necks. She said their heads were too heavy for a neck.

"Support her head. Support her head," Noreen was always saying whenever he picked the baby up. It put a dreadful fear in him—what if Betsy's head popped off and rolled under the table or clean out the door? Toward the end, when he was doing most of the holding and feeding and changing, he'd discovered babies were sturdier than they looked.

Betsy was seven days old when the naval string came off. It was about the same time Noreen lost interest. He noticed her drawing away when they gave the baby her first bath. He thought it would be fun, but the baby just lay in the water with her head resting in the crook of his arm. She didn't splash and coo like he thought she would. And Noreen stood looking over his shoulder as dull as Betsy Lane. He'd dried the baby with a soft cotton towel, being extra careful with all the tucks and folds. Noreen oiled and powdered Betsy Lane, then dressed her and wrapped her in a blanket before putting her to nurse. It didn't go well, though Shade loosened the papoose wrap and tickled the tiny feet. Noreen had sat in the chair like a mannequin with stiffly folded arms. It reminded him so much of his mother.

That's when he'd thought of going to the store to buy bottles and rubber nipples. The baby needed more than the butter and sugar mix she took from Noreen's finger following the sporadic difficult feedings. That trip was the beginning of the end. But now he had a second chance.

He was ready to put the past behind. The house was clean and neat. The windows were closed and shuttered. The icebox was packed with newsprint. The taxes were paid for the year. He'd keep them current by money order for a few more years until the secrets this place held could no longer be a threat. What happened after that was of no consequence to him. He and Betsy Lane would never be back.

He was locking the door when he remembered the bromide of calcium. His fingers wavered back and forth at the black metal plate, the lock click-clacking as he maneuvered the key, undecided what to do. He swore he'd never give such a thing to the baby, but what if she cried and he couldn't get her to hush? It would only be for a short time, just until they got to Cincinnati, and he'd give her only a tiny bit—not the half teaspoon Noreen dosed her with.

His step was light when he crossed the bridge over Tattler's Branch. Once he got to Skip Rock, he'd stash his gear in that old abandoned house he'd found and look for a game—give him something to do this evening. Come morning, everything would change for the better.

CHAPTER 23

LILLY DRESSED HURRIEDLY. It was her half day and she wanted to get to the office early, before the stream of patients arrived. Kip seemed to understand and made short shrift of his business when she let him out.

She cracked the door to the back bedroom and saw that Armina was still sleeping. Good. She'd needed a sleeping draught last night, but thankfully she hadn't slipped back into the fugue state of Saint Vitus' dance. Remembering the baby had left her confused and shaky but not physically unfit.

In stammering bits and stuttering pieces, Armina had told Lilly her story. She remembered climbing through an open window and taking a baby. She didn't remember why—only that it was crying. She recalled running with the baby across a footbridge spanning a deep creek, but she didn't remember where it was or why she was there in the first place. There were giant rabbits and juicy blackberries and grating pickaxes jumbled throughout her account but no understanding of why they were relevant.

When Chanis had stopped by for an evening visit with Mazy, Lilly shared the things Armina had said. "Will Armina be in trouble with the law?" she asked after they stepped outside, beyond earshot.

Chanis rubbed his jaw. "There's way more to this than Miz Armina's able to tell. I talked to the Blair boy yesterday. He saw a fellow hanging around in the alley the same place as I did. He told me something interesting about the man— said he was the guy who'd been in your office a few days before. Said he had long braided hair."

"Yes, Timmy and I talked about it. Remember me telling you about the fellow with the puncture wounds? That was last week on Tuesday. He said he'd stabbed himself gutting fish." Excited, she took hold of Chanis's arm. "I found the baby in Armina's house the night before!"

"That man's the one who broke into your office. It's center as a die." Chanis's eyes narrowed. "He's up to no good, and I aim to stop him."

While they were talking, Mazy had come out. With the white-and-gold scarf draped over her head and across her shoulders, she looked like the woman she was fast becoming. Lilly felt a little glitch in her heart, as if she were going to lose her sister. Chanis's grim appearance had changed the instant he saw her.

Now Lilly slipped into Mazy's room and gently shook her awake. "Mazy, I'm going to the office. Keep a close eye on Armina, okay?"

Mazy opened one eye. "Do I need to get up now?"

"No, just keep an ear bent. I'll come home at noon."

Kip jumped up on the bed. Mazy threw one slender arm over him and pulled him close. He gave Lilly a look, then snuggled down.

"Traitor," Lilly said, smiling at the sweet picture they made. Surely it was only yesterday that Mazy and Molly were mere babies. Mazy was always bubbly—always smiling—while Molly was careful, restrained. Mama would say Molly took after Lilly.

Lilly stopped in the kitchen to finish her breakfast over the kitchen sink. A cold biscuit and jam along with her tea sufficed this morning.

She was halfway to the office when she noticed she'd forgotten to change her shoes. Her attractive new Red Cross high-tops were still in the box, and the sturdy deck shoes peeped outlandishly from under the hem of her skirts. It was a decidedly unfashionable look. She turned to go back but thought better of it. Time was wasting. She'd just keep her feet under the desk. The good thing was her stone bruise was much better.

She opened the clinic door and went in through the back, stopping in the kitchenette to put the kettle on. Another cup of tea would hit the spot as she went through the mail piled on her desk. Lilly sorted through periodicals and business envelopes—and a letter from Tern. The postman had mistakenly left it here instead of at the house. What a sweet surprise. Her heart skipped a beat as she slid the letter opener under the corner of the flap.

How's my sweet girl? he opened as salutation. Tern always got right down to business. Lilly couldn't help herself and went straight to the ending. She couldn't wait to see his proclamation of love for her penned in his distinctive left-handed scrawl. And there it was: *Forever and always, unending love, your husband.*

Husband—how she cherished the thought and word. It was wonderful to be loved and to love. Lilly knew she was blessed.

She backed up and read Tern's account of the men who had died at the mine disaster and of the ones the crew managed to save. Lilly was sad to think of the women whose husbands had gone to work and never come home. Tern told her how much the area reminded him of Kentucky and how the people in Canada were so kind to him and his men. *They talk a little funny,* he wrote, referring to a private joke between them—how no matter where he traveled, folks knew he was from Kentucky whenever he opened his mouth.

The best news was that he would soon be home. Lilly's whole mood lightened. She felt like a girl waiting for cake on her birthday.

When the teakettle shrieked, Lilly fairly floated to the kitchen on her ugly plimsolls.

Turning her chair to face the window, she raised the blind and watched the town wake up while she sipped her honey-sweetened tea. The gaslights winked off one by one like giant exhausted fireflies. Mr. Tippen's wagon rolled past. He would be going to the tracks to fetch the huge blocks of ice a railroad worker would pitch to the ground from the night train rolling through. The elderly black man who sometimes helped Mr. Tippen rode on the lowered tailgate with his legs hanging over the edge. He had his hat pulled down over his eyes as if he were catching a nap. Lilly hoped he wouldn't fall off the back of the wagon.

Every Wednesday, Mr. Tippen restocked the diner, where they stored the ice in the cellar between heavy layers of straw. The fresh-chipped, slightly straw-flavored ice was why the diner's iced tea tasted like a summer day. He also filled the clinic icebox and the one at her house as well as many others in town.

Lilly should check to see if Hannah had emptied the drainage trays yesterday, but it felt so good to sit idly for a moment.

She watched the commissary lights blink on and saw a man drive a mule-drawn cart into the alley and unload the trash bin. As soon as he backed out, there was Timmy swinging his small bucket of cream with his good arm. Just outside the cream station, he paused and wound his arm like a baseball player getting ready to strike a batter out. He swung the tin container around and around faster and faster. Lilly held her breath, praying the lid was secure. Timmy just begged for trouble.

Lilly turned to set her teacup down. She'd make sure the icebox was clean and ready for Mr. Tippen before she pulled charts. From the corner of her eye, she caught a flash of movement in the alley. Her skin crawled with apprehension. As she lowered the blind, she thought of Chanis Clay's warning to never be in the office alone, but who would be watching this early in the morning? She stopped the blind midwindow. There was Timmy coming out of the cream station, counting his change before he headed for home.

Lilly rapped her knuckle on the windowpane as if the lad could hear her. Timmy stopped and stuffed the money into his front pocket, then whipped his head toward the alleyway. Lilly hurried to the door and twisted the knob. Her silly boat shoes tripped her up as she neared the street. Kicking them off, she ran to the alley just in time to see Timmy's feet disappear around the back corner of the cream station. It looked like he was being dragged, but she didn't hear a yell of protest as she pounded up the passage.

"Stop," she screamed when she saw a man hauling Timmy away by the scruff of his neck. "Let him go!"

The man who had Timmy stopped when he heard her. She opened her mouth to scream bloody murder, and that's when he drew the gun. A rush of fear raced through her body like a dash of ice water. He was the man from last week—the man with the puncture wounds. The man Chanis was sure was behind the break-in. They were in trouble.

Timmy bared his teeth and bit down on the man's arm. "Run, Doc, run!" he yelped and struggled free as the man swore.

Lilly ran toward Timmy. She couldn't leave him, not even to save herself, but the man with the gun was swifter than she. He grabbed the boy and secured him with a hammerlock. Timmy's toes scrabbled against the ground. The man was strangling him. With his gun hand, the man motioned for Lilly to come closer. When she did, he let Timmy go, grabbed her, and with a violent motion jerked her around to face a rough tar-paper wall. He pasted Timmy up beside her.

"This ain't exactly what I planned," he said, "but it'll work." With a cord he tied one of Lilly's hands to one of Timmy's. "Now we walk."

Lilly looked around. They were right beside the back door of the cream station and just beyond the grocery's loading dock. On the other side of the alleyway, she could hear carts and wagons on the road. Surely someone would come this way. But there was no time for that.

The man pointed toward the scruffy, untended woods that crept down the bank behind the stores. They plunged into a haphazard stand of spindly sourwood and stubby serviceberry trees. "Straight on," he said from behind them. "Just keep going."

It was hard going through the pocked, stunted forest, where trash cedars seemed intent on taking over and thorny locusts conspired to nip at their arms and legs. Webworms dripped from loose, sloppy nests strung along the tips of the sourwoods like Christmas lights. Lilly brushed one from her hair and felt one squish beneath her heel. She shuddered in distaste. She had to wonder why God created webworms and the aggravating gnats that flew in her eyes and up her nose.

With one arm secured and the other in a sling, Timmy had a hard time keeping his balance. He tripped over a gnarled root and fell hard. Lilly toppled over him. Without a word the man gripped her elbow and helped her to stand.

Timmy scrambled up and looked at the knees of his jean pants. His eyes narrowed and red patches colored his cheeks. "My mommy's gonna be really mad at you, mister. These here are my good britches."

"Shut your trap," the man said. "Keep walking."

For a time they were traveling straight up the side of the mountain. It would have been hard enough if Lilly were climbing alone, but with Timmy attached, it was a strenuous uphill battle with no time to plant her feet or search for an easier way. Fear fluttered in her belly. What did the man want? It had to be about the foundling baby, but why abduct her and Timmy? Maybe he was one of those people who had no conscience. Maybe he would shoot them both just for sport or misdirected retribution. Lilly forced herself to remain calm, to ignore her fear and the stitch in her side by focusing on the farthest tree on the path ahead. *Lord, give me the strength to make it to that tree* became her only prayer.

Finally, after a meandering switchback, they reached the summit. The morning fog was dissipating, burned off by golden sunshine. The air was pure, free of dust and coal

smoke. In the distance a cow's bell tolled. They were standing on a bald knob high above the town. From this vantage
point, the buildings looked like children's blocks. On any
other morning it would have been a beautiful sight.

"Lookit," Timmy said. "There's the church and there's the
store. Wow, you can see everything from up here."

Lilly turned her head to take in the view from all sides.
Suddenly she knew where they were and where they were
headed. The Beckers' homestead was down the mountain
from this point. Anne would be going about her morning:
tending her babies, feeding her chickens, slopping Sassy,
maybe fussing at Cletus over some little something, while,
unbeknownst to her, peril crept its way toward her house like
a cloud of noxious brimstone.

Lilly tightened her lips, choking back questions and con-
cerns. She sensed this was not the time to try to engage their
captor. Better to keep silent and plan how she and Timmy
could escape.

The man gave them a little breather, then herded them
to a steep one-cow path that descended the mountain to
yet another ridge. On one side of the path a green meadow
beckoned, but on the other there was nothing but a sheer
drop-off. A body wouldn't even bounce on the plummeting
way down.

Lilly would not have thought it, but going down was
harder than going up. Since they were tethered together, and
since the path was so precipitous and narrow, Timmy had to
follow behind her, which twisted her arm in a painful way.

Her knees screamed in protest at every downward step. It was probably good that she was barefoot and her hose had long since turned to shreds, for she had to grip the dusty ground with her toes to keep from sliding over the side of the mountain. How did the cows do it? She supposed it would be easier to climb up and down this hill if that was where you wanted to be and if you didn't have a gun at your back.

After a while they came into a clearing and to the back of a boarded-up house. A pleasant, sweet scent tickled Lilly's nose. Honeysuckle abounded on the wire fence that ran along one side of the house. She knew this place from the other side! This was the weather-beaten house she and Chanis had passed on their trip to the Beckers'. Just seeing it gave her a sense of hope.

Surely someone would have missed them by now. Chanis would put two and two together. She began to pray that he would think about the back way to Anne's place. It wouldn't take thirty minutes for him to get here from Skip Rock. Maybe he was already on his way.

"Sit," the man said, indicating the flat porch built low to the ground.

He walked to a metal well pump on a rotted wooden platform and, kicking around in a patch of weeds beside the pump, retrieved a mason jar. After wiping the lip of the jar on the tail of his shirt, he began to pump the handle. The platform creaked under his weight. Rusty water dribbled from the mouth of the well, but he kept at it until clear water gushed forth.

Timmy winged Lilly's side with his elbow. "Maybe he'll fall through and drown like a rat," he whispered.

Lilly wondered what she would do if he did. Would she try to rescue him? It was a terrible thing to contemplate, but she was beginning to hate this man. Lord forgive her, she'd never felt this way before. "Let's pray for him," she whispered back to Timmy.

"I ain't in a praying mood," Timmy muttered, picking at the dried blood on the knees of his pants.

They both kept quiet as the man started their way.

"Ladies first," he said, handing the full jar to Lilly.

She drank gratefully, then held the jar to Timmy's mouth.

"I ain't drinking no skunk water," Timmy said, turning his head away and slapping at a sweat bee in the crook of his sling.

Lilly's arm jerked with his. Water splashed down her front. "Timmy, you need to drink."

"Suit yourself," the man said. His Adam's apple bobbed with each slug as he drank from the mason jar. When he finished, he dashed the rest of the water out at Timmy's feet. He tossed the jar back toward the well. It rolled next to the platform.

The man jerked the pistol at the door. "Inside."

Lilly's stomach sank. There was little hope that anyone would think to look for them inside the house. It would be so much better for them to stay on the road.

A dusky gloom greeted them beyond the door. An animal of some sort skittered away from the sudden burst of light. Lilly's whole body tensed, preparing for the flight she couldn't take.

"It's just a coon," Timmy said. "He won't bother us none."

"Don't try anything stupid," the man said, pocketing his gun.

With swift movements he untied them. Blood rushed tingling into Lilly's hand. She rubbed it vigorously, then started to take Timmy's.

Suddenly the boy launched himself at the man, planting his head in the gunman's midsection. A whoosh of air escaped the man's lips as he doubled over.

Stunned, Lilly headed for the door, sure Timmy would follow. This was their chance to escape.

She stopped and whirled around at the sound of a slap. Timmy's nose dripped blood. The gun was pointed at his head.

The man herded them down a short hall and kicked an interior door open. "In there," he said.

Lilly went in first.

"Not you," the man said, jerking Timmy backward. "I've got a special place for you."

CHAPTER 24

ARMINA'S POUNDING HEAD pulled her out of sleep. The clock on the dresser spoke of eight o'clock. Who lay abed until 8 a.m.? That sleeping draught Doc had insisted on giving her had turned her into a dull-witted sluggard. She wouldn't take it again.

She poured water into a bowl from the Blue Willow pitcher on the washstand. Mazy had chided her for not wanting to avail herself of the fancy indoor outhouse at the end of the hall, but Armina couldn't get used to it. She liked the old ways. She just couldn't see having your water spigot right next to your commode. How'd the water keep from getting all mixed up? Her half-moon toilet with its specific purpose seemed tidier to her.

Now Tillie Tippen, she had it right. Her outhouse had linoleum on the floor and a fancy basket for paper and rags right there on the bench between the two holes, and curtains—lacy curtains on the door window.

Armina paused midsplash. Why would you want a window just there? But Tillie was such a busybody, Armina supposed she wouldn't like a minute when she couldn't see what everyone else was doing.

Armina felt bad for her mean thoughts of Tillie. The woman had been so good to her of late, sending food right to her door while she was laid up and offering to do her laundry for free. Thankfully, she'd had Hannah for that. Doc Lilly could take Hannah's wages out of Armina's own pay. A body didn't want to get beholden to the largesse of others. Soon as Armina was fully well, she'd find some way to give back to Tillie. Maybe shuck a chair seat for her. If it happened to be Turnip's chair, she'd weave a cocklebur in it. Armina tee-heed at the thought.

Mazy had draped the new red scarf on the corner of the mirror; just looking at it made Armina feel squeamish. Why couldn't she remember where she'd found the baby? Doc Lilly had told her about the little thing she called Glory and how no one had claimed her. Armina felt awful over it, but for the life of her, she couldn't make her ornery brain rewind. Doc said she shouldn't push herself. She said it would all come back when Armina was ready.

She finished her ablutions and twisted her hair into a knot. She found a clean cotton shift in the wardrobe and her shoes sitting beside the bed. When she finished dressing, she hurried to the kitchen. Maybe there was still time to prepare Doc's breakfast.

But no, there was Doc's teacup on the drain board. Good gravy, Armina would be glad when she was up to taking care of things again. She could hear Mazy stirring in her room. She'd scramble a couple of eggs to share.

She set the skillet on the stove before fetching some milk from the icebox. Humph, the drain pan was overflowing. Wasn't this Wednesday? She pulled the pan and emptied it in the sink. Usually she'd empty the icebox on Wednesday mornings and wipe everything down with baking soda, but there wasn't time just now. Turnip Tippen would be by any minute with more ice. She'd need to tell him not to leave any at her own house. No sense wasting it. By next delivery date Ned would be home and everything would be back to normal.

Normal—there was a good word. It sort of meant regular, like everybody else. Armina had never thought she'd be a regular person with a regular husband and a regular house. She'd grown up without a mother or a father, bouncing from one kin's house to another, never being wanted. One of the aunts worked her like a mule and another watched every bite she ate like Armina's hunger was her own hair shirt. And then Aunt Orie took her in and things got better.

When she and Ned married and moved to town, Armina

had been at a loss. She couldn't find enough work to keep herself busy; her new little house practically cleaned itself, and idle wasn't in her nature. She was that glad when she started running Doc's house as well as her own. Then her need for busy was like a basket overflowing, just the way she liked it. Plus she liked having her own money. She wasn't a handout sort of woman.

Good grief, speaking of . . . there was Turnip Tippen at the door. Why didn't he barrel on in like he generally did, dripping ice water all over the floor?

"Morning, Armina," he said, holding a big block of ice suspended from iron tongs. "Reckon you could get Kip to move?"

Kip was standing right outside the door, guarding something at his feet. "Looks like he's caught something," Armina said. "I hope it's already dead. Let me get the broom."

Turnip looked around the ice block. "He's got a shoe— just kick it outen the way."

Turnip's bossiness always made Armina's blood boil. Maybe he could get by with that at home, but—

Cold water dripped on Kip's head. He shook it off like he'd just had a bath. Armina saw his catch—it was Doc's new canvas shoe. She picked it up and backed out of Turnip's way. Kip wagged all over, whining and leaping up to rest his paws on Armina's knees. Kip never acted like this. Something was bad wrong.

Armina hurried to Doc Lilly's room and threw open the closet. Her shoes stood polished and waiting. All of them— including the new Red Cross ankle boots. She checked by the bed. There were her slippers peeking out from under the bedspread.

Kip barked and ran to the kitchen door. Maybe Doc was in the garden—that wouldn't be usual of a workday morning, but Armina prayed she was.

"Wait a second, Kipper. Let's see if Doc's satchel is gone." Armina's heart dropped. The table by the front door where Doc kept her kit was empty.

"There, got you all fixed up," Turnip said, closing the door to the icebox. "You all right, Armina? You look like you seen a ghost."

Mazy wandered into the kitchen. "What's wrong?"

"Turnip, you need to take us back to town," Armina said. "There's something bad going on."

"Wait," Mazy said. "I have to get my hat."

Armina was already out the door, shoe in hand. "We ain't waiting. Get a move on, Turnip."

Kip leaped down from the wagon before it was fully stopped in front of the clinic. Armina's sense of alarm didn't lessen when she saw the back door ajar. Doc was strict about not encouraging folks to think they could come in that way.

Hannah stuck her head out. "Where's Dr. Still?"

Another wagon pulled up and Mrs. Blair stepped down. "Has anyone seen Timmy?" she asked.

Kip barked and growled and pulled another shoe from the tall grass beside the sidewalk. It was a match to the one Armina held.

Turnip took it from the dog's mouth. "I'm going to fetch Sheriff Clay," he said.

The room reeled with expectation. Hannah had made coffee and now Armina sat with her strong cup of joe trying to force herself to remember what had happened the day she found the baby. Chanis sat in a chair across from her, his knees nearly touching hers. Everyone else he'd ordered out.

Armina wished she had Kip at her side for a bit of comfort, but he'd taken off like Snyder's hound as soon as she opened the kitchen door.

"It's real important, Miz Armina," the sheriff said. "I think whatever happened to you that day is connected to whatever has happened to Doc Still."

The coffee cup jiggled against the saucer. Armina's nerves were strung tight as catgut on a fiddle. The sheriff didn't help—he looked so starched and official, not at all like the boy who came calling on Mazy. Was he going to write her words down on that pad of paper in his hand? If he did, what would he do with them? She didn't want to wind up some harebrained headline in the paper.

"Wouldn't it be better if I was out looking for Doc? I can't come up with anything else."

The sheriff rubbed his jaw. "Don't be afraid, Miz Armina. I'm just trying to sort things out. Why don't you start at the beginning and say whatever comes to mind."

Armina screwed up her face and closed her eyes tight. It

didn't help—her mind was blank as a blackboard on the first day of school.

Chanis patted her arm. For some reason that light touch made her want to cry. "It's okay," he said. "Don't fret over it. You'll make yourself sick again, and Doc will have my hide."

His kindness washed over Armina. "Maybe—could I talk to Hannah? Like as if we was setting on the porch?"

He went and got Hannah, then put their two chairs side by side facing away from Doc Lilly's desk. "I'll sit here behind you, if that's all right, Miz Armina." He took the desk chair. "Don't pay me any mind."

"Prime the pump, Hannah," Armina said. "Ask me something."

"Remember what a pretty day it was? We had just a little rain that morning. I ran outside to get in the wash, but the rain stopped before I took the first peg off."

Armina rested her head against the chair back. Hannah's soothing voice continued, carrying her back to the misplaced day.

"I recall it well because that night is when you took ill. I remember I was knitting a blanket for my sister's baby. It was the prettiest soft blue."

Armina's hard brainpan split open like a black walnut, exposing the soft meat inside. "I woke up that morning thinking of blackberries." She cracked her neck from side to side, releasing the strain. "I put on one of Ned's work shirts and daubed kerosene around my ankles." Her ankle itched.

She scratched it with the toe of her shoe. "Chiggers are bad around blackberry bushes."

"They are that," Hannah said.

"My walking stick and my berry bucket were in the cupboard. I noticed I needed some flour if I was going to make a cobbler. The berries from up on Tattler's Branch make the best pies you ever tasted."

The sheriff drew in his breath, distracting as a mosquito's whine. But Hannah's soft "Umm-hum" pulled Armina back into the story.

"It had been a long while since I'd been up Tattler's Branch Road, but I went right to the footbridge and crossed to the other side. Those berries were fairly begging to be et."

Armina swallowed hard. "Seems like I must have fell in those bushes because next thing I remember, I was kindly hidden among the leaves and brambles watching a man and woman sort of wrestling down the bank toward the creek. I can't rightly say why this was so, but it seemed like everything was very still—you know, like right before a big storm and even the birds stop their chatter? The air fairly shimmered with forewarning." She rocked back and forth in the chair. Her head felt big as a balloon, like she might just rise up and bang against the ceiling. She clasped the chair arms tightly.

"Next thing I knowed, they was both in the water." She covered her face with her hands. "The man had yellow hair— long yellow hair tied back, and he had a rock—a good-size rock. He raised his hand and the woman went under. That's what I remember."

"Terrible, terrible," Hannah said.

The sheriff's chair scraped against the floor. "You did good, Miz Armina."

"I'm not finished," she said.

He crouched before her at eye level. "Go on. I'm listening."

"There was blood in the water and bloody tracks on the ground. I seen the man on a porch I reckon was at his house. He took a shovel and a pick and disappeared. I heard a pitiful mewling I knew for certain sure was a baby, so I crawled in the window and took the little thing. All whilst I was running back across the bridge over the creek, I could hear that pickax a-ringing on rock. I figured he was digging a grave." Armina gasped. "What if he's digging Doc's grave right now?"

The sheriff handed her his pad of paper and the stub of a pencil. "Can you draw me a map of where you went, Miz Armina? Tattler's Branch is just one mile short of being a river. Lots of folks live other side of it and most have bridges."

"I'll do better than that," Armina said. "I'll take you there."

"Turnip can drive us in the wagon," the sheriff said. "Miss Hannah, you come along."

Half the town was milling around in the road outside the clinic. Mrs. Blair rushed the sheriff when they stepped outside. "Is Timmy with Doc Lilly?" she asked, panic rising in her voice. "Do you think that's where he is? I know he gets into mischief sometimes, but he always comes straight home from the cream station. He hasn't even had breakfast yet."

"Now, Miz Blair, the boy's probably funning around with some of his friends," the sheriff said.

Armina didn't think Chanis meant what he said—he was just coddling the worried mother with words. His mouth was set in a grim line and his eyes had narrowed. The look on his face made her more scared than she already was. She felt like she had set something terrible in motion. But like Pandora and her box, it was too late now.

"You got to level with me," she said as he helped her up to the wagon seat. "It's bad, ain't it?"

Mazy pulled on his arm, distracting him. "I want to go too, Chanis."

"Now, Mazy, it would be best if you stay here."

Tears spilled down Mazy's cheeks. *Bless her heart,* Armina thought. Even scared half to death and with a straw bonnet hiding her curls, she was still pretty as a porcelain doll.

"But everyone else is coming," Mazy said, "and she's my sister."

Armina looked in the wagon behind her. It was full of folks.

"Ever'body out!" the sheriff bellowed. "This is not a hayride." Then he said again, "Now, Mazy. Someone needs to stay here in case Doc Still comes back. I'm just going to look around some. Miz Armina's going to show me something that might be important. Miss Hannah's going along in case Miz Armina takes ill. We'll be back shortly." With a look around at the crowd, he said, "If anybody saw anything the least bit interesting this morning, tell me now."

Mrs. Hill raised her hand. "I'm feeling extra poorly, so I need to see the doctor first. I have a serious disorder, you know. It started in the spring of 1899. It was April 1. I remember because my cousin's husband had a stroke that day . . . or was it my cousin who had the stroke?" she asked in her faltering way. "Well, it was April 1, 1899. I know that for a fact. I ain't been the same since." She pulled a long knit sweater tightly around her body though the day was already warm.

Armina wanted to jump down from the wagon and choke Emma Hill. The foolish old lady never stopped talking, and her talking always concerned some day long past—like her mind was a calendar always flipping backward. It was one thing to yak on when folks had the inclination to listen but, good gravy, not today.

"Come along, Emma," Mrs. Blair was kind enough to say, putting an arm around Mrs. Hill's chicken-wing shoulders. "I expect the sheriff has other things on his mind."

CHAPTER 25

THE ROOM WAS CLOSE and dank with trash and old clothes piled up in the corner. It looked to Lilly like the house had been abandoned years ago. As soon as she heard the man go outside, she tried the doorknob. It didn't turn, of course. The only window was boarded over from the outside, but she could see movement through a space in the two-by-fours. When she peeked out, she saw the man hauling Timmy across the backyard. Timmy twisted and kicked against his captor, screaming like a banshee.

The man opened the door to a dirt cellar carved out of a bank and shoved Timmy in. Timmy churned out before he could slam the door and took off like a shot through the tall weeds. The man grabbed his shirt collar and dragged him back to the hole in the ground. He pitched the boy in head-long and slammed the door, wedging it shut with a metal rod through the latch.

The breath caught in Lilly's throat. Timmy's arm was healing nicely, but it wouldn't stand up well to this rough treatment.

The man was out of her line of sight. What might he be doing? She assumed his goal was to get the baby, but really all he would have had to do was go to the law and claim his rights to her. Neither Lilly nor Anne could do anything to stop him. A sick feeling settled in Lilly's stomach. There had to be something more for him to have gone to such lengths.

She tried to recall how the man had seemed when she treated him last week. He was abrupt and dismissive, but she'd sensed no overt hostility. He'd been clean, except for the bloodstained shirt. She recalled the long braid of his hair and his brown felt hat. He had high cheekbones and a sharp, hawk-like nose. Like Timmy, she would have taken him for an Indian were it not for his fair complexion and blond hair. The only thing odd about him was the reason he'd come in—those wounds to his chest.

She saw the man go around the corner of the house. Everything grew quiet. She thought the man had left, but she suspected that wouldn't last long. In the meantime she might find a means of escape or perhaps a weapon of some sort. With a practiced eye she examined the room. There was a dressing table much like hers, except it had no bench and dust obscured the mirror. A chair bursting springs and horsehair was flanked by a table and a coal-oil lamp. Coal-oil lamps had heavy bases—perfect for conking someone over the head. She pictured herself standing by the door with the lamp raised high.

Getting closer, she noticed something out of place, something coiled around the lamp. She pulled a snakeskin loose and held it up. At least six feet long, it streamed from her hand. The tail end puddled on the floor like a length of ribbon. A blacksnake, she would bet. She hoped it was long gone, but she'd be extra careful when she went through the heap of clothes. Neither she nor the snake had an easy way out.

Lilly took grateful advantage of the necessary pot behind the door—at least she didn't have to worry about her bladder if the snake slithered out and scared her. Then, gingerly, she searched through the clothing, discarding shirt after shirt, dress after dress, finding nothing more interesting than two pairs of moldy shoes. She would sit in the chair and try them on, except the snake might be hiding under the cushion. She'd heard it said that they were more afraid of you than you were of them, but she wouldn't take that chance. Instead she sat on the shelf of the dressing table and examined her feet. They were a mess of abrasions and surface cuts. She hoped Timmy's had fared better; since the boy didn't wear shoes during the summer, she suspected he had a nice protective buildup of calluses.

The first pair of shoes was much too large, but the second

ones would do in a pinch. And Lilly was decidedly in a pinch. She would rather have blisters from ill-fitting shoes than a stubbed toe or a serious cut. After wiping mold from the shoes with a musty shirt from the pile on the floor, she put them on. They'd be okay if she could do up the buttons.

Buttons! Buttonhooks—an unexpected weapon. Frantically aware of the passing of time, she dumped the dressing table drawers out onto the floor. There was no buttonhook but there was a knitting needle. She swallowed hard and slipped it into her pocket, where its presence burned like carbide, like the planning of a sin. What did she think she would do with the needle? Poke his eyes out? Stab him?

One hour turned into two as she waited, afraid to turn her back on the door. Finally she heard his heavy footsteps in the hall and saw the doorknob turn. Now was the time to put faith in action—time to do all things through Christ. She flung the tool away.

"Come along," he said, waving the gun.

"I'm not leaving Timmy here alone," she said.

"Oh yeah, well, what if I shoot you now? Who'll find you or the boy?"

"You are not a cruel man. I don't believe you'd leave the boy in that place to die."

He scraped the barrel of the gun against the stubble of his beard. "Ma'am, you took my child. Alls I want is to get her back."

"And I am willing to help you, but not at the risk of hurting Timmy."

"That boy's brought this misery on himself. He wouldn't stay out of my business."

She raised her hands in supplication. "Sir, he's just a boy."

He whirled and kicked the door so hard it bounced against the frame. She flinched and nearly screamed. His eyes were wild when he looked at her. "Just do as I say and nobody has to get hurt."

"Bring Timmy in here, and I'll go with you." She let her face go soft. It wasn't a stretch to let a few tears flow. She could have cried a river.

He turned on his heel and shut the door. The key clicked in the lock.

Lilly flew to the window and watched him jerk the cellar door open. A subdued Timmy came out and followed the man inside.

"Timmy, you'll be okay here until we come back. Okay?" She held the snakeskin up. "Look what I found."

"Boy, that's a beaut."

"Just think what the boys will say when you show it to them. They're going to be so envious that you've had such an adventure."

"Yeah," he said, wrapping the skin around his wrist. "I can't wait to show them. Maybe I'll find the snake, too."

The man had procured a horse and a two-door carriage, with an ample front bench and a small backseat. Lilly wondered what family was missing theirs.

They'd have to go around the mountain in order to get to the Beckers' house in the buggy. The horse couldn't haul it up the ridge on this road. She was thankful. They were sure to see someone who knew she was missing.

But half an hour later, they rolled into the Beckers' front yard. "I know they have my daughter," he said, his voice as cold as a January morning. "You go get her. Try anything funny and I won't have any qualms about what happens next."

Lilly stepped down from the carriage. She knew she looked a mess. Anne would know something was amiss the moment she saw her. She squared her shoulders, walked up the porch steps with her unfastened shoes flopping, and knocked on the door.

After a moment, Cletus answered. Amy was in his arms. The little girl squealed with excitement when she saw Lilly. She pointed one tiny finger toward the room behind her. "Baba dere," she said. "Baba night-night."

"Is Anne here?" Lilly asked as the Beckers' rawboned hound dog sniffed around her ankles.

"Nah."

Lilly's heart plunged. "Will she be back soon, Cletus? It's important that I talk to her."

"Just left out," he mumbled with his chin tucked into his neck. "Gone to town."

"Skip Rock?"

"Nah, Perry."

Lilly's heart sank. Anne could be gone for hours. She could feel the threat of the weapon pointed at her back. She knew the man could hear every word. "I need to take Glory for some medical tests. Could you get her for me?"

He put Amy down and went back inside. Amy tugged on Lilly's skirt and raised her arms. Lilly swung her up. She buried her nose in the girl's sweet-smelling neck. Tears threatened to overtake her. *Please, Lord,* she silently prayed, *let Cletus notice that something is wrong.*

He was gone for several minutes. Lilly had to steel herself from looking over her shoulder at the buggy. Maybe Cletus was loading his gun, or maybe he'd fled out the back door to run for help. Oh, but the Beckers didn't have a back door.

Amy sucked her fingers and laid her head on Lilly's shoulder. Lilly fought to distract her racing heart. "Does Sassy like her new home?" she asked.

Amy rewarded her with a big, toothy smile. "Oink-oink dere," she said, looking across the yard.

"Yes," Lilly said, bouncing the girl in her arms. "Sassy's in the barn."

"Err-err-err in a barn," Amy chortled.

"Yes, rooster's in the barn too. You're such a smart girl."

"Horsey?"

"Yes, that's a horsey."

Amy pointed at the buggy. "Who dere?"

Lilly turned slightly away from the man's line of vision and whispered, "A very bad man is in the buggy. Bad, bad man."

"Baaa," Amy bleated like a sheep.

Lilly's heart skipped when she heard the buggy door click open and closed. He was giving her a warning. What was taking Cletus so long?

Finally Cletus returned with Glory in her Moses basket. Lilly set Amy down and took the baby. "Thank you, Cletus. Tell Anne I'm sorry to have missed her."

Amy started crying. "Baba here," she sobbed and stomped her little foot. "Baba here."

Cletus swept Amy up and turned his back. Lilly heard the door shut behind her as she stumbled down the steps.

CHAPTER 26

THE WAGON BUMPED and squeaked all the way up Tattler's Branch Road. Armina held herself ramrod straight on her portion of the seat between Turnip Tippen, who was all slouched down relaxed-like, and Sheriff Clay, who was tense as a racehorse at the gate. She clutched the canvas shoes tightly in her lap. Doc Lilly was sure to need them.

Hannah was in the bed of the wagon. Armina hoped she wasn't getting too jostled back there. It had been unnecessary for the sheriff to bring the nurse along; Armina had no intention of falling ill again. Once the awful memories had fully surfaced, her brain clicked along on all its gears. She was kindly glad Hannah was there, though; she was starting to feel like a friend.

Armina watched closely for the narrow bridge as the wagon rolled along. Things looked different from up here. "Stop," she said when she spotted the stately tulip poplar under which she'd waited out the rain that day. "Let me down. I remember that there tree."

Turnip jumped down from the bench and forged ahead like he was chief of the Indians. Sheriff Clay stood back for a moment, taking in the scene. Hannah stayed beside Armina, pinching her elbow lightly as they walked toward the tree.

"This is where I stopped for a break that day," Armina said. "Ye can hear the creek."

Turnip slapped the long, straight tree with the flat of his hand, startling a flock of red-winged blackbirds. The birds burst from the top of the tree, dislodging hundreds of tulip poplar seeds, which pinwheeled through the air. "This here trunk would make a fine canoe," Turnip said while brushing the debris from his hair.

"Weren't nobody talking about canoes, Turnip," Armina said, wishing she could push him off in one. Maybe he'd float all the way to the Mississippi.

The sheriff coughed behind his fist. Armina saw a little smile play around his lips. He must be as weary of Turnip Tippen as she was. The man had not stopped talking all the way from Skip Rock, yet he hadn't said one important word.

"Stand back if you don't mind, Turnip," the sheriff said. "Let's give Miz Armina a little space."

Hannah took the shoes from her. "I'll keep these safe,

Armina." She followed Turnip back to the wagon. The seeds popped like corn under their feet.

Armina stood under the tree with the sheriff. It was definitely the right one. "The bridge is over yonder," she said.

"You all come along—" he motioned to Turnip and Hannah—"but hang back a ways."

She appreciated the young man's effort. It must be hard for him to match his pace with hers. He surely wanted to hurry things up. For her own self she wanted to find Doc . . . and she didn't. She was mortally concerned about what the outcome might be. A body wasn't jerked out of their own shoes without being forced. She didn't think she could bear it if Doc had been hurt. Especially since Armina had started this whole thing.

Behind them, the red-winged blackbirds swarmed the poplar again, screeching and chattering their claim.

Armina stopped just shy of the bridge to get her bearings. "This is the bridge I crossed with my berry bucket. See the gate there among the brambles?"

They trooped across the bridge one at a time. Armina made certain she didn't look down. There might be a pile of bones under there.

When they approached the gate, the sheriff drew his pistol. Turnip carried a shotgun. The sheriff motioned for Armina and Hannah to stay back. Hannah clasped Armina's hand tight enough to cut off her circulation. As soon as the men disappeared among the trees, Armina pulled her forward. They huddled behind the very same tree where Armina had hidden that awful day.

The house looked as tidy as when Armina had seen it last. She didn't see a thing out of place. The flower garden wasn't so pretty, though. The red and orange zinnias drooped, and the yellow marigolds needed a good pruning.

Sheriff Clay sent Turnip around to the back of the house while he went up the porch steps and pounded on the front door. "Sheriff!" he yelled. "Open up!"

When no one answered, he raised his booted foot and kicked the door in. With gun raised, he went inside.

Hannah stood so close behind Armina that she could feel the woman's sharp intake of breath and hear her whispered prayer: "Oh, Lord, please let Dr. Still be okay."

Armina was so thankful for the words that she reached up and patted the hand that Hannah had clamped to her shoulder like a vise.

In moments that seemed like hours, the sheriff came out shaking his head. He called for Turnip, and they stood on the porch together like comrades in arms. Armina and Hannah walked up to the yard.

"Can you be certain this is the right house, Miz Armina?" the sheriff said, his face a study in disappointment.

"I'm certain sure. I even remember the flowers." A shovel sporting a rusty blade had fallen over in the garden and a pickax leaned against the rail. Armina toed the blade of the shovel. "Looks like the tools he carried off that day."

"Show me where you went inside," the sheriff said, following her to the window at the side of the house.

"It was raised that day. I crawled right over the sill."

"Let's go inside. I want to see where the baby was when you found her."

The sheriff poked around in every corner. The house was neat as a pin. There wasn't a cobweb or a dust bunny anywhere that Armina could see. The only thing out of place was a ragged-edged square of paper poking out from behind the kitchen stove.

Sheriff Clay bent to pick it up. He showed the page to her. "Do these pictures look anything like the baby you found?"

"Somewhat," she said, squinting to take it in. "She was an odd-looking little thing."

He examined the page as if it were a bug and he had a microscope. "Hmm. This look like blood to you?"

She looked at a smear on the paper. "Dried up, you mean?"

"Yeah."

"It does."

"Oh, man," he said.

Chanis was reaching for the doorknob when Armina spied something else out of place. On the wall beside the door, a red lard bucket and a sycamore walking stick hung from a peg. She took the stick down and examined it as Chanis watched.

"I can't vouch for the bucket," she said, "but this is my stick. This proves my story."

"It sure does," Chanis said.

Armina took her stick outside while the men searched around the cabin and up to Tattler's Branch. Neither she nor

Hannah felt like talking. They could hear Turnip and the sheriff thrashing around in various places.

Soon Turnip returned for the shovel. His face was white as a sheet. "It don't look good" was all he said before he left again.

"You see any reason we shouldn't make coffee?" Hannah asked.

Armina remembered the grating sounds she'd heard the day she took the baby. "No reason at all," she said, certain as she was that Doc Lilly was not in this place. "It'll give us something to do while we wait."

Armina measured the grounds she'd found on a shelf while Hannah went to the well to fetch water. This kitchen was a puzzle, what with its cheery red-checked curtains at the window and the pink-and-green china so carefully stacked in the cupboard. It was hard to imagine how people who lived in such a welcoming place could wind up wrestling in the creek—much less how one could smack the other upside the head with a rock. Especially if the one that got smacked happened to be the mother of a baby. What would make a woman cleave to a man like that?

She took the lid from the coffeepot and peered inside. It was clean as a whistle. Armina's own sister had a husband mean as a chained dog, always nipping at her with his condescending words. But her sister had hightailed it home the first time he'd shown her the back of his hand. Maybe the baby's mother didn't have anywhere else to go. Or maybe putting up with a man like that felt natural to her—some women didn't have much gumption.

"Looks like a storm's brewing," Hannah said, setting the water bucket on the sink. "That's all we need."

Armina stuck another chunk of wood into the cookstove before putting the coffeepot on the heating burner. "If it ain't one thing, it's another."

The men were glad for the coffee when they came in, their faces set in grim lines.

"We found the grave," Sheriff Clay said. "I figure it to be the mother of the baby you found that's lying there."

"Was her head . . . ?"

"Yeah, just like you said."

Armina bustled around, tamping down the stove, rinsing out the pot, dashing the water Sheriff Clay and Turnip had washed their hands in, while the sheriff jotted things down in his notebook. She couldn't say why it was important, but she didn't want to leave the house in disarray.

Thunder rolled across the mountains and swept up the holler.

"Let's head out," Sheriff Clay said.

"Are we going to leave her like that?" Hannah asked as tears spilled from her eyes.

"We covered her back up," the sheriff said. "That's the best we could do for now."

Armina figured she should keep watch on Hannah. She climbed up into the wagon's bed and settled down beside the distraught woman.

Turnip unfolded a tarp and draped it over them, tucking

the tail underneath their feet. "Sit tight, ladies, and you won't get wet."

Armina found herself appreciating his efforts. Good gravy, was she going to have to change all her opinions?

"Maybe Dr. Still will be waiting when we get back," Hannah said, dabbing at her tears.

Rain tap-danced over their heads as they rode tight as ticks in their temporary tent. "Let's call on the Lord," Armina said as the storm broke.

CHAPTER 27

SHADE HARMON KEPT his eyes on the lady's back. Dr. Still—
what an appropriate name. Even after that steep climb this
morning and then being locked up in that room, she kept her
composure. And then she'd unrolled that snake shed for the
boy like it was no more than a strip of crepe paper, like they
were going to have a birthday party. Still Waters—that'd be
the perfect moniker for her.

He'd need to keep on his toes while around her; that was
sure. He could see she was always thinking of ways to outwit
him. Saying she wouldn't come with him unless he brought
the boy inside—and him holding the gun. Little Miss High-
and-Mighty was about to find out who was in charge of this
roll of the dice.

He pulled at the handkerchief he'd wrapped around the cut on his hand. It was healing well—no fresh blood—but the hankie was stuck like glue. He'd have to soak it off.

Man, he had his share of troubles. And that kid, he'd sure put a crimp in his plans, nosy brat, always sneaking around, spying. Shade's luck had held, though, as it usually did. The boy had become the perfect tool for keeping the doctor in place.

He pushed his hat up a ways with the barrel of the gun. What was taking so long? He watched her swing a little girl back and forth in her arms as she waited on the porch. Talk about your phenomenal luck. Meeting up with Grunt and the boys last night for one last game had been the flukiest thing yet. Hoppy had goaded Grunt about playing with coins instead of bills. Grunt just shook his hangdog head, managing to stutter a few words about a new baby in his house, a foundling his wife had taken in. A lightbulb had gone off then, nearly blinding Shade with knowledge. It all made a perfect, if illogical, sense.

He'd thought of following Grunt home and taking the baby by force, but he didn't want it to go down that way. A gambler's best bet was to stick to the plan—never let them see your hand.

The little girl laughed. Soon, Shade would hold his own baby girl in his arms. He pictured them years from now, Betsy Lane laughing with delight over some little something. Maybe he could find some of those Mother Goose books to read to her. Little Miss Muffet and all that.

Finally the doctor was coming down the steps and heading to the buggy. Shade leaned across the seat and opened the door from the inside. The doctor stepped up awkwardly, then slid inside with Betsy Lane in her basket cradle. He flicked the reins and the buggy rolled out of the yard.

On their way to the Beckers', the doctor had shown a keen interest in the house with the *Quarantine* sign. She was more than likely hoping someone there would notice her through the buggy window. Now as they approached the house again, he ordered her to duck down in the seat.

She gave him a look and stayed as she was. "They're all inside," she said.

He admired her poker face. She was a cool customer. The gun rested with authority in his lap. The horse's hooves clip-clopped along the dirt road. They could have been any family out for a ride.

A family? Why hadn't he seen the possibility before? Nobody would question a family traveling with a baby. He wasn't exactly changing the plan; he was just adding to it, taking advantage of the situation, as it were.

After a few minutes, Shade pulled the horse over into a grove of trees. He wanted to see his daughter.

"Give her to me," he said.

The doctor put the basket on the buggy floor. "Hello, sweetheart," she said as she lifted the baby from her nest of blankets. "Oh, you're fresh as a daisy." She passed the bundle to him, saying, "Support her head."

"I know," he said. "I'm her father, aren't I?"

His hands trembled as he undid the soft flannel wrap. It was her—his baby girl. She yawned and stretched with her whole body, then opened her eyes wide and looked straight at him with her blue all-knowing gaze. She didn't cry or startle. His daughter hadn't forgotten him. The world stood still. Every bit of everything he'd ever gone through was worth this moment.

He traced her cheeks and she turned her face toward his hand. He laughed. "She looks good. Her face is fuller, and her hands—look how plump."

"The Beckers take good care of her."

"Well, I'll be taking care of her from here on out." He lifted the baby to his shoulder and patted her back. "Her name's Betsy Lane," he said.

"That's quite lovely. Is it a family name?"

"Of a sort," he said, laying the baby on his lap so that he could see her face again. He couldn't get enough of her almond eyes and her loopy smile. She began to whimper.

"Cletus put a bottle of milk in the basket. Do you want to feed her?"

"Do I need your permission?" he snapped, the gun resting under the baby giving bravado to his words.

"Of course not," the doctor said with a shrug.

Betsy Lane squirmed and mouthed one tiny fist. "It's not like I've never fed her before," Shade said.

He tipped the bottle. Betsy took the nipple and sucked. There—he knew what he was doing. Then milk flooded from her nose and she turned a frightening bluish color. Without a thought, he handed her over.

The doctor mopped milk with the corner of Betsy's blanket. When Betsy recovered, the doctor handed her back. "Try holding her in a semireclining position while she feeds. See if that helps."

It made the feeding easier, and she didn't strain to suck as she did with the nipples he'd bought at the store. "She likes this better—seems like she doesn't have to work so hard to get milk."

"We enlarged the hole in the tip. The milk flows better that way. You might want to let her rest a bit every few sucks. She tires easily."

"Why is that?" he asked without thinking.

"May I speak frankly?"

A cloud descended. He wasn't interested in her esteemed opinion. He'd had his fill of opinions. "Why should I care what you think? If you were any kind of an expert, you wouldn't be practicing in this backwater town."

"Fair enough," she said.

A ring of bluish-gray circled Betsy's mouth. Her tiny nostrils flared with effort. A sense of urgency flooded Shade. There wasn't much time. The sooner he got Betsy to a big city hospital, the sooner she would get well. He handed the baby over again.

The doctor finished the feeding as Shade drove the buggy back to the boarded-up house. He watched as best he could and noticed that the doctor pulled the nipple frequently, giving Betsy plenty of time. He could do that.

He guided the horse around back of the house. He'd leave the rig at a hitching post once they got to the depot. Someone from the livery would pick it up in the a.m. He liked how that worked. Bunch of hicks—didn't even question his made-up identity. Like every other business, all they wanted was his money.

"What the—!" He jerked the reins.

The doctor inhaled sharply. "Timmy," she said.

The boy was sitting on the porch in front of the open door. A small white dog huddled under his arm. The doctor settled the baby in the basket before pushing her door open and jumping down from the buggy. Shade was left to tote the basket across the yard like some kind of hired help.

The sky darkened. The wind picked up and with it came a hard, slanting rain. He hurried them all inside and slammed the door behind him. After carefully depositing the basket on a table, he turned on the boy, raising his hand.

The doctor stepped between them. "Don't you dare."

"Get him away from me, or so help me—"

She turned on her heel, giving him her back. The dog and the boy followed her. The room looked the same, with the window still boarded, and he knew he'd locked the door. The door key he'd found on the mantel when he first broke in was still in his pocket. He would've sworn it was secure as could be, but the boy had made a fool of him.

"How'd you get out?" He grabbed the boy's arm and gave

him a shake. Timmy puckered his mouth to spit. Shade popped him lightly on the lips. "You want me to kick that dog across the room, smart aleck? Turn your pockets out."

Timmy turned his pockets inside out. A knitting needle clattered to the floor. He'd picked the lock.

Shade pitched it out of the room. "You're quick. I'll give you that. But if you've got a lick of sense, you won't try that again."

He didn't bother slamming the door, just pulled it to and turned the key. Man, he was tired of those two. Back in the kitchen, he searched through his rucksack for the boiled eggs and hard cheese and soda crackers he'd brought to tide him over on the train trip.

Thunder shook the windows. He'd better dash out for some water before the rain got worse. He pulled on the rain slicker from his pack and grabbed a chipped granite bucket. In a minute he was back with the water bucket and the mason jar. The temperature had dropped considerably with the rain, but it was July. Nobody was going to freeze. And it wouldn't hurt the fancy doctor and the boy to suffer some discomfort after all they'd put him through.

He pulled out a chair and ate an egg and a few soda crackers. He wished he had a cup of hot coffee. Maybe when they got to the depot. He looked at his watch. He'd gotten a lot done already; there was plenty of time for him to take a rest. The train didn't pull out of the station until nine. It would take them an hour, maybe two, to get there, depending on the road conditions. He didn't want to be there early.

With his foot, Shade scooted another chair around to face him. He propped his feet up and slid his hat down over his eyes. Things were going pretty much as he'd planned. The boy was a pop-up, but he could be managed. Instead of a sleeper car, they'd sit together in facing seats. He could see how they'd look like a family to the other passengers.

Rain pounded on the tin roof. Otherwise the house was quiet. He closed his heavy-lidded eyes.

He startled awake and looked at his watch. He'd slept an hour. How was that possible? The baby was crying—sitting right on the table where he'd left her. He looked in the basket. Her bottle was still half-full. There were several clean nappies in the space at her feet.

It took forty-five minutes for Betsy Lane to take another third of the bottle. He changed her diaper, being ever so careful not to jostle her so the milk wouldn't come back up. She was asleep before he finished. He picked the basket up and carried it to the bedroom door. After unlocking the door, he carried the basket in and set it down at the lady's feet.

"Could you bring some water and a basin?" the doctor asked. "The dog needs tending."

She had made a pallet of sorts in the corner and the boy slept curled around her like a kitten. The dog was in her lap, its fur bloodied, he now saw.

He would put the dog outside, but it might start a ruckus. Dogs were like boys, nothing if not trouble. Leaving the door ajar, he went back to the kitchen and got the water bucket.

He didn't see a basin, so he took her the mason jar. She'd have to make do.

When he took in the water, the boy sat up and stretched. Shade could hear his belly growl. They were way more trouble to him than they were worth, but he took the eggs, the cheese, and the crackers to them. Nobody even said thanks. How ungrateful could you be? Now he'd have to put out money for food on the train.

"Eat up," he said. "We'll be heading out soon."

Back in the kitchen, he sat drumming his fingers on the tabletop. The rain on the roof mimicked him. Somewhere down the ridge, lightning popped and a tree crashed to the ground. He wished the storm would let up. The road would be a mire of mud. He should figure in extra traveling time for that.

The waiting was making him edgy. The sheriff had probably formed a posse by now. They'd be scouring the hollers for the doctor and the boy. He looked out the window. The gloomy lingering clouds made it seem dark as night already.

Shade's plan took on a sense of urgency. It would have been better to take an earlier train. Too late now; he'd have to play the hand he'd been dealt. Flipping open the blade of his pocketknife, he sliced the oilcloth table cover into two pieces. Now he was ready.

CHAPTER 28

Armina's hopes were dashed when she saw the size of the crowd gathered outside the clinic. They wouldn't be standing there in the rain if Doc Lilly had come back.

Sheriff Clay hustled her and Hannah in through the office door. A deputy was waiting. He looked even younger than the sheriff.

"You find anything?" he asked.

The sheriff filled him in. The deputy shook his head when he heard about the grave. "This changes everything," he said. "We've got a killer on the loose."

"Yep," the sheriff said. "I reckon I should let the folks know so they can lock up tight tonight."

"A killer?" Mazy said, coming into the room. A well-thumbed telephone book drooped from her hand and a yellow pencil stuck out from over her ear. "What do you mean, a killer?"

The sheriff led her to a chair as if she might keel over at any moment. "Listen, Mazy, you have to be strong. I'm going back out right now. I'll find her. I promise."

"Who would hurt Lilly? I can't even believe this."

"And Timmy," the deputy said. "Timmy Blair's missing also."

"But she's been gone too long," Mazy said. "And it's storming. I thought you were going to get her and bring her home."

"She wasn't there, Mazy," the sheriff said. "I think that's a good thing."

Mazy stood and stomped her foot. "You go find her, then. You go get her and bring her home before Mama gets here."

"Your mother's coming?"

"Everybody's coming. I called the post office in Troublesome Creek and the postmaster said he'd send someone to fetch Mama and Daddy. She's already called me back."

Mazy lifted her chin. Armina was proud of her. She hadn't just sat back wringing her hands, waiting to see what someone else would do.

"I've also notified the United States Bureau of Mines," Mazy said. "They're going to find Tern and hasten his homecoming. The telephone's really powerful if you know how to use it."

A man rapped on the door glass. Sheriff Clay let him inside.

"Chanis," Stanley James said, "I got a call from Washington, D.C. I hear the doc is in trouble. My men and I are here to help."

Stanley was the foreman over all the mine workers in Skip Rock. That was a powerful lot of men. Armina hoped Sheriff Clay didn't get all territorial.

"I can use all the help I can get, Stanley," the sheriff said, shaking the older man's hand. "Let me fill you in."

After the men left, Armina watched out the window with Mazy and Hannah. Soon horses were brought in and the men were divided up into groups. "Search crews," she said. "They'll soon find Doc and Timmy."

The deputy came back inside. Rain dripped from the brim of his hat and splattered on the floor. "I'm to escort you ladies home."

A terrible ringing sound made them jump—even the deputy did a little leap into the air.

Mazy hurried into the front room. The ringing stopped and they could hear her shouting, "Hello!" She came back with the telephone cord stretched as far as it would go. "Armina, it's for you."

"It can't be for me," Armina said. "I don't even know how to use that thing."

"It is for you," Mazy insisted. "It's your husband. Now come here before we get disconnected. It's a long way to Boston."

Armina hollered hello like she had heard Mazy do. Mazy adjusted the contraption until Armina was speaking in one place and listening in another. "Ned," she yelled, "you need to come on home now."

"Hey, Armina," she heard him say. She nearly dropped the shiny black telephone it startled her so. "I'll be starting home in the morning. I passed all my boards! Can you believe it?"

"That's good, Ned. You need to come on home."

"Are you okay? Is everyone okay there?"

A blinding flash of lightning stilled Ned's voice. Armina felt a tingle shoot up her arm and down her back. The lights in the office winked and then went off.

Armina let loose of the gadget and patted her head to make sure it was still on straight. They all huddled together in the middle of the room until the deputy said it was safe for them to make a run for home.

The rain lightened until they were in sight of Doc Lilly's house. Then the clouds let loose with a real frog strangler and the wind whipped their big black umbrella topsy-turvy until the spokes stuck out like the bones of a turkey carcass.

Armina put another pot of coffee on the stove. What else was there to do? Mazy kept wandering back to Doc's room like she might have overlooked her before. Hannah peeled potatoes. Other women began to show up: Tillie, Mrs. Blair, poor old Emma Hill, and even the newly widowed Mrs. Clover. Word sure traveled fast in the coal camp.

Tillie brought four frying chickens already cut up for the skillet, Mrs. Blair had half a bushel of green beans, Mrs. Clover had the makings for a four-layer chocolate cake, and poor Emma brought a peck of words.

Armina wished they had stayed away, but this was not her

house, and you couldn't turn folks away in times like this. Plus, the company provided a good distraction for Mazy.

Mrs. Blair said she took comfort that Timmy was with Doc Lilly. Mrs. Clover simply said she needed to be here. Tillie led them in a prayer, and Hannah read the Twenty-third Psalm. Only Emma nattered on until Hannah gave her a pen and paper and asked her to write a list of what they might need to feed Doc's family when they arrived. Everybody petted on Mazy, who was so anxious and scared.

Armina studied the situation. Her mind kept spinning back to the baby—thinking and thinking on where that man would take Doc Lilly. Timmy, she figured, had just got tangled up in the mess somehow. He was a boy searching for trouble, after all.

Despite the rain, she had to get away from the hubbub in the kitchen; all that peeling and stirring and cooking and sharing was making her edgy. She'd put Kip on a leash and take him for a walk. Doc was funny about him being off leash when it was storming.

Doc Lilly's canvas shoes were by the crock in the foyer where Armina had put them when they came in. Armina retrieved her walking stick and fished in the crock until she found Kip's leash. She gave a low whistle. The dog didn't come. And then she remembered seeing his little tail bouncing down the alley across from the clinic. He'd been going to find Doc Lilly. Armina was sure of it.

She stopped in her own house long enough to get a jacket and some mud boots and then hastened down the road to the clinic. She stood where Kip had found the second shoe and looked across the road to where she had seen him running.

The area behind the stores looked forlorn in the rain and the muck, with trash scattered about and discarded papers clinging wetly to the scrub behind the buildings. There was no reason for Doc to have been in this place. But Kip had told her differently. Using her sycamore walking stick, she poked around and struck pay dirt. A bit of colored cloth hung from the branch of a thorny black locust. The ground just beyond the tree looked trampled, and a little ways farther up, a rusty blackhaw sported a broken limb.

Behind her, she could hear horses nickering and men shouting. That would be the search party returning, she was sure. She scrambled back up the slope, using her walking stick for ballast. Maybe they'd found Doc.

The men were gathered in front of the commissary's long porch. Every single face looked long and dejected. Nobody paid her any never mind when she joined in the midst of them. Why did it always take a woman to get things done?

"I need to speak to the sheriff," she said, but the men just talked right over her. She pounded the porch floor with her walking stick. That caught their attention. "I need to talk to the sheriff!"

Sheriff Clay tipped his hat. "Miz Armina."

"You'd best come see what I've found," she said.

Like a pack of hunting dogs, the men all followed her around the building. With her stick she pointed to the piece of fabric impaled on the thorny locust. "There's mashed-down weeds and broken branches down thataway. And I seen Doc's dog heading this way this morning. Kip was tracking her."

"The Beckers' place is on the other side of this mountain," the sheriff said.

"Anne and Cletus," Turnip interjected.

"And the baby I told you about," Sheriff Clay said.

The rain that had held off for a while commenced pounding down. Lightning cracked and a tree crashed somewhere up the mountain.

"Miz Armina, all right if Turnip escorts you home? You don't need to be out in this."

Why was it always Turnip? The Lord was trying to tell her something, but she wasn't about to let her pride slow the sheriff down. "You bring her and Kip and Timmy home this time, Sheriff. Else I'll whack you good with this here staff."

The men got a laugh out of that. They didn't know she was serious as a snake with both eyes open. She was of a mind to thrash the whole lot of them. And one thing was for sure: if Doc Lilly wasn't brought home tonight, Armina was climbing the mountain herself come first light.

CHAPTER 29

USING THE MASON JAR, Lilly dipped water from the bucket and poured it over the soft rag she'd salvaged from a flannel shirt. Kip's ear was torn and he had a gash on his side. He didn't even whimper when she cleansed his wounds.

"Tear another piece of that shirt, please, Timmy. I need to bind his ear."

Timmy ripped a long strip of the material. Lilly bound Kip's ear to his head. If Kip had been his usual feisty self, the bandage wouldn't last a minute, but he lay still in her lap.

"Something got ahold of him," Timmy said, stroking Kip's head. "You're a scrapper, Kip. Just like me."

Lilly slipped her arm around the boy and pulled him close. "Two peas in a pod."

"How long's that man gonna keep us here?"

"He means to take us somewhere else soon." She'd seen a train schedule in his pocket. "We'll be going on a train."

Timmy's eyes grew round. "I've never been on a train."

"Shh," Lilly said. "We don't want him to know we know."

Timmy locked his lips and threw away the key. "What about Kip? I ain't going nowhere without Kip."

"Don't make a fuss if the man says to leave him, Timmy. Kip's a smart boy. He'll make his way home if he has to. He found us, didn't he?"

Timmy peeled another egg and fed Kip part of the yellow. He gulped down the rest. "I was sure glad to see this buddy when I busted out of here. He was scratching on the door like a cat with fleas. Weren't you, Kip boy?"

"Why didn't you leave then, Timmy?"

"I ain't about to leave you behind, Doc. What would you do without me?"

They could hear the man coming. Lilly stood and picked up the Moses basket. Timmy held Kip. They were ready for whatever came their way.

The man draped the basket with a piece of oilcloth and handed her another. Lilly put it over her head like a scarf. He'd pulled the buggy right up to the back porch, with the buggy's door standing open. Timmy climbed in first with Kip. The man ignored the dog. The baby's cradle went in the backseat beside Timmy.

Lilly prayed to get to the train station without incident. There would be lots of people at the depot. Unless the man wanted to shoot them in cold blood, there would be opportunity for escape. She intended to play along.

"Timmy," she said once the buggy was rolling, "take the cover from Betsy Lane."

"Is that the baby's name? That's kinda nice."

"Mind your own beeswax," the man said.

Lilly bit her lip. Stupid man would have let the baby suffocate under the thick oilcloth if left on his own. She chanced a quick glance back at Timmy. He gave a tiny nod of understanding. They were still in cahoots.

The weather conspired against them. The light carriage was no match for the mud. Soon they were stuck. The man got out and packed rocks around the offending wheel.

"We ain't ever getting to the train station this way," Timmy said.

"Shh," Lilly reminded him.

With an oath the man got back in the buggy and flicked the reins. Lilly slipped off her offending shoes and changed positions on the seat. Her feet felt bruised and tender, and the stitch in her side had turned into a dull, constant ache.

After a few miles, the rain and the distant rolling thunder lulled Lilly nearly to sleep. She could hear Timmy's snores and the baby occasionally making smacking noises; she'd want to be fed again soon. Lilly wondered if there was any milk left. It had surprised her when she'd found the bottle and clean diapers packed in with the baby, even though Anne had told her how good Cletus was with little Amy. Around every turn in the road, she expected to see Chanis or Turnip or someone coming to save them, but the road stretched out like a never-ending river of darkness. The horse trotted along as if he'd done this a million times, but when he should have gone straight, he suddenly turned left.

"What the—" the man yelled. The horse took off like there was a bucket of oats and a dry barn waiting. The buggy careened up a narrow trail. Cursing, the man pulled on the reins. "Whoa! Whoa!"

Lilly braced for impact as the horse stopped short. The buggy lashed side to side before it slid from the trail and smashed sideways into a tree. The man smacked against the front of the buggy with a thump and a sound like dry sticks cracking—or ribs. The momentum slammed him back against the seat and left his body in a slump.

Lilly pushed on the door. It was wedged against the tree and gave only an inch or two. She'd have to climb over the man and go out the other way. This was their chance to escape.

"Doc," Timmy whispered, "are we ever gonna get there?"

"Oh, Timmy, is everyone okay back there?"

"I'm all right and Kip's all right; we're good bouncers. But the basket turned over. The baby's under my feet."

"Pick her up and hold her until I get out."

The man sucked in air. "I'm all in," he said.

Disappointment flooded Lilly. Forevermore, would this day never end? She could have cried. She wished she'd kept the knitting needle. "Open the door and let me out! I need to check the baby."

He fumbled around on the floorboard and retrieved the

gun before he opened the door and slowly slid out. He was obviously in discomfort, but she spared him no sympathy. He'd brought this all on himself.

"Do you have any kind of light? I can't see what I'm doing."

Favoring his side, the man shuffled to the front of the buggy and returned with the unlit running lamp. He struck a match to light it and hung it over the open door, then stood back as she examined the baby on the front seat of the buggy.

Lilly cuddled the whimpering child, glad for a pause in the rain. "There's nothing broken. She's only hungry."

"Her mother wouldn't feed her," the man said bluntly.

"Pardon?"

"Her mother wouldn't feed her. I feared she'd starve to death."

Lilly felt a chill of apprehension—maybe the man was insane. She focused on the lunar moth that danced briefly in the lantern's glow. Where had the beautiful creature been hiding during the storm? And what drew it to the light? Fallen leaves provided a slick carpet under her bare feet. Nearly overhead, an owl called for its mate, and in the distance a dog bayed. There was no moon, and it was not a night for hunting. She prayed the dog was searching for them.

"I've ruined everything," he said. "I'm jinxed."

The baby shivered in the cool night air. Keeping her warm was imperative. Lilly climbed back inside the buggy. Timmy was asleep again, and Kip was curled up beside him. After wrapping the baby in blankets, she propped her in the crook of her elbow and tickled her lips with the rubber nipple.

There was not much left in the bottle. She hoped the milk hadn't soured already. All Betsy Lane needed now was a run of diarrhea. Somehow Lilly had to get them all away from this man.

"She was born four weeks ago yesterday," he said from just outside the open door. The light from the lantern distorted his face, casting him in macabre shadow. "How could everything go so far south in just four weeks?"

Lilly gathered her courage. She didn't want to set him off. "Was Betsy's mother ill?"

"I guess you could say so," he said. "Sick in the head. She came after me with a boning knife. Man."

Lilly watched him light a cigarette. He smoked in fast hits. If his ribs were fractured, it would be difficult to take a deep draw. After a minute he launched the cigarette as though it were a dart. Its glowing red tip arced in the dark. Then he got back inside and leaned against the door, turning to face her. He seemed more broken now than threatening.

"What's wrong with Betsy Lane?"

Lilly would bet it cost him a lot to ask that question. "Do you want me to be direct?"

"Yeah."

While Betsy nursed on the bottle, Lilly told him about the cleft in her palate that made her so difficult to feed and about the heart condition that caused her to tire so easily.

"That's bad, right?"

"It makes things hard for her. If her heart gets stronger, then the cleft could be surgically repaired."

"What about that other thing?"

Lilly thought about how to answer. These things were hard for a parent to hear—no matter what the circumstance. "You mean the things you read about in the book?"

"Yeah."

"It's just a circumstance. One doctor calls it mongolism, but what does that mean, really? The Bible says Betsy is fearfully and wonderfully made. You're her father. Do you love her any less?"

"No. I figure I love her more. It's a hard thing to describe." He swiped at his eyes with the heels of his hands. His pain flooded the space around them. "I only wanted the best for her. She's just a baby."

"Betsy Lane can be happy and loved," Lilly said softly. "A life doesn't have to be ordinary or long to be important and respected."

His sigh was long and ragged. "I killed her mother."

Lilly tamped down a momentary panic. "Did you mean to?"

"Things were never right between Noreen and me. She was a hairdresser. Did I tell you that?"

How strange this night had become. The buggy turned into a confessional.

"I told her and told her, 'Don't prop Betsy Lane's bottle.' The milk just leaked down into her bedclothes whenever Noreen did that." He drummed his fingers against the seat and his knee jittered up and down. "That last morning, when I came in from the yard, Betsy Lane was soaked with milk and Noreen was just sitting in the kitchen drinking coffee. I jerked the chair out from under her and told her she was not fit to be a mother. I told her, 'Get your clothes and get out.' She said, 'Fine' and started packing the baby's things."

He took a breath. "When I said, 'It'll be a cold day when you see Betsy again,' she came at me with the knife, crazy as a june bug. I ran out the door and she followed me. She stabbed me twice before we got to the creek. Noreen was stronger than you might have thought. We tussled into the water, me trying to wrest the knife from her hand. When she raised it against me again, I hit her in the head with a rock. . . . I only hit her once, but once was all it took. She's buried up there in the pear orchard."

When he finally stopped talking, the silence felt palpable. His terrible words pierced Lilly's heart like arrows. What could she say that would make any difference? She looked toward the light like the lunar moth had done and prayed for wisdom.

"A family is all I ever wanted," he said. "And now I won't even be able to raise my daughter."

"What are you going to do?" Lilly asked.

"Let me hold Betsy Lane one last time."

Lilly turned on the bench and gave his daughter to him.

He held her for long minutes and kissed each cheek before he handed her back. "It seems there is no hope for me," he said.

"Are you a believer?"

A weary sound escaped his lips—a long, deflating groan. "I'm not sure. What use would God have for a sinner like me?"

"We're all sinners," Lilly said. "The ground at the foot of the cross is even."

The man opened the door. He seemed so lost to Lilly. Was there nothing she could do? The familiar Scripture came to mind: *"Is there no balm in Gilead; is there no physician there?"*

The Lord was indeed in Zion. And Lilly was a physician. She would be His balm.

"I think you cracked a rib," she said. "I should bind your chest."

She put the baby in the basket at her feet and tore diapers into long bands. Rain pattered on her head as she got out and wrapped the strips tightly around the man's chest and tied them off. "This will give you some relief, but you should see a doctor when you get to where you're going."

"You'll see that Betsy Lane gets the best of care?" he asked.

"I will," Lilly said.

"Pray for me," he said. And then he was gone into the storm.

She leaned against the buggy for a minute before crawling back in. She'd rest a moment before she woke Timmy. The night closed in as the stitch in her side, the one she'd tolerated all day, turned into a series of demanding, cramping pains.

"Timmy, wake up."

The boy sprang up, rubbing sleep from his eyes. "Where's he at?"

"He's gone. I need you to go for help."

"I told you already, I ain't leaving you."

Lilly bit back the dark tidal wave of pain that threatened to overwhelm her. "It will be okay, Timmy. I have to stay with the baby. You can take Kip and the lantern."

"Really? All right, then. Which way should I go?"

"Go back up this trail to the road and head toward town. Hold the lantern high and make a lot of noise so nobody mistakes who you are."

Once outside the buggy, Timmy slapped his leg and called for Kip. Kip whined, looking back at Lilly.

"Go on, Kip. Go with Timmy."

She watched the lantern bob away before she gave in to the gripping pain. When Betsy cried, Lilly cried with her. There was nothing to do now but pray.

CHAPTER 30

Lilly wished the noise would stop. She was desperately tired and in such discomfort she only wanted to escape into sleep. But the barking wouldn't stop. Why wouldn't someone get up and let Kip outside? Why must she always be responsible?

Poor little Kipper. She put both hands against the bed, determined to rise, find her slippers and her robe, and put Kip on his leash. But the hard surface beneath her hands was not her soft and comforting bed. She fell back against the buggy seat and sobbed.

Suddenly a slobbering, baying dog pushed his long wet

nose against her shoulder. She could hear the men behind him.

"Praise God," Chanis Clay said when he found her. "Doc Lilly, are you hurt? Where's Timmy?"

Lilly clutched his shirt. "I have the baby," she said, barely recognizing her own wavering voice. She wondered how much blood she'd lost. "Timmy went to get help."

"All right, come on. I'll help you out."

A wave of pain met Lilly's efforts to move. She could see raw fear on Chanis's young face.

"Okay, that's all right, Doc. I'll carry you."

She held tightly to the baby as Chanis lifted her out. She was glad she'd padded herself well with the baby's extra diapers.

"She's too weak to ride," Chanis said when Cletus Becker unhitched the horse from the wrecked buggy.

Cletus swung himself up on the horse's broad back. "Give 'em here," he said to Chanis. "You lead. Go slow."

Cletus held Lilly in his arms as tenderly as he would have held little Amy.

"I'm sorry," she said, barely finding the strength to clasp Betsy Lane. "Thank you."

"Glad to hep," he said and tightened his arms.

It was late morning before Lilly was truly awake again. Her mother stood at the bedroom window looking out. Lilly had slipped in and out of consciousness all night, barely aware of her mother's tender care but grateful all the same.

"Mama," Lilly said, "did I keep my baby?"

When Mama turned, Lilly could see the answer written on her face.

"Oh, sweet girl," she said, climbing into bed with Lilly. "I'm so, so sorry."

Lilly cried on her mother's shoulder just as she'd done so many times as a girl. Finally Mama pulled back, wiping Lilly's eyes and her nose with the handkerchief from her apron pocket.

"There's something wrong with me, Mama. I don't think I can carry a baby. Maybe I'm not meant to be a mother."

Mama patted her cheek in her no-nonsense way. "I suppose we'll find out," she said, moving her hand to rest on Lilly's belly. "I believe there's another one in here."

Lilly fell back against the bolster pillow. "I suspected twins . . . But are you sure? How can you be sure I didn't lose them both?"

"I could find the one, but only one. I have a sense about these things, and you're large for this stage, Daughter." She took a brush from the nightstand and began to tease the knots from Lilly's hair. "Let's get you presentable. Your husband will be home soon."

"Tern . . . and you, Mama—how did you know to come?"

"It seems Mazy is quite the expert with the telephone. I'm proud of her."

Tears leaked from Lilly's eyes. "I think my baby was a boy. I wanted him so."

"I know, honey. Sometimes a woman's lot is hard. And

it's very strange to grieve for one while being joyous for the other."

"Did this ever happen to you, Mama?"

"No, not this particular thing in this particular way, but you recollect, I was carrying you when your own father died."

"How did you stand it? How did you bear up?"

"You just do, Lilly; you just do. Your faith will carry you through."

As her mother gently brushed her hair, Lilly thought of the night before and how God had answered her prayers. She told her mother about the man who had set all this in motion and about how she had felt called to minister to him. "I hope it made a difference," she said.

"I hope so too," Mama said with a final pass of the brush.

"Did you examine the foundling baby, Mama? Is she okay?"

"What a little scrapper," Mama said. "Anne Becker says she's been through a lot."

"You don't know the half of it. It is a miracle that she's alive."

Mama caught up Lilly's hair with a length of blue ribbon. "We'll talk about it later. For now you need to rest."

Lilly was propped up against the pillows, her lunch tray on her lap, when she heard Tern coming. The motorcar was so unexpected that it couldn't possibly be anyone else.

Mazy rushed into the room, clapping her hands. "There's a car coming. Oh, Lilly, it's so exciting. I'll bet this is the first automobile ever in Skip Rock. People are running along behind it, and Timmy's riding on the running board."

"Lilly?" She heard Tern calling from the kitchen before his body filled the doorway.

Mazy took the tray and slipped out, leaving them alone. Lilly felt like she might burst with emotion. She choked on tears. "Oh, Tern, I lost our baby."

He sat beside her on the bed and pulled her into an embrace. "Shh," he said. "Everything will be okay. Just let me hold you for a minute."

Tern was tender and sweet with her, but she could feel his anger just below the surface. "The sheriff filled me in," he said. "I'll never leave you alone again."

"I hope you don't mean that," she said.

"I do mean it! Look what happened because I wasn't here."

"Lots happened, Tern, but not because you were gone. What you do is as important as what I do. Lives depend on you."

"But, honey, yours is the one that matters most to me. Please don't be sad about losing the baby. We can try again."

"I'll need you to grieve this with me, Tern. You'll have to stand some tears."

"I expect I'll shed some of my own," he said, his voice cracking with emotion.

"We'll cry together, darling Husband." Lilly leaned into him, gathering strength. "I suspected there were twins, Tern. Mama thinks I'm still carrying one of them."

"You mean another baby? I don't understand. How can that be?"

"It's not impossible. These things happen, but even if it's true, I could miscarry again." Her tears soaked the front of his shirt.

He kissed her cheek. "Well, seems like we can cry a little and laugh a little. If God intends for us to have this baby, we will. If not, we'll still have each other, and we'll try again."

Lilly relaxed in his arms. His reasoning was exactly what she needed to hear. It was just what the doctor ordered.

Armina slipped away to her own house once she knew Doc Lilly would be all right. She needed to watch for Ned. The doc's house was full of folks, and a public reunion was not on Armina's list of things she wanted to happen.

She raised all the windows in the house, mopped her kitchen floor, and flung the rug from the front room over the clothesline. Dust thickened the air. She'd beaten it to a fare-thee-well with the broom handle and sneezed herself silly before she realized she had her full strength back. Well, how about that?

She raised the broom for one last whack.

"I reckon I'd better stay over here until you put that broom down," she heard Ned say. "Then I'm going to claim a kiss."

Armina nearly jumped out of her skin when she saw him standing there. La, she'd missed her fellow.

"Huh. I reckon that'd be up to me, Ned Tippen," she teased, wishing he'd hurry up about it.

"Surely you wouldn't deny me one little smack."

"Did you get your diploma?"

He waved an official-looking framed certificate in front of her. "I did. Now can I have that kiss?"

"Will you buy me a cow?" she asked, twirling the broom like a baton. "I got my eye on one of Turnip Tippen's Jerseys."

"A cow? Seems like a pretty expensive kiss to me."

"You want it or not? I got things to do."

"Put down that broom and come on over here," he said.

"And a pig," Armina said as the first kiss lingered. "I want me a pig, too."

EPILOGUE

IN THE SPRINGTIME, when the babies were old enough, Lilly and Armina took them up Tattler's Branch Road to visit the Beckers.

Armina was amazed at the work Cletus had done on the place. He'd torn down the old bridge and replaced it with one wide enough to handle their carriage. The brambles and briars had been tamed and a new, wider cattle gate installed.

"Who'd of ever thought Cletus Becker would have turned out to be so handy?" Armina said, guiding the horse up the path toward the house.

Last summer had changed them all, Lilly thought. She had learned a valuable lesson after spending the fall and early

331

winter on bed rest. It was humbling to say the least, being dependent instead of being in charge. Tern had learned from the experience too. He still traveled, but he was never out of touch. They had made a pact to talk every day, convenient or not. And Mazy—who would have thought she'd turn so independent? She still seemed smitten with Chanis, but she was taking it slow. Time and distance would prove if that new love was true.

"I guess Cletus just needed a chance," Lilly said, trying to hold the squirming babies still.

"Like ever'body else," Armina said.

"Yes," Lilly said, her mind going to Shade Harmon, wondering where he was and how he was faring. She had believed the story he told her that stormy night in the woods. Her belief was confirmed when the sheriff discovered a rusted boning knife near the footbridge over Tattler's Branch. Two months after the incident that had nearly taken her life, she'd received a thick packet in the mail. In it was a deed to Shade Harmon's property as well as a legal document ceding the farm to Anne Becker. It was his desire that Anne continue to care for his daughter under Lilly's direction. He asked that Lilly be the administrator of the securities and bonds in Betsy Lane's name with everything to revert to Lilly in the event of his daughter's demise. Lilly could never accept his money, of course; who knew where it came from? But if need be, she'd see that it went to a good cause.

It came as no surprise to her that Mr. Harmon included money for the proper burial of his wife. It was Lilly's opinion that he did love Noreen in his way. She couldn't help but wonder how different things might have been if they had been properly instructed in the care of so difficult an infant. Sadly, no family member ever came forward to claim Noreen's body even though they posted her death in every newspaper in the state and put it over the wire several times. They laid her to rest in the graveyard beside the church the Beckers attended. The granite marker simply read:

Noreen Harmon
?–1911
Beloved Mother of Betsy Lane Harmon

Anne and Cletus took Betsy to visit the grave site every Sunday after service.

It had been a surprise to find a bond in Timmy's name included in the packet. The boy could go to the college of his choice. Timmy teased that he would trade it for a bottle of pop and a candy bar. All he wanted was to be a lawman like Chanis Clay.

Chanis was up for reelection in the fall. Lilly was sure he wouldn't have a problem getting the vote. Folks still talked about how he found "Doc Lilly" by tracking her through the woods with Cletus Becker's old hound dog, using little more than the scent from one of Betsy Lane's blankets. Lilly knew it was a miracle that he found her in time to save two of her babies.

Firstborn Julia Verily and her brother, Simon Inasmuch,

blessed Lilly and Tern every day. But Lilly's heart would always bleed for the loss of the tiny baby she would have named John Cipher if indeed it was a boy. When she was twenty weeks and they'd heard two heartbeats instead of the one that was expected, Mama had told her the miscarriage was for the best—chances of her carrying triplets to term were slim. In her weakened condition, twins had been hard enough. Losing one to save the others was hard to come to terms with, but she trusted that God knew best.

As they rounded a curve in the road, they could see Anne and Amy on the porch. Betsy Lane was hanging from the loop of Amy's arms like a satisfied cat. She was nearly as big as Amy. The baby grew like a weed once her heart murmur had resolved. Sometime this summer, Lilly would take the child to Lexington for her first consult with a surgeon and hopefully to begin the tedious repair of her cleft palate.

Anne waved and started down the steps with Amy on one hip and Betsy on the other. She managed the child care center Lilly had started for employees of the clinic and for local mothers who needed a short break. Bobby Bumble was a frequent visitor. In the fall, when Mazy went off to secretarial school, Lilly also would have a safe place for Julia and Simon when need be. Right now, Armina and Mazy wouldn't hear of anyone else caring for the babies, and she suspected Armina never would.

Lilly knew how blessed she was. She had much more time at home now that Ned had completed his training as a registered nurse. There was little that he couldn't handle when she was absent. Lilly was encouraging Ned to go for his medical degree, but Armina told her to mind her business. Just because Lilly was content with a traveling man didn't mean Armina would be. And Armina wasn't about to move to the city for any man. Facts were facts.

Kip barked and leaped from the carriage before it came to a full stop. The dog rarely let Lilly out of his sight these days. Whatever he'd run up against that day in the woods had cured him of his rambling ways. It didn't hurt that he thought the twins were puppies and that he alone was in charge of their well-being.

The women came together in the middle of the yard with an exchange of babies, laughter, and a few dashed tears. A warm spring breeze showered them with the rounded sweet-smelling petals from the pear orchard just beyond the house.

Anne was all smiles. Armina was strong and ornery again, content with her husband and her Jersey, not to mention one of Sassy's offspring. Lilly had her babies and her traveling man and a job of service to her community. She was exactly where God meant for her to be, and she was thankful. *"All things work together for good to them that love God,"* she thought as she was surrounded by her friends.

Though their lives had been torn asunder and pieced back together like a crazy quilt, each woman was stronger in the mended places and softer for the wear.

Turn the page for an exciting look into
Lilly and Tern's love story in

SKIP ROCK SHALLOWS

AVAILABLE NOW AT BOOKSTORES AND ONLINE.

CHAPTER 1

1908

Stanley James knew there'd been an accident before the blast of the whistle shattered the stillness of the morning. He felt the slightest tremor against the soles of his feet when he bent to lace his high-top work boots. His arm jerked and the rawhide string snapped. Coffee sloshed from his cup and ran across the table like a tiny river overflowing its bank. It dripped onto the knee of his just-ironed coveralls. Stanley swore.

"There's no call for that purple language in my kitchen," Myrtie said in that disapproving way she had. She mopped the spill with a bleach rag before he had a chance to move out of the way.

"Wake the gal," Stanley said.

"It's early yet, Stanley, and she was up late last night."

It would be right pleasant, Stanley thought, if just once Myrtie would do what he asked instead of throwing a wall of words up against him.

Myrtie's eyes grew round as the first warning shrieked. She covered her ears as if it came from right next door and not a mile up the road.

"I'll go get her," she said, folding the rag on the tabletop. Pausing at the door, she looked back. "Will you have time to eat your breakfast?"

Stanley was at the cupboard getting down a box of carbide. "Wrap up some biscuits and fix a thermos. We'll carry it with us."

Myrtie hesitated.

"Wake the gal first, Myrtie. Tell her to shake a leg."

"Stanley, you've got no call to remark on her limbs."

"It's a saying!" Stanley shouted over the alert. "It means hurry up."

"Don't be telling me what to do, Stanley James. I'll go as fast as I want to."

It didn't much matter, Stanley thought. What good would a slip of a gal be against an explosion or a cave-in?

Lilly Gray Corbett was awake. She liked to get up early and climb partway up the mountain to attend to her devotionals under a stand of regal pines. The trees looked down over the valley, where wood-sided shotgun houses jostled each other for elbow room. She leaned against the rough bark of one of the trees, enjoying the fresh green scent of its needles, searching in her Bible for a verse in Isaiah, the one about being called.

When she heard the far-off whistle, her mouth went dry. It was one thing to study about accidents and mangled bodies, quite another to actually attend to one. Carefully, she retraced her steps toward home.

Last night had gone well, though. The baby girl she'd delivered slid into the world without as much as a thank-you. The young mother would have done just as well without Lilly's assistance. If you didn't count the number of births she'd attended with her mentor, Dr. Coldiron, this had been her first delivery—or baby catching, as her mother would say.

Maybe folks were beginning to trust her a little. She'd been here at Skip Rock for two weeks, opening the doctor's office daily, but last night was the first time she'd been called out.

When she reached the end of the one-cow path, Mrs. James met her. "Better hurry, Dr. Corbett. Stanley's in a dither."

Lilly would like to see that—Mr. James in a dither. She'd never seen him break a sweat. He was as deliberate as a plow mule, and he worked just as hard.

Mrs. James ushered her around the side of the house like she was a birthday present. "Lookee here, Stanley. I found her."

Mr. James looked Lilly up and down. "Them skirts ain't going to work."

"Stanley James!"

"Get the gal some overhauls," he said, while fitting pebbles of carbide into a small, round lamp. "We might be going down in the hole."

Dressed and ready, Lilly hurried to catch up to Mr. James. She nearly had to run to match his long stride. He didn't want her there, she knew. In his world, women weren't doctors and they didn't belong in the mines.

Lilly wasn't so sure she didn't agree about the mine part. If her stepfather could see her now, he'd have a heart attack.

The overalls were too long and she kept tripping over the hems. Mrs. James had cinched the waist with a piece of twine, but still they ballooned around her. "I'll fix them proper when you get back," she'd said. "Next time we'll be ready."

Next time? Lilly swallowed hard. What had she gotten herself into?

It seemed to Lilly that she was predestined to be a doctor. Her mother was a natural healer. Her father and his father had been medical doctors. It was in her blood, if not yet in her bones.

She had earned her degree at the end of May and before you could say *whippersnapper* was on her way to the mountains to gain some experience. Sadly, the elderly doctor she was to shadow had died just days before she arrived.

It was no wonder Mr. James's face had fallen when he met her at the train station. He'd stared at the paper in his hand and looked again at her. "Says here you're a man."

She set her hatboxes on the platform and stuck out her hand. "I guess you can see I'm not."

Instead of shaking her hand, he waved the piece of paper under her nose. "Larry Corbett? Larry's not a gal's name, and a gal ain't a doctor."

"I'm Lilly, not Larry," she said. "Dr. Lilly Corbett." *Doctor?* Would she ever get used to using that title?

Mr. James held the paper at arm's length, as older folks do. "Humph," he said.

She picked up the two round, beribboned boxes and lifted her chin. "Shall we proceed?"

What could the poor man do? He stuffed the paper in his pocket and reached for the traveling trunk the porter wheeled out. He said not a word on the buggy ride to her lodgings and kept his face straight ahead. But every so often his eyes would slide sideways as if he was taking her in. It was obvious he found her wanting.

Mrs. James, on the other hand, seemed delighted to see her. She fussed over Lilly as if she were a prodigal daughter as she showed her to the one-room tar-paper shack out behind their house. She even helped Lilly unpack, exclaiming over each garment she hung from pegs beside the door.

"If this ain't the prettiest," she said when she unfolded

Lilly's long silk gown and her matching robe. She laid them across the bed. "I ain't never seen the like."

"Thank you," Lilly said. "It was a gift from my aunt Alice. I guess she thought I was going to Boston or New York."

"I never heard of them places," Mrs. James said. "Are they over round Lexington? My sister's been to Lexington."

"They're just cities. Just big places." Lilly moved to one of the two windows on either side of the door. "Does this raise? Do you have a screen?"

Mrs. James's face colored. "No, I don't have such, but I could tack a piece of greased paper over it, if you want it open. It's clean. I washed it myself."

Lilly felt bad that she had embarrassed her benefactor. The Jameses were kind to provide room and board for her in exchange for a smallish stipend. It was all arranged through the medical school and the mining company. Lilly would be here for the summer practicing her trade.

"Goodness, no, this is fine," Lilly said. "I was thinking I might like some fresh air, that's all."

"Best leave the winders down and the door closed. The air here ain't as unsullied as it once was—it gathers in your lungs and sets up like wallpaper paste. But you know, beggars can't be choosers. We're that glad for the work. As Stanley says, it's a clean breath or a day's pay."

Mrs. James took a snow-white rag from her apron pocket and wiped the windowsill. "You can push it up after dark if you want. Seems like the night dew settles the dust. I'll have Stanley see if the company store carries ary winder screens."

Opening the door, she shook the rag out over the stone stoop. "We're saving up, though. I got a money jar hid behind the grease can." A wistful note crept into her voice. "Soon's as we get a bit together, we're fixing to buy a place over to Stoney. They ain't any mines besmirching the mountains there."

Coming out of the memory, Lilly stopped for a second and rolled up her pant legs. She would take scissors to them herself when she got back.

About the Author

A FORMER REGISTERED NURSE, award-winning author Jan Watson lives in Lexington, Kentucky, near her three sons and daughter-in-law.

Tattler's Branch follows *Skip Rock Shallows*, *Still House Pond*, *Sweetwater Run*, and the Troublesome Creek series, which includes *Troublesome Creek*, *Willow Springs*, and *Torrent Falls*. Chosen Best Kentucky Author of 2012 by *Kentucky Living* magazine, Jan also won the 2004 Christian Writers Guild Operation First Novel contest and took second place in the 2006 Inspirational Reader's Choice Award Contest sponsored by the Faith, Hope, and Love Chapter of the Romance Writers of America. *Troublesome Creek* was also a nominee for the Kentucky Literary Awards in 2006. *Willow Springs* was selected for *Library Journal*'s Best Genre Fiction category in 2007.

Besides writing historical fiction, Jan keeps busy entertaining her Jack Russell terrier, Maggie.

Please visit Jan's website at www.janwatson.net. You can contact her through e-mail at author@janwatson.net.

Discussion Questions

1. In the beginning of the story, Armina seems drawn to the house where she finds the abandoned child. Have you ever felt God's hand pulling you toward a decision? Did you comply? Why or why not?

2. Armina is reluctant to accept Lilly's help when she falls ill. Why do you think she tries to push Lilly away when she needs her most? How do you feel about accepting help? In your mind, is it a virtue or a luxury?

3. Lilly has her hands full with her sister Mazy visiting for the summer. Where do you see similarities between the two sisters? What are the major differences in their characters?

4. Mazy is enthralled with the advances of the time, especially the telephone. Do you share her enthusiasm for new technology, or are you a skeptic like other residents of Skip Rock?

5. After observing Chanis and Mazy together, Lilly worries her younger sister is acting too old for her age. If you were Lilly, would you tell Mazy your thoughts or let her make her own choices and live with the consequences?

6. Lilly struggles to keep up with the responsibilities of her practice while taking extra care of herself and her unborn child. Do you agree with her ultimate decision about what is most important? Have you ever struggled between two conflicting obligations? How did you solve the conflict?

7. Shade Harmon is disturbed by what he learns about mongolism, an early term for Down syndrome. What did you think of how Betsy Lane's condition was treated or referenced throughout the story? How have modern advances in the medical field changed the general public's perceptions?

8. After a particularly tiring day at work, Lilly longs for her husband to come home and rub her feet but chides herself for her "silly vanity—wishing niceties to come her way when there was so much sorrow all around." Do you ever struggle to stay thankful in your everyday life? What do you do to maintain perspective?

9. When Lilly and Timmy are taken, Lilly is struck by her feelings of hatred toward Shade. How do you feel about Lilly's struggle? Do you ever find it difficult to leave judgment up to God?

10. Shade made many mistakes in his life and in the search
    for his child, but in the end, he truly desires the best
    for his daughter. How did you feel toward Shade by the
    end of the novel? Did he redeem himself?